PRAISE FOR BARRY EISLER

"Eisler is at the top of his game."

—RT Book Reviews

"Eisler combines the insouciance of Ian Fleming, the realistic detail of Tom Clancy, the ennui of Graham Greene, and the prose power of John le Carré."

—*News-Press*

"Furious and creative . . . Rain's combination of quirks and proficiency is the stuff great characters are made of."

—*Entertainment Weekly*

"No one is writing a better thriller series today than Barry Eisler. He has quickly jumped into my top ten best American mystery/thriller writers, along with Michael Connelly, Lee Child, Walter Mosley, and Harlan Coben . . . Rating: A."

—*Deadly Pleasures*

"Written with a delightfully soft touch and a powerful blend of excitement, exotica, and what (ever since John le Carré) readers have known to call tradecraft."

—*The Economist*

"Barry Eisler serves up steamy foreign locales, stunning action and enough high-tech weaponry to make for an A-plus read."

—*New York Daily News*

ZERO
SUM

ALSO BY BARRY EISLER

A Clean Kill in Tokyo (previously published as *Rain Fall*)
A Lonely Resurrection (previously published as *Hard Rain*)
Winner Take All (previously published as *Rain Storm*)
Redemption Games (previously published as *Killing Rain*)
Extremis (previously published as *The Last Assassin*)
The Killer Ascendant (previously published as *Requiem for an Assassin*)
Fault Line
Inside Out
The Detachment
Graveyard of Memories
The God's Eye View
Livia Lone

SHORT WORKS

"The Lost Coast"
"Paris Is a Bitch"
"The Khmer Kill"
"London Twist"

ESSAYS

"The Ass Is a Poor Receptacle for the Head: Why Democrats Suck at
Communication, and How They Could Improve"
"Be the Monkey: A Conversation about the New World of Publishing"
(with J. A. Konrath)

BARRY EISLER

A JOHN RAIN NOVEL

ZERO SUM

THOMAS & MERCER

Published by Thomas & Mercer, Seattle

www.apub.com

Amazon, the Amazon logo, and Thomas & Mercer are trademarks of Amazon.com, Inc., or its affiliates.

ISBN-13: 9781477824481 (hardcover)
ISBN-10: 1477824480 (hardcover)
ISBN-13: 9781477824467 (paperback)
ISBN-10: 1477824464 (paperback)

Cover design by Edward Bettison

Printed in the United States of America

First edition

Lasciate ogni speranza, voi ch'entrate.

chapter
one

Whoever said "You can't go home again" didn't know how good he had it. At least there was a home he couldn't go to. All I had was Tokyo. And no matter how many years I spent there, that bitch of a city was never going to be any kind of home to me. More an unrequited love.

So it was probably less from nostalgia than longing that I found myself back there in the fall of 1982. Or maybe it was something deeper and more stubborn still. Why do salmon swim upriver to the place where they were spawned? All animals have programming. What makes humans special is our need to rationalize our actions, rather than just accept them.

Of course, I didn't understand any of that at the time. I told myself that life in the Philippines had grown stale for me, my work with the insurgency in Mindanao too dangerous to continue. A change in venue would be good. The question was, a change to where? And for an exiled mercenary with no family, no connections, and no friends outside the country that begot him, it was a question with only one answer.

Or maybe it was all just fate. At least, that's how it felt that morning as I strolled along the gravel paths of Tokyo's Hamarikyu Gardens, waiting for my contact, Miyamoto, a Liberal Democratic Party fixer I had once helped with a problem, and who I hoped might now help me in return. Certainly the weather was auspicious: a deep-blue sky; a cool, dry breeze; everywhere ginkgo and maple leaves lit by the sun in flaming yellow and orange and red. The city's soundtrack played all around me, as familiar as a favorite album heard after a long hiatus: the buzz of *higurashi* cicadas in the trees; the rumble of truck traffic on the overcrowded roads surrounding the garden; the chimes of an incoming Yamanote train in the distance. It felt good to be back. It felt easy.

Yeah, I know. Stupid. But remember, I was barely out of my twenties at the time. Blooded, but not yet seasoned. There was still a lot I didn't want to accept about the permanence of the path I had embarked on ten years earlier, when I had gone to war with the yakuza and the CIA, and then "died" to protect the girl I had fallen in love with, who was innocent of all of it. She was safe now, in America, which meant Tokyo would be safe for me.

I know. Stupid again. But, in retrospect, apparently not ineducable. And is there any teacher better, more patient and determined, than fate?

For an hour or so, I strolled and snapped photos with an Instamatic camera, blending with the tourists and Tokyoites around me—one of the lessons I had learned from my late and unlamented CIA handler, Sean McGraw. I wasn't worried about a threat from Miyamoto. Ten years earlier, he had taken a huge risk to warn me that his superiors wanted me dead. I wouldn't soon forget that, or stop looking for a way to repay him.

It was nearly noon when I saw Miyamoto enter the garden from the Otemon Bridge gate. His hair was thinner and grayer, and he was more portly than I remembered. But I would have recognized him from his tie alone—a floral design probably five inches across, and as incongruous in conservatively dressed Tokyo as a giggle at a funeral.

I waited until he had almost reached my position before emerging from behind a cluster of retirees enjoying the foliage. Urban concealment hadn't yet become second nature to me, and I was still deliberately practicing it.

His face lit up with a broad smile when he caught sight of me, and when we were closer he bowed unnecessarily low. I would have matched the bow, but knew he would then have felt compelled to go even lower to show his appreciation and respect. So I remained at a more ordinary angle until he had straightened.

"Rain-san," he said, still beaming. *"Hisashiburi desu ne."* It's been a long time.

"Sō desu ne," I said, returning his smile. Indeed it has.

"It gives me such pleasure to see you," he continued in formal Japanese. "And you haven't changed at all. Other than your tan—you look like a surfer! The climate in the Philippines is to your liking?"

"I can't complain. You look the same, too. Things at work are agreeable?"

He laughed. "I look older, balder, and fatter. But yes, things at work are agreeable. Thanks to you."

He was referring to an introduction I had brokered—a contractor, who had removed an extortionate LDP functionary. We both understood the contractor was, in fact, me, but continued to maintain the polite fiction that we were talking about some mysterious third party.

"As always," I said, "you are being far too kind. I wish I could have done more. And regardless, your introductions in the Philippines were more than repayment."

Miyamoto had been an officer in the Imperial Japanese Army. Stationed in the Philippines, he had maintained contacts there after the war, contacts that had led to my work with the insurgency in Mindanao. It had been satisfying, and reasonably lucrative, to be on the side of the guerrillas for a change—using what I had learned the easy way with American Special Forces, and then the hard way at the hands of the Vietcong.

He gave a half bow. "I am so pleased my minor service proved useful. Now, what brings you back here? Was there no judo in the Philippines?"

I laughed. I had been obsessed with judo training at the Kodokan, the birthplace of the art, when I'd last lived in Tokyo.

"I couldn't find a dojo," I told him. "But I'm sure I'll get back into it in Tokyo if I stay."

"So this visit is more than a vacation?"

"Well, that's something I hoped you and I might discuss."

"That would be a great pleasure. Perhaps over tea?"

A short distance away was the Nakajima Teahouse, famous for nearly three centuries for its potent *matcha* tea and its views of the garden surrounding the pond over which it was built. Ten years earlier, it had been the site of a fateful conversation between Miyamoto and me, and an even more fateful decision. If I'd been more superstitious, or maybe just smarter, I might have proposed somewhere else this time. But ten minutes later, we were kneeling on the tatami mats, savoring small sips of strong green tea and wordlessly contemplating the beauty of the pond and the garden.

Miyamoto broke the silence. "I am struck by your mindfulness. As I grow older, I find my own sometimes slipping. It is kind of you to so gently remind me."

The mindfulness he spoke of was called *nen* in Japanese—an acknowledgment, an appreciation, of the importance of small things. The things that make living more worthwhile. And that, in my work, make it more probable, as well.

I smiled. Once upon a time, I had thought Miyamoto's humility to be entirely straightforward. Now, I recognized that while the quality was still genuine, he used it also to communicate concepts for which a more straightforward approach might cause offense, and therefore incomprehension.

"It was kind of you to teach me to be more mindful in the first place," I said, carefully setting down my cup of tea. "And that you continue to teach me now."

He dipped his head as though embarrassed. "If I had anything to teach, I could not ask for a better student."

I smiled again. I had the feeling Miyamoto had a lot to impart, and not many people to impart it to. Someone else's loss was my gain.

For a while, we sipped our tea and engaged in pleasantries about the unusually fine weather. I noticed that the cloth and cut of his gray suit were considerably finer than the rumpled bureaucrat's uniform I remembered. He had risen within the ranks, it seemed, and, his taste in ties aside, wasn't inclined to hide it. Good for him. And good for me—the story a person's clothes might tell would have been lost on me the last time we had seen each other. *Nen* applied to so many things.

Presently, the conversation turned to politics. Miyamoto told me it had been decided that Yasuhiro Nakasone would be the next prime minister, in part because Nakasone was eager to deepen Japan's military alliance with America under President Reagan. A lot of money would be made, he said, and the LDP would control all of it.

"So the whole party is behind Nakasone?" I asked.

"Not all the factions, no. In fact, Nakasone faces substantial opposition."

"Then how do you know he'll win?"

He smiled, a warm smile with perhaps just a hint of patient affection for his younger friend's naïveté.

"Because money makes the world go round," he said.

"Not love?"

I thought I saw a twinge of sadness in his eyes. Then it was gone.

"Both are powerful forces. But if there's a conflict, money always wins."

"Always?"

He shrugged. "There may be unforeseen circumstances. And frequent setbacks. But in the end, yes. Money always wins."

I was impressed by his knowledge and his confidence, if not his cynicism. Miyamoto was no longer anyone's flunky. He was an insider now, and I realized it was fortunate I had treated him well when there had been no obvious reason to. And fortunate, too, that he was the kind of person who would remember such a kindness with gratitude, rather than resentment.

We were quiet again for a moment while I considered how to broach the topic that had brought me here. But he must have sensed the opening I was struggling to find, because he said, "You mentioned this might be a longer stay?"

"It might be. If I could find a suitable position."

He smiled. "Well, we have no insurgency here in Japan. Although some might find such an absence regrettable."

I laughed. "I had imagined something lower-key than a full-blown insurgency. Perhaps something more akin to the service my contact performed for you before. If you have any such work now, I could put you in touch again."

He nodded slowly, and I sensed the request had made him uncomfortable. Was it the continued fiction that the service in question had been performed by a third party?

After a moment, he said, "It is very kind of you to make this offer. In fact, there is a great deal of such work, and, if it were up to me, I would be grateful to accept your kindness."

I wanted to press, but sensed I would do better to respect his circumlocutions. "I fear my directness has put you in an awkward position," I said, bowing my head. "Please accept my apologies."

"No!" he said quickly. "The one who must apologize is I. The awkward position has nothing to do with you. You see, as a result of your previous kindness, I find myself in a quite different position today than that of a decade ago. A position to make decisions about . . . delicate matters."

He paused, and then went on. "And yet, the kind of service your contact performed for me earlier is now the one thing about which I am . . . not free to decide."

Okay. Whatever was making him uncomfortable, it seemed it wasn't our fiction, which in any event felt more like habit than necessity.

I waited, letting the silence draw him out, the way I had learned from McGraw.

"You see," he said after a moment, "the matters for which I would otherwise be so grateful for your help . . . they must now all be funneled through a single outside party."

I didn't know what that meant, or even how to proceed in the face of it. Feeling I was missing some subtle point and certain I was blundering, I said, "I'm . . . not sure I understand."

He grimaced. "Only because of my failure to adequately explain. Rain-san, we have known each other for a long time. Helped each other. And trusted each other with confidences. Is this not so?"

"It's very much so."

"Then I will trust you with one more."

I nodded once, sensing my silence was more eloquent thanks for his trust than anything I might have said aloud.

He took a sip of tea, looked into his cup for a moment, and then set it down. "For a while, after you left Tokyo, I found myself in charge of certain . . . personnel decisions. Well, not the decisions as such. But when some worthier person decided that, due to unfortunate circumstances, an individual had to be . . . terminated, the termination was left to me."

He paused again, then went on. "I managed to develop several contacts to carry out those terminations. They were not as reliable as the contact you generously put me in touch with, but they were reliable enough."

I was still young, and wanted to show him I was grateful for his trust by reciprocating. So I said, "Miyamoto-san. I think we both know who that contact really was."

He nodded. "Yes. Though I would not acknowledge it without your permission."

"You have it now."

He bowed his head for a long moment, then looked at me. "I used my new contacts from time to time to carry out my superiors' orders.

7

Things went well. Then, three years ago, I was approached by a man. A very dangerous man, as I learned. He calls himself Victor."

"A foreigner?"

It was strange to refer to someone as a foreigner, as though Miyamoto and I were both Japanese. Miyamoto was, of course. But my mother was American, so I was only half. And as a cruel teacher had once told me when I was a child, when you mix dirty water and clean water, you are left with . . . dirty water.

Still, the basis of in-groups and out-groups is always relative. And there was something about Miyamoto that made me feel Japanese. Which I suppose was part of my affection for him.

"He is of mixed parentage. One Asian, judging from his features, the other Russian, I believe, because of his accent. His Japanese is quite good, so I believe he spent at least some time here as a child."

There was no need to point out that this man Victor had some traits in common with me. Either Miyamoto hadn't noticed, or he didn't care. Or he was being characteristically polite.

I waited, and he went on. "Victor told me he had been watching me for some time. And the people I worked for. He told me henceforth I would funnel all . . . terminations exclusively through him."

"How did he learn so much about you?"

"This I have never been able to discover. I can say only that he has proven himself exceptionally resourceful. And, as I have said, dangerous."

"Dangerous how?"

"When I told him I needed no new assistance with anything involving my governmental responsibilities, he assured me that this would soon change, and that he would approach me again when it did."

"And?"

"And two days later, one of the three contacts I employed for terminations was dead. A day later, the second was dead. I warned the third—younger than the first two, but still very tough and capable,

8

though regrettably perhaps a bit hotheaded. He told me he knew of this man Victor, and would take care of him. And yet the day after this conversation, he, too, was dead. After which, Victor approached me again, offering his services. At which point it was quite obvious to me that if I were to decline, he would kill me as he had killed the men I employed."

He frowned and took a sip of tea. "I discussed the situation with my superior. He told me Victor would be taken care of. And yet, three days later, my superior was himself dead. Since then, I have done as Victor demanded."

We were quiet for a moment while I considered all he had said. Then I asked, "These men Victor killed . . . how did they die?"

He winced. "All beaten to death."

His expression was answer enough, but still I asked. "You saw the results?"

He nodded.

"Well," I said, "I imagine you were supposed to."

We were quiet again. Then I said, "It's new to me in the particulars, but overall what we're talking about is a pretty standard racket. You know, you want to open a massage parlor, you have to agree to send all the linens to a yakuza service. Or the parlor gets torched. Want to open a restaurant? Fine, as long as you hire a yakuza outfit to haul away the garbage. Victor's just taking the concept and adapting it to a new area. Want to remove political problems? Fine, as long as you contract it through Victor, Incorporated."

Miyamoto sighed. "Yes. I believe your analysis is unfortunately accurate."

"I'm surprised your people let him muscle his way in like this."

"His introduction was most persuasive."

"Of course. And I'm sure his prices are reasonable, too. For now. But have you considered what happens later? Violence is a currency, and you're letting this guy monopolize it. How long before he decides to move into other areas, too? At that point, how would you stop him?"

"I believe some of my superiors share your concerns. But, perhaps understandably, they prefer to treat Victor's monopoly simply as a new cost of doing business."

"Just as long as you understand the cost will go up. Is he charging you a monthly minimum, regardless of whether you require his services? If not, it's coming."

He looked at me. "Rain-san. How do you know so much?"

I shrugged. "I just ask myself what I would do if I were a guy like this Victor."

"And what is he like?"

"From what you've told me? Ambitious, ruthless, not at all risk averse, and disdainful of the existing order."

"Yes. All those things. An unfortunate combination."

"What is he charging you?"

"He prefers to be paid in US dollars. Fifty thousand per job."

I laughed. "He's robbing you guys. I worked for a fifth of that. Albeit ten years ago, but still. Why don't you pay me that much to make him go away? And then I'll charge you half his amount going forward."

He lost a little color at that. "Do you really need the money this much?"

I shrugged. "Well, I've managed not to spend everything I made in the Philippines, but my savings aren't going to last forever."

"Still. This is not a good idea."

"Why?"

"If you met him, you would understand why."

"Then I'll meet him. He's got a crew, right? He has to, if his intel is as good as you say and he's able to act as quickly as he does. Tell him you have someone who might be interested in working for him."

He shook his head. "I don't think so."

"Why not? Could be a lot of upside for you. And . . . I need the work, my friend. I don't know what I'm going to do here without it."

He sighed. "Was life in the Philippines really so bad?"

I considered that. "Did you read about what happened on Pata Island last year?"

What had happened was a massacre of over a hundred Philippine army soldiers by guerrillas—guerrillas I had helped train.

"Of course."

"That debacle led to a lot of pressure, and eventually someone gave me up."

"Who?"

"It doesn't matter. I handled it. What matters is that I lost my anonymity. I can't go back."

None of that was untrue. But the aftermath of the Pata massacre was really more an excuse than a reason. For months, I'd been getting restless, the unspoiled tropical paradise of the southern Philippines coming to feel like a timeout, a purgatory. The danger inherent in my work seemed no match for a growing ennui. And while I supposed it was sad in some ways that coming back to Tokyo to work for Miyamoto felt like a purpose by comparison, it did.

We sat in silence for a moment. Then he said, "How do I reach you?"

The mention of logistics felt like progress. "Remember the answering service we were using last time?"

He nodded.

"I kept it. Same number. Same name. You can reach me there. I'll check in at least twice a day."

He nodded again, but his expression was still reluctant. Another long moment went by. Finally, he said, "I want to help. And you know I will. But this man . . . I'm concerned you're underestimating him."

"Is it possible you're underestimating me?"

"It's possible. But one of the advantages of being as old as I am is that age enables greater clarity about the true motivations of one's youth. Things we once told ourselves were matters of principle are revealed instead to have been driven by pride. Risks we judged as the product of reason, we later understand were in fact an outgrowth of insecurity."

I smiled. "Are you saying I'm insecure?"

He didn't return the smile. "All young men are insecure."

He might have added that all young men are stupid. Which would have explained why I didn't listen to him.

"Can you set up a meeting?" I asked.

He sighed. "I suppose I could tell Victor I know a capable young man looking for work for which he is well suited."

"Then do it. And obviously, my real interest is between you and me. We don't know where Victor has been getting his intel. But if there's a leak in the LDP . . ."

"Please don't worry. If I discussed this with any of my superiors, they would immediately instruct me to stand down. And probably to see a psychiatrist, as well."

"Well, at least they care about your mental health."

"The point is, if you move against Victor . . . it has to be without my knowledge. And presented to my superiors only after the fact. A kind of fait accompli."

"Would I still get paid?"

"I would of course find a way to make sure you were."

"Okay, it's a deal. Anyway, I just want to assess this guy. If he's as formidable as you say, I'll walk away. If I see an opportunity to break up a monopoly, I'll take it. What's the worst that could happen?"

chapter two

Two days later, I was standing in the entranceway of a nonde-
script, four-story concrete building in Kasumigaseki, one of
the city's government districts, announcing my name to a security
camera and intercom. After a moment, a buzzer sounded. I took this
to be my invitation and went inside, where I encountered one small
lobby and two large Japanese gangsters. I raised my eyebrows and
looked at them.

"Stay there," one of them said.

I glanced around. A tired-looking, mustard-colored upholstered
couch. Two similar chairs. No receptionist. Well, other than the two
gangsters. The stairs were blocked by a ceiling-high sliding metal gate,
no doubt in contravention of city fire codes. So other than an exte-
rior fire escape, which I assumed would also be blocked, the elevator
was the only access to the upper floors. Victor liked his security, it
seemed, and was more concerned with manmade threats than with
natural disasters.

The elevator doors opened. Two more Japanese gangsters and a
sour-looking, heavily muscled white guy in a gray suit got out. The
two new gangsters frisked me while the white guy watched. When they
were satisfied I wasn't carrying a weapon, they nodded to the white
guy, who inclined his head toward the elevator. Okay, the two Japanese
were labor; the white guy was management. I got on, the three of them
right behind me.

We got out on the fourth floor and walked down a short corridor, the white guy in front of me, the two gangsters behind. At the end of the corridor, we came to a door with another camera and intercom outside it. Someone must have been watching from inside, because the door opened. We filed in, past another gangster, who closed the door behind us.

The room was as much of a mustard-colored afterthought as the lobby. Four upholstered chairs. A glass coffee table. An end table with a metal lamp on it. Soot-covered windows with a view of the elevated-toll-road traffic outside.

In one of the chairs was another large white guy, a shiny scalp showing through the dark razor stubble on his head. He remained sitting as I was brought in, not even looking up. Instead, he concentrated on a persimmon he was quartering with a small knife. The other men watched him, apparently afraid to do anything to get his attention, not even a cough or cleared throat. If the other white guy had been management, this was clearly the boss. Victor.

He looked about forty, with broad Slavic cheeks and pale skin. Apart from his shaved head, his most distinguishing characteristic was his solidness. I estimated a little short of six feet and in the neighborhood of two hundred thirty pounds. He wasn't muscled like a weightlifter, and in fact he was thick around the middle. But then, all of him was thick—his arms, his chest, his neck, even his fingers. His nose was flattened like a boxer's, and there was a heavy scar running from the left side of his forehead down to his cheek. Whatever had caused it, he was lucky not to have lost an eye when it happened.

He was wearing a lime-green polo shirt, beige slacks, and a heavy gold chain around his neck. Markedly casual attire in eighties Tokyo, where an ill-fitting suit was the uniform of the day. Maybe with his mixed-Slavic features, he figured why bother trying to blend? Or maybe it was a calculated insult to the existing order. A declaration that he played by his own rules.

Or no rules at all.

He said nothing, continuing to cut his persimmon in lieu of a greeting. I assumed the ostentatious fruit carving was theater, intended to demonstrate power over me, if only the symbolic power to make me wait. I had learned the routine from McGraw, who had taught me a lot before I killed him.

Or maybe he just wanted me to know he was good with a knife. But I'd spent a decade in the Philippines, where I worked with men who had grown up with knives, who from not much past infancy were drilled in *kali*, and who had more real-world experience killing with knives than any sane person would ever want. If Victor hoped to impress me with his edged-weapon skills, he was going to have to do more than take on a piece of fruit.

Only after he had cut each persimmon quarter into several smaller pieces did Victor finally ease back in his chair and look at me. His eyes were my first glimpse of the Asian ancestry Miyamoto had mentioned. They were muddy brown, with prominent epicanthic folds. His nose, too, in addition to having been flattened and spread, most likely by repeated breaks, was set low enough on his face to suggest Asian parentage.

"So you are famous tough guy," he said in Russian-accented English, looking me up and down. "Former US Special Forces. MACV-SOG. Many, many confirmed kills."

MACV-SOG was the Military Assistance Command, Vietnam–Studies and Observations Group. A deliberately bland name for a highly classified joint Special Forces–CIA task force that operated in North Vietnam, Laos, and Cambodia, and of which I'd been a part. Miyamoto must have briefed Victor on my credentials.

I waited a beat before saying, "Not famous, no."

He stopped his up-and-down look and held my gaze. "You are, what, now contradicting me?"

"Just telling you I'm not famous. I wouldn't be much use to you if I were."

"And this is what you want? To be of use to me?"

"I need work."

"What kind of work?"

"The kind I'm suited for."

He looked left and right at his men, and then started laughing. His men chuckled nervously, apparently unsure of whether it would be appropriate to join him in his mirth.

"This guy," he said, still laughing. "Listen to this guy. He answers in riddles."

I was getting irritated. "If you don't like the answers," I said evenly, "maybe the problem is the questions."

This only made him laugh harder. He wagged a finger at me and said, "And funny, too. Funny guy. You know what, funny tough guy? I like you. I think maybe you have balls. You know why I like this?"

I said nothing.

He leaned forward. "I like my men to have balls because it takes balls to do what needs to be done."

He speared a slice of persimmon with the knife, fed it into his mouth without looking, and chewed and swallowed it. "And also because, if they don't do what needs to be done, I cut balls off." He speared and swallowed another persimmon slice, presumably to emphasize his point. And maybe to suggest that he liked to eat balls, as well. Whatever.

"Do you have anything for me?" I said. "Miyamoto thought maybe you did. But if he was wrong, I don't want to waste your time."

He set down the knife, leaned back in his chair, and stared at the ceiling while he tapped his fingertips together as though in profound contemplation. "Anything. Do I have anything. Good question, I think." He leaned forward, then said to the other white guy, "Oleg, bring Kobayashi."

I didn't like the sound of that—it seemed like the setup for a joke Victor was enjoying. The question was, what was he going to do for a punch line?

Victor gestured to one of the empty chairs and smiled. "Sit?"

His teeth were unnaturally white and even. Bridgework, I realized. The scar, the nose, the teeth . . . this guy's face had endured some serious trauma.

I glanced around the room, noting the presence of weapons of convenience—the metal lamp; a Lucite clock; the paring knife, of course. And the coffee table in front of Victor, which I would kick into him to buy myself time to make it to the door.

If it came to that.

A minute later, Oleg returned with a lean Japanese guy in gray slacks and a white dress shirt. His sleeves were rolled up, and the corded muscles of his forearms were covered in yakuza tattoos. He looked at Victor, then at me, then at Victor again, the turns of his head quick and precise, as though he had a tic. Or was jacked on *kakuseizai*—amphetamines.

"Meet Kobayashi," Victor said. "He was soldier with Gokumatsu-gumi, but sadly also he was fuckup. I gave him chance with me anyway, but I think maybe now this was mistake. What do you think, Kobayashi-kun? Do I make mistake giving you chance?"

Kobayashi gave a single quick shake of his head. "No. It was an accident. I can do better. I will do better."

"I give you simple job. Detailed dossier. Photos. All information. And you kill wrong man. This is bad enough, but worse is that right person is still alive. And now being more careful."

Kobayashi's head twitched toward me, then back to Victor. "I'll take care of him. I'll make it right."

"Maybe you will," Victor said. "Or maybe we need new blood." He gestured toward me. "This man Rain-san comes highly recommended. Should I give him your job?"

Kobayashi's head twitched. "No."

"No? You want to keep job?"

Kobayashi nodded.

Victor looked at me. "But you want work, yes?"

I returned his look, trying to see where this was leading. "I told you I do."

He threw up his arms. "But I have only one position available. Right now, this position is Kobayashi's. And he says he wants to keep it."

Kobayashi looked at me, then back at Victor, the movements jerkier now, more nervous. I noticed his hands were shaking slightly.

Victor sighed. "So I guess question is, who wants position more? This you two men must show me."

While I was trying to process that, he added, "Show me *now*."

And while I was trying to process that, too, Kobayashi lunged for the paring knife.

Fuck.

A half dozen micro-thoughts flashed through my mind. That I'd been comforting myself with the unsupported notion that Victor was a buffoon. That Kobayashi had seen this game before, and knew how to play it, while I was still trying to figure it out. That a problem I assumed could be addressed with reason later needed to be solved by instinct *now*.

Kobayashi snatched up the knife and began to turn in my direction. Time slowed down. Hearing faded out. Combat reflexes kicked in.

I spun toward Oleg, grabbed him by the sleeve, and yanked him past me. He tried to twist around, but before he could find his footing, I got hold of the back of his belt and collar and shoved him forward like a lineman hitting a football sled, bellowing a war cry, driving him into Kobayashi. Kobayashi stabbed at me, but Oleg was in the way, and Kobayashi succeeded only in slashing the other man's arm. Oleg screamed something in

Russian and tried to break free, but I kept bulldozing him forward, not giving Kobayashi a chance to regroup or find another angle of attack.

As he backpedaled, Kobayashi tried to reach me with the knife but couldn't get around Oleg, and Oleg, unable to break loose, began grabbing at Kobayashi's knife hand. Somehow he got hold of Kobayashi's wrist, but Kobayashi broke the grip and slashed Oleg across the arm again. Oleg howled and Victor laughed harder and I screamed and kept driving Oleg forward. Kobayashi crashed back into the wall, Oleg's body pinning him in place. He made one last effort to get to me with the knife, but with the wall behind him he couldn't generate speed or power, and as the blade snaked past Oleg's side, I stepped back and blasted my palm into the back of his hand, forcing his wrist inward and past its natural range of movement. He howled, and as his fingers reflexively opened, I swept in with my other hand and snatched away the knife. I shoved Oleg aside, and suddenly there was nothing between Kobayashi and me but a length of sharp steel.

Kobayashi's eyes bulged and he tried to pivot away. I grabbed him by the shirt with my free hand and, bellowing another war cry, drove the blade into his stomach. He screamed and flailed and I thrust my shoulder into his sternum, swept my free arm up under both of his, jammed him back against the wall, and stabbed him in the stomach again, and again, and a half dozen times more. My vision was tinged red and I didn't even know where I was. All that mattered, the only thing that was real, was that I was killing a man who was trying to kill me, the primal consciousness the same in that room as in the war. Kobayashi's shrieks went falsetto and his flailing more spastic but I didn't relent at all.

All at once, I realized I had lost track of my perimeter. I was seeing Kobayashi through tunnel vision, but he was no longer any threat. The threat now, if there was one, was around me.

I released Kobayashi, took a long step forty-five degrees from him, and brought the knife in and my free hand up. I scanned the room for danger, but saw none. Victor was still sitting, slapping his thigh and laughing uproariously. Oleg was cradling his wounded arm. Victor's other men were frozen in place, wide eyed.

I looked back at Kobayashi. He had collapsed and fetaled up, his arms crossed uselessly across his belly. He was panting and bleating, and his feet kicked feebly in place, as though some part of his mind believed he was running away. His shirt had gone crimson, and the carpet around him was dark with his blood.

"Horosho!" Victor cried out, clapping delightedly. *"Ochyen horosho!"*

I had gotten some control over myself, but my vision was still tinged red. I looked at Victor and felt rage surging up. Without warning, he had just thrown me into the ring—not a fighting ring, a combat ring. With a little less experience, or a little less luck, it easily could have been me bleeding out on the floor. And now he was laughing about it.

He stood and walked over to Kobayashi, still laughing. When he reached the downed man, he paused and looked at him for a moment, his laughter slowly subsiding. He blew out several breaths as though trying to compose himself.

He was only ten feet from me. Oleg was injured. The other men looked half in shock. I watched Victor, trying to rein in my rage. I thought I could take him out, and probably the others, as well. But that was just it: it needed to be the product of thought, not emotion. And in that instant, I wasn't sure which was driving me.

"Oh, Kobayashi," Victor said, shaking his head and wiping his eyes. "Kobayashi. So, okay. Giving you chance with me was mistake. You are fuckup! Can you even deny this? Nothing but fuckup."

In response, Kobayashi only twitched and whimpered.

Victor remained still for another moment, looking down at Kobayashi as though in anticipation of a response. Then, with no sign of escalation, no apparent switching of gears, no warning at all, he raised a leg and stomped Kobayashi full force in the side of the face. Kobayashi screamed and his arms flew up to protect his head, and Victor, laughing now, stomped his face again, and again and again, adjusting his position from time to time to ensure the stomps were landing where he wanted. Kobayashi's efforts to protect himself grew more feeble, his twitching diminishing, his screams fading to moans. Finally, his arms flopped open and he stopped moving entirely, but this seemed only to encourage Victor, who stopped laughing and continued the vicious stomping with even greater determination, like someone whose life depended on smashing through a basement storage door.

I looked at Oleg and the other men. All were wide eyed, and had gone pale. I'd seen enough petrified faces in the war to recognize the look here. These men were terrified of Victor. Obviously with reason.

I'd never experienced anything quite like this. The rapturous joy this man obviously experienced from killing at such intimate distance. The instantaneous transition from buffoonery to savagery. The incongruity, the sheer abnormality and unexpectedness of his behavior. It didn't terrify me. But it confused me. It threw off my confidence in my understanding of the enemy, the environment, and my ability to manage both.

In retrospect, the opportunity had been there. At that moment, I could have—should have—ended him. But also, at that moment, I was gripped with too many doubts to do so.

Finally, Victor stopped. He stood over Kobayashi for a moment, panting from exertion. Kobayashi's face was an unrecognizable ruin of blood and bone and brain.

Victor looked up as though remembering there were other people in the room. "You believe this guy?" he said, glancing down at Kobayashi. "Always he makes a mess. And look at this one! Biggest mess yet! But also last one, yes?" He laughed as though he'd just said the funniest thing of all time.

He walked back to his chair and collapsed into it, leaving a trail of bloody footprints along the way. "Oleg," he said. "Call doctor. Get arm taken care of. We don't want blood all over the place, do we?" He laughed again. "And get couple more guys in here to get rid of mess."

Oleg nodded and walked out, his face still ashen. The other men remained rooted in place, plainly unsure of what to do and afraid that, whatever they did, it might be the wrong thing.

Victor sighed. "Congratulations, Mr. Rain. You're hired."

I said nothing. I was pretty sure the danger had passed—or the immediate danger, at any rate—but I wasn't ready to put down the knife regardless. There was one less man in the room now, too. I'd missed one moment, but maybe this was another one.

"What are you going to do?" Victor said. "You want to stab me? Go ahead, try. You wouldn't be the first. You won't be the last."

He was unarmed. And sitting. I had a knife. I was paralyzed between the urge to do it, and the fear that I was overlooking something.

"Good. I like this. Not just funny. Not just balls. Also smart. Only stupid man would try to kill me now, without first hearing about job he's hired to do."

Was he reading me right? Was he deliberately reinforcing, or even planting, the notion that no move was now the safe move?

It didn't matter. What mattered was that all at once, the notion of working for, with, or anywhere near this guy seemed like an extremely bad idea.

"You're right," I said. "I haven't heard anything about a job. And even if I had, you haven't hired me. Because I haven't accepted."

A bit of the good humor disappeared from Victor's expression. "No, you did accept. I asked who wanted job more, you or Kobayashi. You answered this. Very persuasive answer, too, congratulations to you, my friend. But now Kobayashi is gone. Now you take his place. This is not negotiation. This is reality. Money is good. Fringe benefits also good. You like very much. But don't say no again to me. Not after you say yes. Otherwise, I think you are unreliable guy. Like Kobayashi. And man who recommends you, too. Miyamoto. He sends you here for work, to me this is guarantee of you. If you turn out to be unreliable guy, then so is Miyamoto."

Oleg returned with two more Japanese gangsters, one of whom was carrying a large roll of contractor's plastic sheeting and a roll of duct tape. When they saw what was left of Kobayashi, one of them turned away. The one with the plastic and tape managed not to, but his face blanched and he had to clench his jaw.

"What is problem?" Victor said. "Go ahead. Clean up mess. And maybe new carpet, too, yes? What do you think, maybe red this time is better." He looked at me pointedly. "In case anyone else turns out to be unreliable guy."

chapter
three

After leaving Victor's office, I did a long SDR—a surveillance detection run, tradecraft I'd learned from McGraw. I didn't know how large Victor's organization was, the level of resources he could bring to bear, how far he might go if he decided I posed a threat. What I did know was that he had spooked me.

For the moment, of course, there was no reason for him to come after me—if he'd wanted me dead, he could have done me there in his office, and had his men carry me out in plastic sheeting alongside Kobayashi. But the notion of a good SDR was comforting. Before missions in Vietnam, I had learned to steady my nerves by checking my gear. An SDR, it seemed, was the urban equivalent. It was cheaper than a drink, and more effective, too.

When I was satisfied I was alone and began to feel a little calmer, I found a bench in Hibiya Park and opened the file Victor had given me before I'd left.

The target was named Koji Sugihara, an LDP Diet member. There was a work address, a home address, and a newspaper clipping from ten years earlier that included a photo of Sugihara, tall for a Japanese, posing with some students from the University of Tokyo the article described as "the future of Japanese government."

A work address, a home address, an old newspaper photo. Not the most complete dossier I'd ever seen, but that was okay. The file was usually only a start, even when the contents were as top grade as McGraw's.

The file I really wanted was one on Victor. I had to learn more about him. At the moment, what I knew was all jumbled and impressionistic. I started trying to sort it out.

It wasn't something I was excessively proud of, but I did find a certain amount of grim satisfaction in how well I could handle violence, which for most humans presents the most toxic, traumatizing, paralyzing environment a person can be faced with. I had killed countless Vietcong and NVA regulars who were doing everything in their power to do the same to me. I had outmaneuvered the son of the most powerful yakuza in Tokyo, a guy who had earned the sobriquet "Mad Dog," picking off his soldiers one by one as they tried to hunt me down. I had spent a lifetime learning and implementing the lessons of guerrilla warfare—first, as a half-breed kid bullied in Japan and in the working-class American town my mother brought me to after my father had died; then in Vietnam; and then again, most recently, in the Philippines. I was good at violence. Exceptionally good. Exceptionally unfazed by it. There's a cost to that kind of aptitude, and maybe the cost isn't worth it. But for the moment, the cost wasn't the point. The point was, I was good.

And yet, I'd never encountered anything like Victor. The closest analogue was my blood brother, Jimmy "Crazy Jake" Calhoun, who more than anyone I'd ever known was capable of taking a life without compunction or regret. But there was a stillness in Jimmy's approach, a focus, a professionalism. No matter how much satisfaction he found in war and killing, no matter how addicted he was to the high of combat, he never found outright joy in gratuitous butchery. Even at Cu Lai, where we had lost control and massacred civilians, there had been more a "get it over with" aspect to Jimmy's actions than what I would classify as joy or delight.

Jimmy, I knew, was what the army had classified in World War II as an *aggressive psychopath*—a man who needed no particular conditioning to overcome an innate reluctance to kill, and no particular comforting afterward. He could just do it. Historically, about two percent of military men have fit this category, and the majority of killing in war has been their handiwork. But because they pose no danger to society outside of war, maybe the term *psychopath* isn't really suitable. Or maybe I just didn't like it because I'd been similarly classified myself.

What I did know was that Victor was different. If the term *psychopath* had any real application, I thought it was what I had witnessed in his office. I didn't know what to make of the behavior beyond that. But it had unnerved me.

I decided that was all right. The real problem would have been if it *hadn't* unnerved me. When you recognize something is dangerous, it automatically becomes less dangerous. So recognizing Victor's nature was something. But it wasn't much. What I needed, and fast, was intel. And that meant Miyamoto.

I called him from a payphone and asked if he could come to the same place we had met last time, in one hour. I didn't want to say too much on the phone. Paranoid, maybe, but with someone like Victor, I decided paranoid was practical.

An hour later, we were sitting on a bench in one of the shady sections of Hamarikyu, away from the teahouse and other attractions.

"You might have been right," I told him. "Victor is dangerous."

"You've changed your mind, then? About trying to remove him?"

I smiled. "Would that be a welcome development for you? Or unwelcome?"

He didn't return the smile. "My people would of course be delighted to see him go. But that is of little interest to me compared to your well-being."

"Thank you for that," I said, strangely moved by the sentiment. "But I think we're a little past the point where changing my mind is even an option." I told him what had happened to Kobayashi, and how Victor had decided on the spot that I had taken Kobayashi's place.

By the time I was done, he looked grimmer than I'd ever seen him. "I wish you had listened to me," he said. "But . . . it doesn't matter now."

"I wish I had listened to you, too."

But even as I said the words, I realized they weren't entirely true. I'd gotten bored in the Philippines. And whatever else Victor might be, he wasn't boring. A part of me was excited by . . . what, the challenge? The distraction? The danger? Was I actually glad things had turned out this way, so I could involve myself in this thing while telling myself it wasn't my choice?

Exactly, I could imagine Crazy Jake saying. *And nothing to be ashamed of, either. You like the game, John-John. You're good at it. One of the best, maybe. But you can't be the best at a game you won't play.*

I pushed aside the thoughts because they were subordinate to the matter at hand.

Or maybe because I didn't like the implications.

"What will you do?" he asked.

"Well, I think I'd better do the job, don't you?"

"Not at all. I would instead recommend that you leave Tokyo. Disappear again. You've done it before."

I had hoped not to burden him with Victor's threat, but I was beginning to see that was going to be difficult.

"I'm afraid it's a little more . . . complicated than that," I said.

He paled a little, as though he already understood, or at least sensed it. "What do you mean?"

I told him what Victor had said about Miyamoto being my guarantor. And how if I didn't do what Victor wanted, he would conclude Miyamoto was "unreliable guy."

When I was done, he had paled a lot more. "I'm sorry," I said. "I just . . . I hadn't imagined anything like that. I should have. But I didn't."

He shook his head. "It's not your fault. It's mine. You didn't know Victor. I do. I should have seen that he would do something like this."

27

"You told me it was a bad idea. And you were right, even if you didn't foresee all the specifics. I'm the one who insisted. And I'm the one who's going to fix it."

He nodded—in relief, it seemed, as much as agreement. "How?"

"Well, for starters, by following up on this guy Victor wants dead. That ought to buy us some time, at least."

"Who is he?"

"You don't know?"

He frowned. "At the moment, there are no outstanding contracts with Victor. At least none that I know of."

I hadn't seen that coming. The twist worried me, along with the fact that I'd missed it. "Shit, I just assumed . . . but that was dumb of me. You're not Victor's only client."

"Not if your description of his monopolizing violence in the Tokyo underworld is correct, no."

"Well, then I better not tell you more. It could just put you more at risk."

He laughed. "Rain-san. Is that really possible at the moment?"

I didn't care to admit it, but he had a point. "All right," I said. "The guy I'm supposed to take out is LDP. Which is part of why I assumed the contract went through you. His name is Sugihara. Koji Sugihara. Do you know him?"

"Of course I know him. He controls patronage for the Fukuda faction."

"Well, who would want him dead?"

"A man of his power? Many people. A Fukuda faction member who feels Sugihara has overlooked him. A rival, hoping to take over his network. Another faction, hoping to weaken Fukuda. But . . . to go after a man in his position is very bold. Unprecedented. Something like this would never be sanctioned by my superiors."

"Are you sure? Maybe whoever wants it knew there would be problems if it were handled through the usual channels. So they went around you. Directly to Victor."

He nodded. "Yes. I suppose this is possible."

"Victor said Kobayashi killed the wrong man. That mean anything to you?"

"The wrong man? No."

"No other Diet members killed recently? Or even just died?"

"No. None."

"Because Victor said that, as a result of Kobayashi's screwup, Sugihara had upped his security."

"I can look into that. But no matter what, this is bad business. It's one thing to pound down the nail that sticks out. This has to be done from time to time, and besides, is not the nail's own behavior to blame? But as far as I know, Sugihara has done nothing wrong. He plays by the rules."

"Maybe he's played too well."

"Yes, that is my point. Punishing a cheater preserves the system. Punishing a winner undermines it."

"Maybe that's what someone wants."

"Who?"

"Victor himself, maybe. I don't know."

He shook his head. "I don't like this."

It wouldn't have been productive to tell him that I didn't care one way or the other. Instead, I focused on the aspect we could agree on. "Better Sugihara than you, my friend."

"Yes, if it comes to that."

"Then let's make sure it doesn't."

"What do you propose?"

"Tell me what you know about him."

He sighed. "I can do better than that."

"Yeah?"

"The grandson of the minister of agriculture will be married this weekend at the Hotel Okura. Sugihara will be there."

I knew the Okura. Opened in 1962, just ahead of the Olympics that marked the end of the postwar era and the beginning of Japan's economic rise, it was the top hotel in Tokyo, frequented by celebrities, captains of industry, and heads of state. For a government official hoping to demonstrate his power and success while networking with the who's-who guests, nothing else would do.

"All right," I said. "But how do I get in? I'm guessing there's going to be security. Probably a lot of it. I can't just hang around in the lobby."

"No, I think you'd do better with an invitation."

"And how do I get that?"

"I'm going to give you mine."

I shook my head, annoyed that I was missing something. "Don't you need to be there? I mean, it might look suspicious if—"

"Don't worry about me. I'll be there."

"How are you going to get in?"

"The ceremony itself will be small, held in the hotel chapel, but there will be almost a thousand guests at the reception afterward. I'll simply tell the security people checking the invitations that I seem to have misplaced mine. I'm sure we'll be able to find people to vouch for me."

"All right. But I'm not going to do it there. You'd be too much the focus—the guy who said he lost his invitation. We don't want to take that chance."

"But how long do you have before Victor concludes you are unreliable?"

"I don't know. But I'm not doing this half-assed. The Okura will be just an opportunity to observe. Maybe to follow, see if a secondary opportunity presents itself. Most of all, to buy some time. Victor told me he wants progress reports. No fewer than once a day, until I've taken care of business. If I go through the motions on Sugihara, I'll have reasons to meet with Victor. I'll be better prepared than I was the first time. I'll find an opening."

I considered for a moment, then added, "I think you should start being a little more careful. Just as a precaution. Do you know how to tell if you're being followed?"

"It isn't something that's traditionally been a concern, no."

"Look, it's not just for you. It's for me, too."

He shook his head as though perplexed, and I went on. "I'm not easy to get to. No fixed address right now, and I know how to watch my back. If I were Victor trying to get to me, I'd start with the guy who made the recommendation."

He nodded slowly. "I see your point."

"Don't worry. None of it is complicated. Mostly just common sense. Along the lines of, 'If I were trying to follow me, what would make it more difficult?' That kind of thing. Besides, after all you've taught me? It would be nice to be able to teach you something in return."

He gave me a wan smile. "I have a feeling what you propose to teach me will have considerably greater value."

I returned the smile. "I wouldn't go that far. *Nen* hasn't just changed my life. It's probably saved it. But yeah, knowing how to spot surveillance, or an ambush, if it comes to that, wouldn't be the worst thing right now. I'll teach you the fundamentals, but then you have to practice, too, okay? Think of it as a game. That's always the best way to learn."

"Not a very fun game, I fear."

"No," I said. "But it beats the alternatives."

chapter
four

Two days later, I stepped out of a black cab in front of the Hotel Okura, and paused for a moment to review the unfamiliar surroundings. Dozens of other guests were arriving at the same time, some turning over their Mercedes sedans to swarming valets in hotel jackets and caps, others released by uniformed drivers rushing around to open back doors, the men in tuxedos, the women in the latest Paris couture or formal kimonos.

I strolled toward the entrance, my rented tuxedo as comfortable as a straitjacket, my hair slicked back, my posture military-straight. I reminded myself that I belonged here, I was invited. The secret to making a cover work, McGraw had taught me, was to believe it, to *feel* it. Here, though, McGraw's dictum was going to be something of a challenge, because there was only so much I could do to create and inhabit the role. I was too young to pass myself off as one of the government grandees, and, even if age weren't a problem in that regard, a moment's conversation with any of my supposed peers would have instantly ended the subterfuge.

So I had decided instead that I was a childhood friend of the groom. Miyamoto had told me the groom's father, himself a bureaucrat with the foreign ministry, had been posted overseas while his children were young—London, Riyadh, Accra, and other far-flung locales— taking the family with him as he was transferred from one continent to another. To the extent the groom had stayed in touch with any childhood friends, therefore, it was unlikely any of the friends would have closed the loop with each other. I'd do what I could to avoid conversation, but if avoidance failed, I'd ask a lot, reveal little, and use whatever I learned to tailor a background unlikely to raise red flags. I tried to think of it as a game, as I had advised Miyamoto with regard to countersurveillance. But the tuxedo was stiff, and the hair gel felt fake, and the rented shoes were just tight enough to make me aware of how eager I'd be to get them off by the end of the evening.

But shit, was my awkwardness really a problem? Everyone around me looked to the manor born, yes, but how many of those tuxedos were rented, how many of the stunning dresses and sumptuous kimonos had been borrowed from a sister or mother or aunt? Many of these people, maybe most, must have been feeling as uncomfortable and pretentious as I was. Which meant feeling that way would only make me blend that much better.

The thought settled me a little. I flowed with the crowd through the entrance, flanked by doormen in stiff caps and jackets with embroidered epaulettes, kimonoed hostesses bowing and greeting us *"Irasshaimase"*— Welcome—in unison as we passed.

Getting past the doormen outside the banquet hall was almost comically easy. Faced with an inflow of hundreds of people, they were barely glancing at invitations, let alone asking for identification. It interested me that they seemed to be reacting more to patterns—the clothes, the posture, the sense of purpose—than to the invitations that should have been their focus. It reminded me of an article I'd once read, about an experiment some social scientist had done. He'd put a person in a room with two strings hanging from the ceiling. The task was to get ahold of both, but the strings were too far apart for the person to reach one while holding the other. There was a hammer in the room, though, which a few clever subjects realized they could tie to one of the strings, push away, and catch on the backswing while holding the other string. The thing was, subjects who first used the hammer for a few simple tasks involving nails suffered a diminished ability to realize that the hammer could be used as something else—as a weight to make a pendulum, for example. Context had reinforced familiarity, and familiarity had blinded them to new possibilities. Watching the reactions of the doormen, I thought this was a principle I might learn to exploit.

Pondering peripheral matters reaffirmed my conviction that I wasn't going to kill Sugihara tonight. And not just because I wanted to keep Miyamoto clear of it. The person I really wanted to kill was Victor, and to that end, going slowly on Sugihara seemed tactically sound. Maybe while I dragged things out with the one, I'd get a chance at the other. If I was wrong, I could always kill Sugihara later. But I didn't really want to. Why would I? I'd promised myself ten years ago I would never be someone's employee again. And Victor had told me I'd be paid five thousand dollars for the hit—presumably a tenth of his monopolistic finder's fee. I was doing all the work, and he was going to keep ninety percent of the profits. It was enough to put a young contract killer off capitalism forever.

For a while, I drifted along at the edges of the massive banquet hall as it grew increasingly crowded, the sounds of conversation and laughter loud but not unduly so, the twenty-foot ceiling, thick carpet, and silk-screened walls combining to keep the din tolerable. I wasn't hungry, but made sure to take a few samples of finger food from the servers working the room, barely noticing what I ate. The space was enormous—the size of a football field, at least—and with only the one old newspaper photo to go on, spotting and confirming Sugihara amid the dense, shifting crowds was going to take some luck. At one point, I caught a glimpse of Miyamoto, wearing a black bowtie in lieu of the more febrile designs he ordinarily favored, but per the plan we ignored each other.

An hour passed. The good news was, I had managed not to talk to anyone, so my story hadn't been tested. The bad news was, though I saw several men who might have been Sugihara, I couldn't be sure. The single photograph, the intervening decade, and the uncharacteristic and interchangeable tuxedos . . . it was all making my job harder. That was fine, up to a point. I could explain my difficulties to Victor, and tell him it was worth going slowly because we had to be certain, following Kobayashi's failure. But it was bothering me that I couldn't accomplish something as simple as ID'ing a target. It was making me feel like as much of a fuckup as Kobayashi. And Kobayashi's story hadn't ended particularly well.

So I must have been scanning the room pretty hard when I heard a voice coming from right alongside me—a woman's voice, speaking Italian-accented English. "Who are you looking for?"

I nearly jumped, managing through some vestigial social instinct not to leap back and get my hands up. An absolutely stunning brunette was looking at me with a friendly smile, her eyebrows raised quizzically. "Sorry," she said. "I didn't mean to startle you."

I don't like anyone ghosting up on me, and ordinarily I'm sufficiently aware of my surroundings to prevent it. But in my search for Sugihara, I'd gotten tunnel vision. I was lucky she seemed harmless. Letting someone less well-inclined flank you like that can easily be the last mistake you ever make.

"No, it's okay," I said, trying to shake off my discomfiture. "I was just . . . people watching. Lost in thought."

She was wearing a black gown, I noticed, cut maddeningly low in front with thin straps across the shoulders, and though I was concentrating on her face, I was aware of a long neck, delicate clavicles, and the kind of décolletage wars have been fought over.

"You didn't look lost," she said, the friendly smile widening slightly into something better described as dazzling. "You looked . . . mmm, how to say, intent."

Damn. She'd ghosted up on me, and before that, she'd been assessing me—and assessing me well, I had to admit. It made me feel foolish, like the amateur McGraw had always accused me of being.

I laughed uncomfortably, trying to focus on her face, which was distracting enough, and not glance down at her body. She had beautiful cheekbones, a fine, straight nose, a tiny cleft in her chin, and absurdly sensuous lips. Her hair was a luxurious jet black, wound tightly and pinned off her neck in a way that made me wonder instantly what it would look like cascading down her back. She was wearing a multi-tiered pearl choker, long shimmering earrings, and a lot of eyeliner. I'd never seen a woman as beautiful, voluptuous, and glamorous, at least not in person, and in addition to the way she had initially spooked me, just her raw physical presence was throwing me off whatever game I might otherwise have had.

"I don't know about that," I managed to say. "Were you watching me or something?"

She took a sip of champagne from a glass she was holding. It was the first time I'd noticed her hands. Again, stupid. She wasn't a threat—at least, not an immediate physical one—but hands are what hold weapons, and only an idiot fails to automatically check them, however discreetly. Well, I'd been distracted, obviously. But that's never a good excuse for being dead.

A massive diamond ring encircled her fourth finger. Which made sense. She was so beautiful I couldn't be sure of her age, but she was older than I was—Forty? Forty-five?—and, a decade or two earlier, she must have been inundated with proposals. But who was her husband? I hadn't seen many foreign guests, though maybe I hadn't noticed because I was looking for Sugihara—the same way I had likely managed to overlook her, because she was anything but overlookable. There was another lesson there, I thought distantly, about pattern recognition and distraction.

She smiled again—not coyly, I noted with a surprising pang of disappointment, but more the way you might smile at something awkwardly cute, like a puppy. "Maybe a little," she said. "You looked so earnest."

"Oh. Well, I don't know many people here. Friend of the groom's, from a long time ago."

"From America?"

I was immediately on guard, and looking for a way to avoid a detailed conversation. "Why?"

"Your English, of course. You sound American." She looked at me more closely. "You're not fully Japanese, are you?"

I tried not to be irritated, tried not to slot her doubtless innocent and perfectly reasonable question into a lifetime of slights and rejection. "I'm fully Japanese," I said in Japanese, my annoyance cutting through the spell of her beauty. "And also fully something else. A person doesn't have to be only part this and part that."

She frowned ever so slightly—not in incomprehension, I thought, but as though I had finally said something interesting. As she did so, I noticed a small network of wrinkles around her eyes. Forty-five, I decided. Somehow the wrinkles made her even more beautiful, perhaps because they suggested the beauty's impermanence. *Tsukanoma no koto* is how it's said in Japanese. The fleetingness of things.

"You're right," she said in Japanese. "That's a nicer way of putting it. After all, when you acquire a new language, you grow a new soul. But the previous soul isn't, mmm, diminished, yes? If anything, it grows."

I liked that I'd said something she agreed with. And those little *mmm* pauses, while she searched for a word, were charming. "You sound like you would know," I said, switching back to English. "Where are you from?"

"*Roma*, of course, could you not tell?"

"I thought Italian, but I couldn't have specified Rome."

"You didn't know from the style? That you can tell instantly. The arrogance and impatience it takes longer to appreciate."

I laughed. Hoping to keep the focus on her and not on me, I said, "Who are you here with?"

"My husband. He gets invited to so many of these functions and it would be rude if his wife didn't join him."

"Does that mean you would prefer not to be here?"

She gave me the intriguing frown again. "Did I say that?"

"No. I asked if you meant it."

She laughed. "Let's just say it's an unexpected pleasure to meet someone who is fully more than one thing."

She glanced past me and raised her glass, then finished her champagne. A second later, a waiter appeared with a tray. She placed the empty glass on the tray and took two new ones, handing one to me as the waiter moved off.

"Salute," she said, raising her glass.

We touched glasses. *"Alla tua,"* I said.

She cocked her head. *"Parli italiano?"*

I took a sip of champagne. "Only English and Japanese. But I can toast someone's health all over the world. Order a beer, too."

She looked me up and down. "You seem young to be so accomplished."

I couldn't tell if she was teasing me, or flirting with me. Or maybe it was both.

"I was thinking the same about you."

She laughed. "What do I call you?"

I wasn't sure if it was an English-as-a-second-language thing, or if by asking what to call me rather than for my name she was implying I might be working a cover.

But maybe I was overthinking it. Maybe I was just buzzed on her beauty. *Mabushii* is the Japanese word for it—glaring or dazzling like the sun, but used more commonly to describe the effect of a woman like this one.

I sipped my champagne. "John. And you?"

"Maria." She held up her glass and we toasted again.

"Well, John," she said, taking a sip, "if you want to blend at mini–affairs of state like this one, you have to know the little things."

I wasn't sure what she was talking about, but it made me uneasy. "The little things?"

"Yes, of course. Such as, you hold a champagne flute by the stem, not the bowl. This keeps the champagne cold."

"Oh," I said, looking down at the way I was holding the glass—the flute—as though I needed visual confirmation. "I didn't know."

She shrugged. "It's the kind of thing you don't know unless somebody teaches you."

I adjusted my grip. "Thanks for telling me, then. Is there anything else?"

"Well, since you mention, your tie is too wide for your lapels, and in any event a proper tuxedo never has notched lapels, only shawl or peak. And no flaps on the pocket or vent in back. Or cuffs on the pants. But I wouldn't worry too much about any of that. If you look at the way these other men are dressed, you fit in very nicely."

"Thanks. I think."

She laughed. "You asked."

I was more intrigued than irritated. "You remind me of a friend of mine, who also takes note of little things that aren't really little. He calls it *nen*—mindfulness. What else should I be aware of?"

"Ah, well, you seem a little stiff. A little too, mmm, eager. Not so much like a normal bored wedding guest. I'm guessing there's some regulator here, or banker, or someone you hope to ask about a job, and you're trying to find him. That maybe this is why you accepted a wedding invitation from a friend from a long time ago."

I was relieved she had constructed a plausible reason for my awkwardness. It reminded me of another of McGraw's lessons: sometimes it pays to confess to the commission of a lesser crime to conceal the commission of a greater one.

"That's pretty cynical," I said, deliberately not denying it.

"Am I right, though?"

"Well, not wrong, exactly. I've been away for a few years and just got back. I guess you could say I'm figuring out my next move." To change the subject, I added, "Anything else you noticed?"

"Well, I haven't seen you talking to anyone else the whole evening. For most people at a party, this would be unendurable. They would find some way to make small talk even with strangers, to prevent the embarrassment of being seen alone."

I raised an eyebrow. "So . . . you've been watching me for a while."

She laughed. "Long enough. You don't mind being alone?"

In fact, I preferred it, but not if it was going to draw attention when I was supposed to be operational. Although attention like hers was something I sensed I could probably live with.

"Not usually, no. But this is a nice change of pace. Was I doing anything else wrong?"

She smiled. "Not that I noticed."

"Well, that's good. Since you seem to notice a lot."

"Only when I'm interested."

Okay, she had to be flirting with me. Though I was aware I should discount the conclusion because I wanted a lot to believe it.

I took a sip of champagne from my properly held flute. "What else interests you?"

"Ah, so many things." She turned and gazed out at the room. "Have you noticed the lamps?"

I followed her gaze and took in the scores of long vertical lamps hanging from the ceiling across the great room. "Not particularly, no."

"Well, then, you are missing something important. Each lamp is a hexahedron. The shape is inspired by gems discovered in burial mounds from the Kofun period, when they were used in necklaces. Do you see how each is only slightly lit, diffusing light through the paper screens?"

I was intrigued that she would know something like this, and notice it, though I wasn't sure I agreed it was important. It also seemed noteworthy that she had so smoothly used a word like "hexahedron." Several times earlier in the conversation, she had paused for one of those delightful *mmm* moments while recalling an unfamiliar word. She must have known this subject quite well.

"Now that you mention it," I said, "I do."

"When you go through the lobby later, be sure to look at the walls. The light-brown stone is called *Tako Ishi*. It's found only in Gunma Prefecture, and the designers of the hotel chose it not just for its unusual color, but also because the afternoon sun creates delicate shadows on its uneven surfaces. The shadows are said to resemble the dark brushstrokes of old Chinese landscape paintings."

I was beginning to feel slightly in awe of her. "Who are you?"

"Just a person who tries to appreciate her surroundings."

"I'd say you're doing more than trying."

She smiled and took a sip of champagne. "Well, life isn't only about the present. Everything in our present also is connected to the past, and hints at the future."

I was aware I was feeling quite buzzed, whether from the champagne, or her, or both. "How do you know all this?"

"I make it a point to know it."

"Yes, but you're a foreigner."

"Ah, but the things we're born to are often the very things we most take for granted. Sometimes it takes a foreigner to appreciate what locals can't see. Isn't this why it took a Frenchman to write *Democracy in America*? No American could have had such perspective on his own culture."

"I'm sure that's true, but even so, I think you must be . . . exceptional. Do you study these things?"

"Of course."

One of the hotel's discreet waiters, seeing that we were nearly done with our champagne, appeared like a magic trick, refreshed our glasses, and moved off. As he did so, I glanced around and saw Miyamoto watching from a distance. I couldn't be sure, but I thought he looked displeased. Did he think I was more interested in this woman than I was in spotting Sugihara? If so, he wasn't completely wrong. I needed to extricate myself. But I didn't want to.

"But why?" I said, sipping the champagne. "Are you a professor or something?"

She laughed. "I think you're trying to flatter me, John."

"I'm glad if I did, but I wasn't trying to."

She shook her head as though dismissing a silly notion. "I'm not a professor. I just do a little work for one of the local museums."

"What kind of work?"

"Oh, are you interested in museum work?"

"Not usually, but I think it's growing on me."

She laughed.

"Why did you come over to me?" I asked. "Why really."

She sipped the champagne. "Maybe I was bored. Is that a crime?"

"No. But I'll keep it a secret."

"Oh, are you good at keeping secrets?"

Suddenly, the tuxedo wasn't the only thing feeling stiff. I wanted to volley back, but had no idea how.

A man's voice just behind me said in Japanese, "Ah, there you are."

I turned, and saw a distinguished-looking Japanese man, his black hair steel gray at the temples, walk up and touch Maria's arm. "I was looking for you."

"Ah, I'm sorry," Maria said in Japanese. "I met a fellow aficionado of Japanese crafts. We were talking about the hotel. This is John. And John, this is my husband, Sugihara Koji."

I automatically bowed low—in recognition of his rank, and to hide the surprise and confusion I was afraid might show in my expression.

I hadn't recognized him at all—the photo had been too old, and not a great likeness in any event, and even beyond all that, he looked different in the tuxedo.

And, I had to admit, I'd been too distracted by his wife.

"It's good to meet you, sir," I said, straightening and nearly stammering. "Are you enjoying the reception?"

"Indeed, a lovely affair," he said.

From his tone, he might have been describing a bout of hay fever rather than a party. I assumed that, as a top LDP politician, he would be capable of better artifice, so he must have judged me not worthy of the effort.

I struggled to think of a way to kick-start a conversation, and lead to something operational. But so many conflicting currents were crisscrossing my mind—his sudden appearance; the fact that he was this woman's husband; my attraction to her, now that I had just learned she was his wife; my fear that he might have noticed said attraction making its presence known beneath my ill-fitting tuxedo pants—that I couldn't come up with anything.

He turned to Maria. "The ambassador is here. It's best if we meet him together, so . . ."

She nodded. "Of course." Then she turned to me and extended her hand. "It was a pleasure chatting with you," she said in English. "I'd like to put you in touch with the museum director. Find me before you leave, all right?"

"Of course," I said, not knowing what the hell to make of that and totally on autopilot. "Thank you."

Sugihara gave me a slight bow of apology and took his wife's arm. I watched as they strolled away, unable not to notice that she looked every bit as fantastic from behind as she did from the front.

I wanted to gulp the rest of the champagne, but I needed to clear my head. I hit the restroom, then walked out to the pool deck, which was mercifully empty. Reflections of ambient light from the surrounding city rippled on the water, and the loudest sound was the hum of the filtration motor.

His wife? She was Sugihara's *wife*? It was so awful it was almost funny.

Why had she approached me? And why that bit at the end about a museum director? She must have wanted to see me again. But why? Was she interested? In what, an affair? I was half-horrified at the thought, half-hopeful.

And what about Sugihara? I'd been disinclined to kill him from the start, but I'd at least known I could if I had to. Sugihara had been an abstraction for me, an equation, a cost/benefit. And that was good. Killing is built on dehumanizing the target—look, I did it right there, referring to a "target," like something inanimate. It's why the military refers to *engaging the enemy*, not *murdering your fellow humans*. It's why UN peacekeepers typically don't wear helmets—the sight of a human face is itself a powerful deterrent to killing.

But now I'd met his wife. Talked to her. Flirted with her—or at least that's what it felt like.

I considered. I didn't care about Sugihara. Our meeting had been brief, and to the extent I knew him at all, he struck me as something of an aloof prick. I imagined it, and realized I could kill him if I had to. That hadn't changed.

So what's the problem? Stick to the plan. Play for time. Look for the opening to take Victor out. If you run out of time, you drop Sugihara. You just said you could.

But that was just it. I could drop Sugihara. But I didn't want to drop this woman's husband.

What are you going to do, then, just stand down? If that psycho decides Miyamoto is an "unreliable guy," Miyamoto's death will be on you.

Damn it. Miyamoto had been good to me. Kept my secrets. Warned me about a plot to kill me. He was one of the few people I called friend. Protecting him had to be the priority.

Exploit her, then. She could be an intel gold mine. Is there anyone who could help you fix Sugihara in time and place better than his wife?

Logically, there was no arguing with any of that. But the thought made me feel worse. Now I wasn't just considering killing Sugihara, but also making his wife—Maria—an unwitting accomplice in his death. Turning her into the instrument of her own tragedy.

How do you know it would be a tragedy for her? He's older. Cold where she's warm, aloof where she's charming. A politician. Gone half the time, visiting his home district, wining and dining cronies at night, an absentee husband. Why are you so sure she's even attached to him? Maybe she wouldn't care. Maybe it would free her. Hell, for all you know, she might even want him *dead.*

It was a rationalization, I knew.

It's not a rationalization. It's rationality.

Bullshit.

It's not bullshit, either. It's just math. She's pretty and you liked her. But get your feelings out of the way and add up the numbers. There's only one right answer. You just don't want to see it.

I heard the pool gate squeak and looked up. It was Miyamoto, silhouetted against the hotel.

"Rain-san," he whispered loudly. "Is that you?"

I looked around, concerned by his breach of the operational security we had agreed on.

"Yeah," I whispered back. "What are you doing? How'd you know I was here?"

He walked over and whispered more quietly, "I imagined where I might go if I wanted a moment alone."

Despite the mild breach, I was pleased. "It sounds like you've been practicing the countersurveillance mentality I taught you."

"I have indeed. Most useful. Now, what in heaven's name were you doing with Sugihara's wife?"

45

Of course. I should have realized—he hadn't been looking at me disapprovingly because I was chatting up a woman. It was because I was chatting up Sugihara's wife.

"I didn't know who she was. She just started talking to me."

"But is that wise?"

"I don't know if it was wise or not. It just happened."

"But won't this create difficulties?"

I wasn't sure if he was referring to logistical difficulties, or emotional ones, or both.

"I'm not sure. Probably. Yes. I need to think it through. That's why I came out here. Hey, Victor said Sugihara had beefed up his security, but I didn't see any bodyguards or anything like that. Did you?"

"He has a man outside the reception. A dozen guests brought bodyguards tonight, but none to the party itself."

I nodded, thinking Sugihara's security wasn't very secure. He was lucky Kobayashi was dead, and that someone a bit more reluctant, if not quite so incompetent, had been sent to kill him instead.

Miyamoto glanced around nervously. "What are you going to do?"

"That's what I'm trying to figure out."

"I'm sorry. I'm pestering you. And we shouldn't be talking anyway. I was just . . . concerned."

"Don't worry. I'll handle it."

He gave me a slight bow and went back through the gate. A moment later, the area was quiet again.

I knew I had sounded reassuringly confident when I'd told Miyamoto I would handle it. But the truth was, I had no idea how.

I imagined setting up a meeting with Victor. I could tell him I'd made some progress—established contact at the wedding. I'd leave Sugihara's wife out of it, of course. Completely out of it. But the wedding itself would be a morsel to toss the psychopath. And maybe while he was chewing on that morsel, I'd see an opening and take him out.

That settled me a little. I sat in the shadows on one of the lounge chairs for a while, just thinking, enjoying being away from the party. What I'd told Maria was true: I didn't mind being alone. I'd been alone before Sayaka, and, a few pretty Filipinas aside, I'd been alone after. The things I did in the war had felt like a wall after I'd come back, and now, after another decade of war in Mindanao, it was as though that wall was even higher and thicker. I knew it would always be there, between the world and me. It didn't feel wrong, or tragic, or even unfair. It felt appropriate, like some moral version of Newton's third law, a force cutting me off from the living in reaction to the lives I myself had cut short.

And yet there I was, sitting in the dark and thinking about this woman.

That's okay. She's a lead. An asset. You should *be thinking about her.*

The problem was, I wasn't thinking about her . . . that way.

I told myself I was being stupid. She was too old for me, too worldly, too married.

And too close to the mess I was in. Look what had almost happened to Sayaka, from no more than being near me. The wall wasn't simply punishment for the man on this side of it. It was protection for the people on the other. I needed to remember that.

Then knock it off about how you feel about her. She's an asset. A piece on the board. Stop mooning and play the fucking game.

Right.

I headed back inside and spotted her almost immediately. She was alongside her husband, smiling like the perfect politician's wife as he held forth to a group clustered before them. I looked around, and confirmed that the bride and groom were far off. It wouldn't do to have Maria ask me to introduce her.

I maneuvered through the crowd so she could see me pass, then stopped by a buffet tray along the wall and began filling a plate with multicolored *mochi* desserts. In my peripheral vision, I saw her excuse herself.

"Ah, John," she said, walking over. "I didn't see you for a while. Did you leave the party?"

Had she been looking for me? "I . . . you were right. I guess I'm more comfortable by myself than at parties."

"But did you meet the person you were looking for? I could probably help, you know."

I didn't know how to answer that. So I just said, "I'm glad I met you."

She looked at me closely, then smiled. "You're sweet."

"I'm not, actually." I hadn't meant to say it. I wondered if I was trying to warn her or something.

"Well, we're all complicated people. Maybe you're sweeter than you know." She reached into the tiny black purse she was carrying and removed a business card. "Here's that information I mentioned," she said, handing it to me. "I hope you'll follow up."

I glanced at the card. It was for Maria Sugihara of the Tokyo National Museum in Ueno. I glanced at the back and saw the words *Monday. 2:00 p.m. The Honkan entrance.*

I knew the museum. It was Tokyo's largest, and had been my mother's favorite. She had taken me there any number of times when I was small. The Honkan was the main building, with dozens of exhibition rooms.

I slipped the card into my pocket and nodded. Was this about the museum director? Or something else? "Thank you. I'll . . . make sure to follow up."

She held out her hand and smiled. *"Prego."*

We shook, and she turned and walked back to the group, her posture businesslike, someone who had performed a promised kindness for a stranger and was now done with him.

But she wasn't done. That much was clear. What wasn't clear was what she was doing with me.

Though no less clear than what I was doing with her.

chapter five

I spent the next day reconnoitering Sugihara's home and workplace per Victor's dossier. Neither venue was at all promising. Sugihara lived in a condominium in Minami Azabu with a gated garage. The neighborhood was entirely residential, and there was no good place to set up outside the building. I could envision several ways of accessing the garage and waiting for him there. None was low-risk, and the chance that I might be spotted by Maria enhanced the difficulty.

Work was even worse—a gated facility in Kasumigaseki with high walls and a guard post. Again, not impossible, but difficult and high-risk.

The good news, I supposed, was that I could use the dossier's shortcomings as an excuse for why the job was taking a long time. Excuse, hell, it was an actual reason.

You can do better than that. Tell the psycho if he really wants you to drop Sugihara, he should get you a gun.

I considered. Guns were rare in Japan, but if anyone could get me one, I figured it would be Victor. Though if his instincts were as good as I sensed, he wasn't going to let me anywhere near him armed.

There was one other possibility. My friend Tatsuhiko Ishikura. Tatsu. We'd known each other in Vietnam, and ten years earlier he'd helped me solve my yakuza problem, and then disappear. But Tatsu was with the Keisatsuchō, Japan's National Police Force, and while he had always prioritized the imperatives of justice over the niceties of law, I thought asking him for a gun so I could drop a Russian gangster might be a bridge too far.

Not a bridge too far. Just farther. A kind of . . . plan C.

All right. I'd keep Tatsu in mind, as a kind of backup. But first, I needed to check in with Victor.

I spent the night in one of the city's thousand love hotels—short-stay institutions designed for romantic liaisons, but useful, too, for anyone trying to avoid being tracked—and called Victor the following morning. As I dialed the number from a payphone, I realized I wasn't exactly eager to get together. As the saying goes, if the enemy is in range . . . so are you. But I didn't see another way to play it.

Someone picked up and said, "Hello." Oleg. I recognized the voice, and the accent, from last time.

"It's me," I said. "I made contact last night. If he wants to hear more, I'll come in. If not, I'll just get on with it."

"No, for sure you should come in. You can be here in half hour, yes?"

I thought about what that might mean. Most likely they were there now—assuming the number I was calling was to a phone in Victor's office. In theory, the number might have been for a phone in a different location. But Oleg didn't strike me as someone Victor had hired for his subtle spy skills. Surprised by my call, communicating over the phone in his weak English, he wouldn't have been sharp or focused enough to say "here" to mean the office if he was taking the call somewhere else.

So it seemed they spent a fair amount of time at the Kasumigaseki office. Not actionable intel yet, but another piece I might in time be able to combine with other pieces.

"I can be there."

"Good." He hung up.

A half hour later, I was back in Victor's office, having repeated the drill from last time—the wait, the pat-down, the escort by Oleg and two Japanese gangsters. Victor was a careful man.

He was sitting when I came in, and he clapped theatrically when he saw me. "Good to see you, my friend, good see you. Glad you have progress to report. Sit, sit! I want you to be comfortable."

No persimmon this time, I noted. And no knife. The polo shirt was now blue. The carpet had been changed—to red. I'd thought he was joking about that, but it seemed his men had decided it was safer to act as though he'd meant it.

"I'm fine standing," I said. "I don't want to take too much of your time."

"No problem," he said. "No problem. I want you to sit." He gestured to an empty upholstered chair. "*Pozhaluista.* Please."

I would have been more comfortable standing. But I supposed if the plan was to kill me, the four of them, presumably armed, would probably manage it regardless of whether I was in a chair or on my feet. So I sat.

"Very good. Thank you, my friend." He leaned forward. "Now. Tell me about Sugihara."

"There's not much to say. I would have told Oleg over the phone, but he said I should come in."

"Of course, it's better you're here. Face to face, always better. So. Sugihara. He is dead, yes?"

I looked at him. Was he serious?

He waited a beat, then laughed uproariously. "All right, all right, still alive, then. No need to worry. Just give details."

"There was a wedding last night. The grandson of the minister of agriculture. I managed to get in to the reception. I met Sugihara briefly. No opportunity to do more than that, but I'm more certain of who he is now than I was from that old newspaper clipping. Which ought to reduce the chances of another fuckup like Kobayashi's."

Victor looked at me, his expression unreadable. "You met him." Not a question, a statement.

I returned the look. "As I said."

"You met man. But you didn't kill him."

"I considered it. But in the end, the thousand or so witnesses stayed my hand. You have a problem with that?"

He stared at me, his eyes like empty pools. I wondered if I was getting under his skin. He was certainly getting under mine. I needed to shut that shit down. Stay detached. But deep within myself, I felt a realization locking into place.

One way or another, I was going to kill this asshole.

"His security wasn't even with him. Bodyguard stayed outside."

I wondered whether he knew that, or whether he was fishing.

"I didn't say his bodyguard was the problem. I said it was the witnesses. Look, if you want this done right, it might take a little time. If you want me to be hasty, you're risking another fuckup, and that would make the job even harder, maybe even impossible. Is that what you want?"

Again he stared at me for a long moment. If he lunged at me, I would come up under him and go for his eyes while shoving him back into Oleg, then fight to get to the door. Though the odds wouldn't be great.

"Hasty," he said, scratching his neck. "I thought I knew this word. But maybe not. Does it mean spending half of party making sexy eyes with Sugihara's Italian wife?"

That confirmed it—he had someone on the inside, someone at the wedding. Probably the same someone who'd been feeding him intel about his opposition in the LDP and on the street, enabling him to quickly acquire the targets who stood to thwart him, and have them beaten them to death.

But his gambit, and what lay behind it, didn't throw me off. I might have been awkward at a wedding reception, but Victor was tripping all my combat triggers, and combat for me is like coming home.

"You knew he had a wife," I said, my tone dropping a notch, "and you didn't tell me? That's a solid operational lead. I could have sought her out as a route to Sugihara instead of having to stumble upon her by accident. I got lucky. You want this job to depend on luck, or do you want to work with me by telling me what you know?"

But probably he hadn't known. Not before. Probably his inside man apprised him of what happened at the reception after the fact. In pushing back, I concealed this suspicion. And put Victor on the defensive.

Though I had to be careful. If I made him too defensive, things could get ugly fast.

Victor's eyes narrowed and he nodded slowly. "You are not . . . afraid of me, are you." Again, not a question. A statement.

I watched him, wary. "I'm just trying to get the job done. And done right."

"This is interesting. I like man who isn't afraid of me."

I thought he was full of shit about that. It seemed to me this guy wanted everyone who ever even heard his name to be afraid of him, and in general he was doing a reasonably good job of pulling it off. Although whether he was lying to me or to himself, I wasn't sure.

He leaned back in his chair as though to look at me in deeper focus. "But maybe also true that man who isn't afraid of me . . . is dangerous."

"You scare a man enough," I said, "and you'd be amazed at how dangerous he can become."

He looked at me for a long moment, the pressure of silence in the room building as though something might explode. In my peripheral vision, I saw his men watching. Oleg's right hand drifted to his waist—in preparation to access a weapon, no doubt. I braced to intercept him.

Then Victor threw back his head and laughed. It went on for maybe a half minute, peals of hilarity filling the room. When it finally began to ebb, he leaned forward again, still laughing and wiping his eyes. He pointed at me. "Like I said. Funny guy. I really like you, funny guy. Okay, so it's good thing you're not afraid of me, yes?"

"I guess so. Now, do you have any other leads you're planning to hold back? Or do you want me to get this job done?"

He laughed again and clapped. "All right, funny tough guy. You don't worry. I get you good lead. Where can Oleg call you?"

"I don't have a phone."

"Where do you stay?"

"With a friend. But I don't like to disturb him with calls that aren't for him."

He looked me up and down, his face expressionless. I could feel the tension in the room again.

"You know, funny tough guy, I like you. But fuck with me is big mistake. You know this, yes? You want me to show? Show you right fucking now?"

The tension in the room intensified. I wasn't afraid, though. More . . . interested. This psychopath seemed to have a certain amount of self-control. And he was exercising it now because he wanted something from me. Something I wouldn't be able to do for him dead.

"How about if I call you?" I said. "Just tell me when you want me to."

I figured letting him tell me when to call might make him feel like he was in control again, and get him to overlook the fact that I had ignored his demand, and made my own instead.

It seemed to work, because after a moment, he said, "You call Oleg tonight. Five o'clock. If we don't have lead then, you call twice a day. Nine o'clock, five o'clock. Don't miss call. Don't be unreliable."

"You know, this whole thing would be easier if you could get me a gun."

Victor smiled as though he recognized exactly what I wanted that gun for. "Guns are . . . difficult to get in Japan. Oleg has one, but I like him to be only guy to have."

Was it true that Oleg was carrying? I hadn't seen any telltale signs—a bulge under the arm, a sagging waistband. When his right hand had drifted to his waist earlier, he might have been going for a pistol, maybe something small enough for good concealment by his jacket and his bulk. But my gut said the weapon he'd been reaching for was a knife. Even if he hadn't read Sun Tzu, Victor was smart and experienced enough to know that when weak, you feign strength, and when strong, you feign weakness.

And what about Victor's other men? I hadn't seen any other hands drifting in a telltale move for a weapon. And beyond that, if Oleg, who was clearly Victor's right-hand man, wasn't carrying, it was hard to imagine the flunkies would be.

And even if I'd been wrong—even if Oleg were carrying, and even if I could disarm him before the others converged on me—I'd be pinning everything on the weapon itself. A weapon that, for all I knew, might be improperly maintained and could easily jam. Probably it would be operational, but if not, I'd be dead a few seconds later.

So I waited.

"Besides," Victor went on, "you know where Sugihara lives. Where he works. With what I give you, you should be able to club him in head with rock it's so easy."

"Yeah, I made a few runs past his building and where he works. They're both low-percentage places to try to get to him. That would be the case no matter what, because of the layout, the neighborhood, the access control, and the guards at work. But it's even more the case because, as you've said, he upped his security after Kobayashi, and unless it's the least competent security in the world, they would have explained to him that he has to be extra careful coming and going from home and work because these are the known, predictable places where someone would try to drop him. Now, he wasn't being super careful at the wedding, so we know he's going to be vulnerable somewhere. But I need solid intel to figure out where that somewhere is."

"Excuses."

"No, obstacles. Does he have a hobby? A mistress? A dog? Something like that. If he has a dog, maybe he walks it at night because his wife doesn't want to get out of bed. That kind of thing. That might be an opportunity."

"I don't know about dog."

"Look, I'm the weapon, but I need your help acquiring the target. And if you can't help, okay, but then I'm going to have to develop the intel myself. That's going to take time, or luck, but probably some of both."

He looked at me with his blank eyes. "You call Oleg tonight," he said. "Don't be late. Don't be unreliable guy."

chapter
six

The National Museum was in Ueno Park. I was staying at another love hotel, this time in Ikebukuro, which was a straight shot to Ueno on the JNR Yamanote line.

It was odd to be back in the city after a decade away. Of course, it all still felt like the Tokyo I remembered—the sounds of trains and traffic; the smell of rice and ramen; the overall energy of the place. But so much had changed, too. The Ikebukuro skyline was dramatically different, with high-rises going up everywhere—one of which, the giant Sunshine 60 building, was currently the tallest in Japan. So many of the stalwart wooden houses, browned by decades of alternating sun and rain, were being supplanted by concrete. And the war had receded, too. When I was a boy, there had still been signs of it—craters, empty fields, the skeletons of buildings immolated by American incendiary bombs. By the time I was back, in 1972, the physical scars were gone, but somehow their memory lingered, a ghostly presence in the increasingly prosperous, ever more cosmopolitan city. But now, it seemed, even the ghosts had departed, and the war had come to feel less like memory, and more like history.

The train was fine—clean and fast and efficient. But it made me miss Thanatos, the Suzuki GT380J I'd abandoned when I left Tokyo ten years earlier. Maybe I'd get another, if I took care of Victor and wound up staying. But probably it wouldn't be the same. There's no love like your first.

I got off the train and strolled through the park, avoiding Shinobazu Pond, the place where I had "died" ten years earlier. Remembering the gunshot, and the splash among the lotuses, and the cries of startled birds, I thought the spot would feel haunted now. I wouldn't mind if I never saw it again.

It was a warm day, and sunny, and the park was full. I saw groups of schoolchildren in their blue uniforms and yellow safety caps, chattering and holding hands as their teachers ushered them to whatever shrine or museum was next on their itinerary; tourists, cameras hanging from their necks, consulting maps and guidebooks; mothers with strollers, out for walks; salarymen with newspapers out for illicit *saboru* breaks; pensioners on benches out to kill time. The air was light with laughter and the sounds of relaxed conversation. The leaves of the gingko trees were tinged with yellow, and the *kōyō*, fall colors, made me think of my mother, and how much she had loved autumn in Japan.

I walked past the fountain along the esplanade in front of the museum, then stood for a moment, watching as a foreign tour group gradually filed into the massive stone structure. As the last of them disappeared inside, I saw Maria, standing alone under the main entrance portico. She waved when she saw me, and started down the steps.

"John, hello," she said as she reached me, kissing my cheeks in the Italian fashion. "I wasn't sure you would come, you know, but I'm so glad you did."

She was wearing an over-the-knee black skirt, a white button-down blouse open at the neck, and black pumps. Small gold earrings, a simple pearl necklace, and a bit less eyeliner than she had at the reception. I wouldn't have thought it possible, but she struck me as even more beautiful in the understated business attire than in the black gown.

"I wasn't sure, either. It was a little hard to know what this is about."

"Well, a job, of course."

"A job?"

"Isn't that what you were looking for at the reception? Someone to talk to about a job?"

That had been her interpretation. I hadn't denied it, but neither did I think I'd confirmed sufficiently for her to try to actually offer me something.

"I . . . don't know what to say."

"Was I mistaken? You're not looking for work? The way you answered, I thought you were being, mmm, euphemistic."

"Maybe a little. What kind of job are we talking about?"

"Recently, the gentleman who was leading English-language tours had to return suddenly to Australia. So when I met you, I thought maybe you could be a good fit."

I glanced over at the imposing bulk of the museum behind her. "Maria, it's nice of you to think of me, but pretty much everything I know about art is from a conversation with you at a wedding."

"Of course, you would need a teacher. Luckily for you, as you can see, I'm a good one."

I laughed. "Why didn't you just tell me you wanted me to come here?"

"Honestly, I was afraid if I told you without also showing you and introducing you to Director Kurosawa, you might not realize you were interested."

"Might not realize? I guess that's one way of putting it."

"Look, you've come this far, so you must be at least a little intrigued, yes? Why don't I introduce you, show you around a little, and then, if you're still not interested, at least you'll have made an informed decision, isn't that right?"

I tried to think it through. Was she telling the truth? Did she really invite me to the museum about a job? Because it occurred to me that, if there was something more she was interested in, or something else, the job pretext would have made excellent cover for action. Everything aboveboard, including a meeting with the museum director himself. Everything deniable. A much safer way to proceed than, say, a drink in a bar or a rendezvous on a park bench.

Or maybe the cover for action was more for her than for potential third parties. It wasn't until years later that I read Reinhold Niebuhr's *Moral Man and Immoral Society*, where Niebuhr talked about how the baser self has to deceive the better self to get the better self's buy-in for behavior it would never otherwise agree to. But even before I read the book, I grasped the concept, and I wondered if maybe she was interested in me for something other than a job, but had convinced herself it was about a job because she wasn't ready to accept the true nature of that interest. I certainly knew enough about the kinds of rationalizations involved with killing to understand something similar might come into play in the context of forbidden attractions.

Or maybe that was all foolish hope on my part. Projection. Maybe I was just overthinking it.

It didn't matter. I needed to develop her for information about her husband. And one pretext for that was probably about as good as another.

A formation of chattering, blue-sailor-uniformed high-school girls flowed out of the museum and past us. I watched them go, then threw up my arms in surrender. "Okay. I guess what's the harm."

We walked inside, and I paused for a moment in the foyer, craning my neck to look around. I tried to recall the last time my mother had taken me here—probably when I was seven or so. I didn't expect to remember it well, and was surprised to find that I did. The imposingly high ceiling with its elaborate carvings. The tall marble walls. The massive split staircase, twenty feet across, and the metal carvings on the huge bannisters. And of course the solemn echo produced by all that stone and space.

Maria smiled as I took it all in. "Impressive, yes? There's talk of designating this building a *jūyōbunkazai*. I think they will."

Jūyōbunkazai, or Important Cultural Properties, were places so designated by the government because of their significance to Japanese culture, and thereafter subject to restrictions on alteration. There was an equivalent for people—the *ningenkokuho*, or Living National Treasures—masters of arts the perpetuation of which the government considered critical to the continuity of Japanese culture.

"I think that would be appropriate," I said, still staring all around.

"Come, let's meet Director Kurosawa. He's expecting us. And then I'll show you around. There's so much to see."

We went around the huge stairs, past a sign declaring in English and Japanese "Museum Staff Only," and came to a massive doorway, mahogany with a glass transom on top. Maria knocked loudly on the open door. "Director Kurosawa?" she called out in Japanese. "I have someone I'd like you to meet."

We walked into a room cluttered with hanging scrolls and folding screens and enough artifacts to strain the building's foundation, with a single large window looking out onto a tranquil garden. In the middle of it all was a tiny man in a rumpled suit, his hair and wispy beard both entirely white, sitting at a wooden desk so massive it made him seem a child alongside it. He looked up from a book, pulled off one set of wire-rim spectacles and pulled on another, and used a cane to come to his feet.

"Yes, of course," he said, adjusting his glasses and squinting at me. "You must be the gentleman Maria-san told me about. So you're interested in museum work, is that it?"

I bowed, a little bewildered at how fast this all seemed to be happening. "Well, sir, I . . . yes, I'm certainly interested."

He cupped an ear and inclined his head toward me. "Say that again, please?"

He was hard of hearing. I should have already realized that, from the way Maria had knocked and then called out to him. I repeated myself, louder this time, bowing again.

He gave me a small bow in return. "Where did you get your degree?"

"Sir, to be honest, most of my education is . . . informal." That seemed a fair way of describing what I'd learned as a soldier and mercenary.

"Ah, well, a formal education is sometimes overrated. Maria-san herself is elegant proof of that. But your English? This would have to be top-level, because you would be conducting tours. Not just for tourists, mind you, but also for visiting dignitaries. The National Museum is a window onto the Japanese soul, you understand? It's a first impression for many very important visitors to our country"—here he paused to glance at my faded jeans and scruffy boots—"and we want that first impression to be a good one. As our economy grows ever more international, much depends on that."

"I grew up in Japan and America, sir," I said, wishing I'd bothered to iron my shirt, if only for the sake of appearances. "My English is as native as my Japanese."

"Good, very good. I wish I could say the same about mine, but it's almost too embarrassingly weak to use. Yet another reason the museum needs the support of young, internationally minded people like Maria-san. Well, I'll turn you over to her now." He looked at Maria and beamed. "Maria-san, he seems like a good young man."

We bowed and walked out. As we rounded the stairwell again, she said, "Do you not already adore him?"

"He seems . . . very nice."

"I love him. He took a chance on me ten years ago even though I have no formal degree, and it practically saved my life."

We maneuvered around a tour group and started up the stairs. "That's a pretty strong characterization for a job opportunity," I said, wondering if she thought she was doing something similar for me.

"Well, not literally. But it's what I needed at the time. And he's backed me ever since."

At the top of the stairs, we turned in to one of the exhibits—*Fashion of the Edo Period*, featuring stunning examples of formal silk kimonos. The smell of the old wood flooring, the sound of footsteps echoing off the high ceiling . . . it was all making me unaccountably sad. Maybe because the last time I had been here, I'd been so innocent. And not nearly so alone.

"I started just as a tour guide," she said quietly as we walked. "The first *gaijin* guide the museum ever had, because I speak English and Italian and Japanese. And some French and German, from university. But Director Kurosawa has given me more and more responsibility. In fact, later this week, we open a new exhibit that I curated—*Treasures of Azuchi Castle and Nijo Castle*. It's a collection of sliding door panels and folding screens depicting views from the castles at the end of the Sengoku period. With cassette tours I narrated in Italian and English, and an accompanying coffee-table book I wrote. I could never have done any of it without Director Kurosawa."

I liked that she honored him by calling him Director—*kanchō*, in Japanese—even when he wasn't present.

"That's amazing," I said. "I'd love to see it."

She smiled. "I'm glad, because we're on our way."

We left the fashion exhibit, and came to a red-velvet rope at the end of the corridor. She lifted it, replaced it behind us, and unlocked a small door—a rear entrance, I supposed, to an exhibit room. We went inside, but it was too dark to see anything. She turned on the lights and closed the door behind us.

Displayed before me were some of the most spectacular gold-leaf screens I had ever seen—enormous, evocative depictions of mountains and lakes and birds of prey, the gold leaf catching the light beautifully. Some of the sliding panels stretched to the ceiling, wooden dividers creating the illusion that we were looking through a window at a garden surrounding an ancient cypress tree.

"It's . . . breathtaking," I said, shaking my head slowly in wonder.

"Ah, *grazie*. I won't deny, I'm very proud of it."

"You should be."

"Now you can see why I'm so fond of Director Kurosawa."

"Yeah, I think I get it."

"And that's who you'd be working for. Interested?"

"I'm flattered. Really. But I think I'd disappoint you."

"Shouldn't you let me decide that?"

"My concern is, I think you *would* decide that."

She laughed. "I'm not usually wrong about these things. Now, how about a private tour? I haven't done a tour in a long time and it would be my pleasure."

We spent an hour just in her exhibit. I was amazed by her knowledge of the art and the history behind it, and even more by her insights into the cultural forces that had produced the works on display.

When we were back in the corridor, she said, "What else can I show you? *Zen Scrolls of the Kamakura Era? Ukiyo-e of the Edo Era? The Dawn of Japanese Art?*"

I smiled. "When my mother took me here when I was small, she would always ask me the same questions. And I would always tell her I wanted to see the swords and armor."

She laughed. "For some reason, I can so easily imagine that. But the *Attire of the Military Elite* exhibit is being refurbished, so it's temporarily in storage. I can still show you, though, if you like."

We took the stairs to the basement. Unlike the floors above, the corridors here were narrow, the ceilings low, the lighting barely adequate—clearly a part of the museum not intended or maintained for public consumption. At the end of the hall, we turned a corner, where Maria slid a key into an ordinary lock on an ordinary door. She flipped a light switch and I followed her in.

The room inside looked like a treasure cave—shelves crammed with artifacts; paintings and prints carefully aligned in cubicles; warrens of boxes containing who knew what. We moved left and right down the mazelike aisles, and there, in the very back, a corner crowded with swords and armor, none of it behind glass or otherwise inaccessible.

"You're not worried about someone breaking in here?" I said, amazed at the lack of security.

She shrugged. "There's a guard at night. Besides, this is Japan, have you ever heard of a museum, mmm, heist here? Anyway, no one outside the museum knows where out-of-exhibit items are stored." She cocked an eyebrow. "Only you now, so if something goes missing, I'll know who took it."

We walked over to the swords. There were at least a dozen, each resting on a wooden stand holding two components. On top of each stand was a *koshirae* scabbard and *tsuka* hilt, suggesting a sword at rest within. But the gorgeous lacquered scabbards and *tsukaito* ray-skin-and-silk grips were for combat, not storage; for the latter, on the lower tier of each stand was a *shirasaya*, a plain wooden scabbard, with the blade inside and a plain wooden hilt attached. Nearby were some white cloths alongside a couple of glass jars—probably *choji*, a mixture of mineral oil, clove oil, and powder employed to protect the steel from corrosion and mold. These swords were spectacular, and it was good to see they were well cared for.

"Do you remember any of them?" Maria said. "They've been with the museum for a long time."

I nodded, feeling a little wistful, and pointed to the one I was already looking at—a classic *katana* resting in its *shirasaya* scabbard below a gold lacquer *koshirae*. "This one was always my favorite."

"Would you like to handle it?"

I glanced at her, remembering how badly I'd wanted that as a boy. "Are you kidding?"

"Just please be careful."

"Don't worry, I won't hurt the exhibits."

"I'm more worried about you than the exhibits. They're extremely sharp. I know you know, but still."

I gripped the *shirasaya* in my left hand and the wood *tsuka* with my right, lifted the sword from the stand, and then, taking care to draw the *mune*, the back, along the inside of the *shirasaya* so as to protect the *ha*, the edge, unsheathed the slightly curved blade. I held it horizontally at eye level, manipulating it with my wrist, watching the expertly worked steel catch the light, dazzled by the perfect weight and balance, the sudden sense that what I held in my hand was more than mere metal, but was instead alert, purposeful, almost alive. I gazed at the *hamon*, the temper pattern along the edge, wondering how many battles this weapon had seen, how many lives taken, and for a moment, I felt a strange connection to it—both of us born in Japan, both of us forged for killing.

"It suits you," Maria said, her voice slightly strange.

I blinked, realizing I'd been gone for a second. "Hmm?"

She was frowning slightly. "Just . . . you seem very comfortable holding a sword. Not like when you wear a tuxedo."

I didn't know quite what she had seen, but instinctively wanted to conceal it. I looked at the blade again. "I just always liked the *kotō*, the old swords, better than the *shintō*, the newer ones. The *shintō* were expertly made, of course, with beautiful tempering patterns. But I think I liked the more utilitarian presentation of the classic blades. They were less about beauty, and more about business."

She laughed, and the odd moment vanished. "Ah, listen to you, you are a tour guide already!"

We spent another hour touring the museum. She obviously loved showing off its treasures, and I could easily see why Kurosawa had supported her as she said—it would have been hard to imagine a more knowledgeable, passionate, and charming guide. As we walked and talked and I stole surreptitious glances at her hair and face and body, I became aware that I was grappling with what was becoming a fairly serious crush. I wasn't sure what I should do about it.

No, that wasn't quite right. I knew what I should do. I just wanted to do something else.

She walked me out when we were finished. The sun was lower, the air slightly cooler, and the crowds had thinned. A team of gardeners in traditional denim *momohiki* pants and *hanten* coats and conical bamboo hats had deployed across the grounds. I watched for a moment as they went about trimming bushes; edging the grass; most of all, raking and sweeping the brightly colored *ochiba*, fallen leaves, the gentle scraping of their bamboo rakes and brooms like a little aria of autumn in old Tokyo. It made me nostalgic for the days when my mother had taken me here as a child, when I'd also seen the gardeners, always late in the day, I supposed because working at closing time and probably after made them less obtrusive.

When we were clear of the museum, Maria took my arm. I was acutely aware of the warmth of her hand through my shirtsleeve. Was she flirting with me just to get me to take the job? Or was it something more? Or both?

Or worst of all, was I just reading too much into it?

"I have to tell you," I said as we walked. "I think it's amazing you learned all this yourself. I mean, people go to college to acquire this kind of knowledge. Graduate school, even."

"Well, I'm not completely self-taught. I majored in Asian art at Sapienza University for two years, but didn't get my degree."

"Why not?"

"My husband was a visiting lecturer there. I came back to Japan with him and we got married."

There must have been a whole history, a whole world, beneath that bland statement. Came back with Sugihara when she was what, twenty? Dropped out of college? Did they have an affair? Had she gotten pregnant or something?

But her face had been carefully expressionless as she said it, her tone as neutral as someone delivering a weather report. It was clear she didn't want to discuss more than the bare facts of it.

Still, because it related to her husband, I couldn't resist probing a little. "Do you . . . are there children?"

"We had a boy. But he's gone."

The way she said "gone" left no ambiguity as to her meaning. I stopped and looked at her, suddenly aware of how much pain surrounded and emanated from those seven simple words, and moved by the dignity and self-control behind them.

"I'm sorry," I said.

She shook her head. "It was a long time ago."

"I don't think something like that can ever be a long time ago. It's not how time works."

She looked at me as though trying to decide whether to advance or retreat. In the distance, I heard the sound of a Yamanote train's arrival bells.

"No," she said quietly after a moment. "That's true. And thank you."

"Thank you for telling me. And I'm sorry for bringing up something so painful."

"No, it's all right. Sometimes it's hard to avoid. Because it's attached to everything, you know? It affects everything."

"But your husband," I went on, feeling dirty for pressing for something operational at the very moment she had shared something so intimate and so painful. "What was a politician doing lecturing on art in Rome?"

She smiled, and I could see she was glad I had changed the subject. Or at least changed the focus.

"This was a long time before he was a politician. In his first, mmm, incarnation, he had a graduate degree in fine art. He was a professor in the conservation of historical property and historical culture at the Kyoto University of Art and Design."

"I'm not even sure what that is. Still think I'd be right for this job?"

She smiled. "It means he was an expert in restoring and preserving relics—sculptures, paintings, ceramics, those kinds of things. It's an important field and the background is unusual—typically some combination of chemistry and art history. Anyway, now you know. See how fast you can learn with a good teacher?"

I laughed. "So how did an expert in restoring and preserving relics become a politician?"

She took my arm and we started walking again. "His father was the Diet member for Yamanashi Prefecture. My husband never wanted anything to do with politics, but when his father died, a lot of LDP people pushed my husband to run for his father's seat. And his mother pushed him, too. He was the only son, and these Diet seats . . . well, you know how it is. The samurai are gone, but politics in this country still has a lot to do with inheritance and lineage."

"So he ran for office?"

"Yes, he was elected in 1960 and we moved to Tokyo. I was so sad to leave Kyoto. Because you know, where else in the world would a lover of Japanese art want to live? But Tokyo isn't so bad. My husband has to go back and forth to Yamanashi, of course, to stay close with his constituents, but I spend most of my time here."

I wondered whether there was anything in there that might be useful. I wasn't sure yet.

"But it wasn't quite what you wanted."

She glanced at me, and again I had the sense that she was trying to gauge how much to say. After a moment, she smiled with what seemed a little effort and said, "Not exactly. And what about you? Where did you go to school?"

She was changing the subject. I wanted to press, but sensed I'd do better to wait.

"I didn't. I didn't even finish high school. Still want to hire me?"

"It's like Director Kurosawa said—formal education can be over-rated. Still, I'm surprised. You seem, I don't know, educated."

I laughed. "I don't even know how to hold a champagne flute."

"No, you do. I taught you, remember?"

I laughed again. "That's true. But still."

"It's the way you carry yourself, I think. You were uncomfortable at that party, weren't you? That I could tell. But you didn't seem, mmm, insecure. You know, some people without a formal education feel like less because of it. You don't strike me that way."

I considered. "That's fair, I think."

"Which makes me think you got an education elsewhere."

"Fair again."

"May I ask where?"

I glanced at her. "Is this part of the interview?"

"Definitely."

"I dropped out of high school and joined the army at seventeen. Then spent three years in Vietnam."

"My God."

"Surprised?"

She looked at me closely. "No. Maybe not. I thought there was something about you. I just didn't know what."

I was intrigued. "What do you mean?"

"The way you were alone at the party, but also comfortable with it. Like you hold yourself, mmm, aloof. Like you know something, or feel something, or did something that separates you from the rest of society."

That was insightful enough to unnerve me. "Fair again."

"You saw things in the war?"

A beat went by. "And did things."

"I'm sorry."

"It was a long time ago."

She smiled. "That's no more true when you say it than it was when I did."

I didn't answer, and she squeezed my arm, as though to comfort me. "I think trauma can make you feel so separate from people who haven't experienced it. As though they live in a different world."

She had too good a read on me—much better than I had on her. I felt like I was doing *randori* with someone I expected was new to judo, and who turned out to be a black belt.

"Maybe there's a silver lining," I said, thinking of Crazy Jake. And of Tatsu, who I had known, and bonded with, in the war. "The few people who do know . . . they get it. Really get it."

She nodded. "I can imagine that."

"But isn't there someone . . ." I stopped, not knowing how to finish the sentence.

"Ah, you know. It can be a little isolating, being a foreigner in this country."

"Yeah, I know. But what about your family?"

"That's a long and sad story. I'd rather you tell me about yours."

We moved off the paved path, gravel crunching as we walked. There were still people around, and the park remained fairly animated. But it also felt somehow as though there was no one else but the two of us.

"Not much to tell. My mother was American. My father was Japanese. He died when I was eight, and my mother took me back to the States. So I grew up in both countries."

"But never felt at home in either."

That was certainly true, but I didn't want to confirm it. "Why do you say that?"

"Just a feeling. Your mother, she's still in the States?"

"She died. That was a long time ago, too."

I said the last part ironically, but she stopped and looked at me anyway, the sympathy in her eyes making her almost impossibly lovely.

"Sure it was," she said softly.

To that, I only nodded. My father had been killed in the street riots that rocked Tokyo when the Kishi administration ratified the 1960 US-Japan Security Pact. My mother died of cancer about ten years later, while I was away at war. And Maria was right, none of it was really a long time ago. I just kept it all in a box, along with memories from the war. Along with Sayaka.

We were both quiet for a moment. Then she said, "Well. Maybe that's enough sad stories for one day?"

"You're right. I'm sorry for pressing."

"Not at all. I was pressing, too. When we get to know someone, there are light things we can see, and dark ones we bump up against, isn't that so?"

"Apparently it is."

"So! Do you want the job?"

"You think I'm ready for it?"

"No, of course not. Director Kurosawa will follow my recommendation, but he'll still want to interview you at some point. For that, you need to know more than you do now."

I cocked an eyebrow. "Well, if only there were someone willing to teach me."

She laughed. "So? Can you come by again this week?"

I wasn't sure what made sense. I wanted to see her again, that much I knew, though I also knew I was badly mixed up about why.

"This week isn't great for me during the day," I said, on impulse. "But how about a drink one night? I mean, there's a lot you have to teach me, but it doesn't all have to be at the museum, does it?"

"Oh," she said with a little frown. "I thought your days would be okay if you're, you know, not in a job right now."

Shit. She had good instincts. And next time, before I opened my mouth, I'd need to be sure my story would seem consistent with whatever she already believed.

"It's a long story. Just . . . a little tied up."

"Maybe interviewing someplace else? How could anything compare to working with Director Kurosawa and me?"

Not for the first time, she'd given me the opportunity to confess to a lesser crime to conceal the commission of a greater one. I shook my head, relieved. "I doubt anything could compare. But . . . still."

She looked at me with those dark eyes, and I had no idea what was going on behind them.

"Well," she said after a moment, "actually, tomorrow night could work for a drink. The museum closes at five. Maybe after that."

I thought quickly, trying to push aside the bolt of pleasure and excitement I felt at the prospect of a drink with her. I didn't know many bars in Tokyo. There was Kamiya in Asakusa, of course, one of the places McGraw had used for our meetings. But that was a big, boisterous, neighborhood kind of place. Not what I had in mind. The Orchid Bar at the Okura would have been good, but she might be known there, and that could make her uncomfortable.

Back when I'd first been getting to know him, Miyamoto was always talking about bars—a passion of his. And there was one, new at the time, he'd taken a particular fancy to, because the owner was a student of *sadō*, the tea ceremony, as was Miyamoto himself, and had built a bar informed by *biishiki*, an aesthetic consciousness, an awareness of beauty. Bar Radio, that had been the name. In Minami Aoyama. I wasn't sure it would still be there, but I could call, and if it had closed, I'd figure out something else.

"Have you heard of Bar Radio?" I said.

"I haven't."

"I haven't been there, but I have a friend—the same one I mentioned at the wedding, who taught me about *nen*—and he loves it. So I think it would be worth seeing. If you like, I mean."

She smiled. "Well, that's a very attractive proposition. I'd like to see what this *nen* is all about. Especially in a bar."

"So would I. It's in Minami Aoyama. What time is good for you?"

"Why don't we say six o'clock? I'll just take the train to Omotesando."

I had a sudden image of myself riding Thanatos from Ueno to Minami Aoyama through twilight Tokyo, Maria on the saddle behind me, her arms around my torso. But I'd left Thanatos ten years ago by the lotuses of Shinobazu Pond.

"What is it?" she asked.

That jarred me from my reverie. "Oh, nothing. I was just . . . remembering something from a long time ago. I used to have a motorcycle here. I would have picked you up."

"Ah, that sounds lovely. I actually have a little Vespa. But to Minami Aoyama, maybe the train is easier."

"Okay. So . . . six o'clock tomorrow."

There was an awkward pause. Then she smiled and held out her hand. I would have preferred one of those Italian double cheek kisses, but I guessed the main thing was the drink.

We shook. *"Ciao,"* she said, and headed back toward the museum.

I watched her go, thinking *No good can come of this, John.*

I really should have listened.

chapter seven

I called Oleg that evening from a payphone. He had no leads on Sugihara. That was fine with me. Anything that delayed the endgame and gave me more time to figure out how to take out Victor was a welcome development.

I pressed him again about a gun. I didn't think he'd go for it, but I wanted to be able to use the refusal as an excuse for not being able to quickly drop Sugihara.

"Gun won't happen," Oleg told me. "Stop asking."

"Why? It would make this whole thing a lot easier. And faster."

"You don't need gun."

"Yeah, but—"

"You want to kill guy? You go to hardware store. You buy rat poison, okay? You know rat poison?"

"I know rat poison, yeah."

"You dip knife in rat poison. Any knife. You don't need long blade. You come behind guy, you stab. Three, four, five times. Kidney. Liver. All over. Happen very fast. Guy can't stop you. Probably, guy bleeds to death. But even if ambulance is right there, doesn't matter. Because rat poison. Now stop asking stupid questions."

"I don't—"

"And another thing. You and Kobayashi. Twenty stitches for me from that. You're lucky Victor thinks you can be useful. But if he changes mind, you and I have long talk."

He hung up. For a moment, I stood staring at the phone.

Long talk? I don't think so, asshole. When I have that kind of talk, I keep it short. And right to the point.

I put the receiver back in the cradle and walked away, imagining visiting a hardware store exactly as Oleg had suggested. And then setting up outside the Kasumigaseki office until Victor emerged.

It was a pleasing thought, but not realistic. Sugihara might have some security, but he was no hard target. Victor, on the other hand, was a man who knew he had a lot of enemies, and understood he had to live in a way that would deny them opportunities. Not very likely he would just blithely stroll out of his office one evening to smell the autumn air, with no escort, and pause without checking his surroundings while I moved in behind him. Not impossible that it could work, but high-risk. I wasn't that desperate.

Though I supposed that could change, if I didn't play things right.

That night, I walked from the hotel in the direction of Zōshigaya Cemetery. Once I was clear of giant Ikebukuro Station, the area quickly became residential, all dim lamplights and narrow streets and old wooden houses fronted by lovingly tended potted plants. I passed a few people shuffling along in slippers to the neighborhood *sentō* for a post-work soak. The ritual of the public bath was one of the things I loved about Japan, and that made me hate my birthplace for not loving me back. Still, the quiet helped to settle my mind.

The cemetery was even better—empty, dark, and silent. I found a tree among the markers and sat with my back to it, listening to the crickets, feeling like I should be holding and contemplating a skull. And maybe in a sense I was, because this was the very spot where, ten years earlier, I'd put a bullet in McGraw's head. The memory of that moment was satisfying, even comforting. I realized I had probably come here for more than just the solitude and silence.

I tried to step back, to see the board rather than simply the pieces. Not just Victor, but the organization around him. And his place in it.

They didn't seem to have a particularly large crew. Both times I'd been to Victor's office, it had been the same people. And Victor had delegated an important job to a fuckup like Kobayashi. Who Victor had been comfortable getting rid of only once he knew he had a new guy to replace him.

This felt like a squad-sized unit to me. Not even a platoon. Certainly not a company.

Organizationally, Victor was the principal, Oleg the muscle, enforcer, and overall right-hand man. Victor had met me at his office so he could assess me, and then smoothly turned me over to Oleg, who was now acting as a buffer, inhibiting direct access to Victor. It was obvious a significant part of Oleg's job, his function, was to protect Victor.

But who was protecting Oleg?

I chewed on that.

Losing someone like Oleg would scramble Victor's organization. Likely force him to change his routines, make him more vulnerable.

It wouldn't be easy. But if I could make it work, it could open up one of Victor's flanks. Not for long, probably, but maybe long enough.

What was missing, though, was intel. And intel meant Tatsu.

The last time I'd seen him, he told me he thought we would work together again. But I didn't think what he had in mind was exactly a partnership. Tatsu would be in charge. Or, at a minimum, he'd demand something in return for whatever help he offered. I didn't want to put myself in a position where I would have to provide it.

But maybe my reluctance was stupid. The situation was reasonably stable at the moment, but that could change at any time. If it did, I'd want to be ready, not scrambling. I could talk to Tatsu, tell him a little, feel him out, see how much he'd be willing to offer, and how much he'd require in return.

I knew it was the right call, but still it felt fraught. Tatsu was a wily bastard, with great cop instincts coupled with an unusually flexible attitude regarding means and ends. But the cop instincts I'd have to risk. It was the flexibility I needed right now.

chapter eight

I headed back to Ikebukuro Station and called Tatsu at home. At that hour, a lot of cops would have been out for a post-work drink with their cronies, but I knew Tatsu. When pressed, he would respond gruffly, but he loved his wife and doted on his daughters, and I knew nothing gave him more pleasure than a quiet evening at home with them.

His wife answered. I said I was an old friend and asked for him. A moment later, he was on the phone with a curt *"Hai."*

"It's Rain," I said in Japanese. "It's been a while."

There was a pause. "Yes, it has," he said. "Why do I sense this isn't a social call?"

"Well, it's also a social call."

"Of course. You are back in Tokyo?"

"I am. And it feels like I never left."

Based on our dealings ten years ago, he would know exactly what that meant.

"Indeed."

"So . . . if you have time at some point, it would be great to see you."

"I imagine sooner would be better than later."

"Well, I do miss you."

I pictured him smiling. No one needled Tatsu—he was too formidable a presence for that. But somehow I got away with it, and I imagined he found it refreshing.

"It's kind of you to say," he replied. "Perhaps we could enjoy a beer tonight."

"I'd be grateful for that. Are you still in Nihonbashi? Name a place you like, and I'll be there in a half hour."

He gave me an address in Yūrakuchō, not far from his neighborhood. It was a straight shot on the Yamanote, and I arrived to find an old-school *izakaya*, the Japanese institution dedicated to cheering tired salarymen on their way home from work with ice-cold beer and yakitori chicken and the ear of a sympathetic *masutaa* at the bar. This one was sandwiched under the Yamanote tracks, and had the feel of a secret subterranean haven—a low ceiling, cramped tables, the rumbling of overhead passing trains in lieu of recorded music. Steam rose from an open stove behind the bar, the sounds of fat dripping and popping on the charcoal below, and the air was pungent with the smell of grilled meat. There were about forty people jammed inside, laughing and talking, and it took me a moment to confirm that Tatsu hadn't arrived yet. A waitress saw me and cried out, *"Irasshai!"*—Welcome!—and I bowed slightly to acknowledge the greeting. I found a table alongside a wall, ordered us each a *nama* beer, and waited.

Five minutes later, I saw him come in. He'd aged a little since the last time I'd seen him, with some gray scattered through the black hair, and he'd put on some weight. But the gait—a bulldog barely held back by an invisible leash—was impossible to miss. And ditto the smile, which always seemed like it had overcome some urge to suppress it, when he saw me.

I stood and watched as he worked his way through the tables. "Rain-san," he said when he'd reached me. And then, as though responding to some contradictory inner thought, he added, "But it's always good to see you."

I bowed, then shook his hand. Maybe it was that we'd first known each other overseas. Or maybe it was that he was so Japanese he made me feel American by comparison. But I always liked to shake his hand.

We squeezed into our seats and I raised my mug. *"Kanpai."* He raised his own and grunted in agreement, and we clinked the glasses and drank.

He set down his mug, let out a long sigh, and wiped his chin. "Well, then. What kind of trouble have you gotten yourself into this time?"

"You know, Tatsu, if I were a little more sensitive, I might be hurt by what you're implying."

He gave me a cop stare that might have caused someone who didn't know him to confess to the Great Chicago Fire.

"I mean, never even a 'How've you been? How's life?'"

He sighed. "How've you been? How's life?"

"Fine, thanks for asking. And you?"

"Good."

"Your wife? Your daughters?"

He sighed again, but I thought I detected the trace of a reluctant smile. "Fine. Teenage girls can be a puzzle. But"—he paused, and the smile broke through—"very fine. Thank you."

I returned the smile. "I'm glad. Thanks for coming out tonight to meet me. And if you deny you'd rather be home with them, we're just going to have an argument."

He grunted a laugh. "Okay, okay. Now tell me what kind of trouble you're in. Nothing to do with Mad Dog Fukumoto, I trust? You know he's long gone."

He was talking about the yakuza kingpin's son I had taken out ten years earlier—the reason I'd had to flee Tokyo, leaving my bullet-ridden "corpse" floating in Shinobazu Pond. But the son had long since joined the father, and I didn't expect the underlings who had deposed him would recognize me even if our paths crossed, or care one way or the other.

I took a swallow of beer, then leaned forward so I could speak more quietly. The tables were mostly full, and conversation around us was loud enough to provide good cover. "I don't even know where to start. Maybe by asking you a question. You know a guy named Victor? I don't even know his last name, but—"

"Karkov. Victor Karkov. Half-Russian, half-Japanese. A former colonel in *Spetsnaz*, Russian Special Forces. Arrived in Tokyo a little over a year ago. The yakuza families are still reeling from it. Unless I'm mistaken, of course, and you're referring to a different Victor."

I knew Tatsu made it a point to be knowledgeable about these things, but still I hadn't expected him to be quite that dialed in.

"Uh, no. That's him."

"And you're mixed up with this man?" He managed to sound only mildly disapproving. But I sensed he was at least equally intrigued.

"Well, 'mixed up' might be a strong way to put it."

"Indeed. And how would you put it?"

I took another sip of beer to give myself time to think. I realized I should have gamed this out better before seeing him. Winging it with Tatsu was a dangerous strategy.

"He's . . . put me in a difficult position."

Tatsu said nothing. I knew he was using the silence to draw me out, and I had to resist the urge to just keep talking.

"Let me ask you this," I said. "If Victor were to take, say, early retirement, would you have a problem with that?"

He shrugged. "I think the world would be fine without Victor. On the other hand, there's always another one like him."

It almost slid right by me, but for some reason I didn't quite buy it. Tatsu was as coldly rational an operator as I'd ever known, but he was still Japanese, a people intrinsically suspicious of, even hostile to, foreign interference. They closed the country for 250 years during the Tokugawa shogunate, opening it only when Admiral Perry's black ships arrived and left no choice. So even someone as levelheaded as Tatsu was unlikely to be blasé about a guy like Victor Karkov in Tokyo.

I took another sip of beer, deliberately casual. "If you say so. I mean, a foreigner waltzing into Tokyo and pushing out the local gangsters. Just seems . . . embarrassing. But okay."

There was a long pause. If he thought the silence was going to draw me out any more, he was mistaken. McGraw had been as good at that shit as anyone, and he'd trained me.

"Well," he said after a long moment. "I wouldn't call it embarrassing. But . . . a foreign criminal organization does present certain intelligence challenges. And cultural ones. The yakuza has always been an unfortunate part of Japanese society, but a part nonetheless. There are many unspoken rules. With Victor, many of these rules seem not to apply."

It was a subtle concession, but still a concession. There was room here for joint action. I just didn't know how much.

"What rules are we talking about?" I said.

"Rules about public violence. Leaving the mangled bodies of enemies in the street as a message, for example. The yakuza shy away from such tactics out of respect for public harmony. For Victor, violation of public harmony is itself a weapon."

The word he used for public harmony was *wa*, a concept integral to Japanese culture. *Wa* implies an elevation of the needs of society over the needs of the individual, the primacy of peaceful unity and conformity. To violate *wa* is to invite some form of correction—possibly quite strict correction. I wondered if, in his reference to *wa*, Tatsu was also hinting at the need for that kind of reaction.

"I'd like to learn more about him," I said.

"For example?"

"Well, whatever you know."

He looked at me with an *Is that the best you can do?* expression.

Yeah, he wasn't going to reveal what he knew until I revealed what I wanted. I couldn't blame him. I would have done the same.

"I want to be frank with you," I said. "But I need to know the parameters."

"One parameter would be limiting yourself to Victor. No other early retirements, is that correct?"

He was telling me no civilians. No mistakes. I said, "What if someone else in his organization were to retire, too?"

He nodded with slightly exaggerated gravity. "Well, these things happen, I suppose. Changing personnel. Simultaneous departures. Who do you think might also retire?"

"You know his guy Oleg?"

"Oleg Taktarov."

"Okay, you know him."

"He is former *Spetsnaz*, like Victor himself. Both of them took part in the Soviet invasion of Afghanistan three years ago. Operation Storm-333, I believe it was called. Several hundred Soviet Special Forces soldiers, dressed in Afghan army uniforms, stormed the palace, killed the president and his two hundred personal guards, and then installed a handpicked successor. A very impressive operation."

"Hasn't been going so smoothly since then."

"True, but I don't think the larger geopolitical problems Russia faces in Afghanistan are the fault of men like Victor and Oleg. Any more than the outcome in America's war in Vietnam was the fault of men like you."

I nodded at the fair point. "What are they doing in Japan?"

"I was very much hoping you might be able to tell me that."

"You don't know?"

He took a sip of beer. "These Russians aren't like our yakuza. They don't keep regular office hours. They don't have business cards. They conduct themselves more like the black-ops soldiers they were than like the criminals they've become. That said, I have some information. Most of it obvious."

"They seem to have cornered the assassination business."

He looked at me. A beat went by, and I thought he was going to ask how I would know that. But all he said was, "That would be the obvious part."

When Tatsu was disappointed I wasn't keeping up, he wasn't shy about showing it.

"Okay, right. But why? Was it just an opportunity for a hostile takeover? And where are they getting their intel?"

He nodded. "Those would be the nonobvious parts."

"You don't know, then."

"No."

"My understanding is, when they got here, they faced a certain amount of opposition. Which they wiped out more or less as smoothly as it sounds like they took the presidential palace in Kabul. Okay, fine, they're experienced and ruthless. But still, an operation like that means pinpoint intel."

"Of course."

"Shit. I was really hoping you might know."

"I've been able to find out some things about the beginning. And some things about the present. But the connective tissue so far has eluded me."

"You wouldn't happen to know how big his organization is, would you?"

"Not precise numbers. Victor and Oleg, of course, but only a few local soldiers under them. Their strength is military experience, ruthlessness, and of course highly accurate intelligence."

I nodded. "That tracks with my assessment."

He frowned. "Tell me, how did you get mixed up with these people, or however you would prefer to put it?"

I supposed it was too much to hope that he wasn't going to push on that.

I took a sip of beer. "They're insisting I do a job for them. With the implicit promise that, if I don't do it, they'll kill me."

"And this is what brought you back to Japan? Where have you even been?"

"It's a long story and it doesn't really matter now. I went back to war. I got tired of it. I came back hoping for something better. An old friend introduced me to Victor, and from there it went straight to shit."

He nodded as though considering all that. "What do you propose to do?"

"What do you think I'm going to do?"

"Eliminate the source of the trouble."

"Am I really that obvious?"

He grunted. "You can get to him?"

"Not easily. Not now. But if I open up a flank . . ."

"Oleg."

"Exactly."

"If something happens to Oleg, and Victor just met you, he'll come at you. I don't think you want that kind of fight."

"Yeah, I already thought of that. And agreed, I'd prefer the kind of fight where I come at Victor from a blind spot. You know, no fight at all."

"This is no soft target. We're talking about a former *Spetsnaz* soldier. How are you going to do this?"

"That depends on the intel, I guess. All I know right now is absent a hell of a lucky break, my best bet is to peel a layer off Victor's defense. And then get inside."

"Take out the colonel's best soldier."

"Yes, and in doing so, force the colonel to take the field himself."

He took a sip of beer. "I imagine I can get you operational information about Oleg. But this plan of yours . . . wouldn't it make more sense to just walk away? Leave Tokyo. You have before."

It probably should have concerned me more that first Miyamoto and now Tatsu—both smart, savvy players, both older and more experienced than I—were telling me the same thing.

"It's a little more complicated than that," I said.

"Why not tell me how?"

"I . . . have an acquaintance in the picture who would probably bear the brunt of Victor's retaliation if I were to skip town."

"The person who introduced you, I imagine."

I looked at him, not for the first time appalled by the keenness of his instincts. "Why do you say that?"

"Well, you don't have many friends."

"Thanks."

"And if it were me, you would tell me."

I nodded. "You can count on that. Always."

He grunted an acknowledgement. "And the last time we met, you mentioned you were dating someone. But I don't imagine she's still in your life."

He was talking about Sayaka. I had to work for a moment to keep the box closed.

I didn't want to ask, but I did. "Why do you say that?"

"It's not inconceivable you came back here for her. But . . . ten years is a long time."

"She's not here anymore."

Whatever he saw in my eyes or heard in my voice must have made him understand not to push any further on that.

"So," he said. "Just a process of elimination. And proximity. Someone introduced you to Victor. Presumably, someone you know well enough to care about. And Victor is treating that person like the surety on a loan."

I nodded, a little chagrined at how easily he was able to see through something I thought would be opaque. "That's about it."

We were quiet for a moment, just sipping our beers. I tried to imagine what he was thinking. How much more he might extract from me. How far he'd go to help.

"What else do you know about Victor?" I said.

He set down his mug and rubbed his chin. "The enemy of my enemy is my friend. Quite a number of yakuza are willing to share what they know of Victor with the authorities, in the hope that in doing so, they will enable us to help with their problem. Some of this information has enabled me to confirm other details. Beyond those details, I am forced to speculate."

"I'll take whatever you have."

"All right. I believe Victor was born of a Japanese mother, and that he spent his childhood in Japan."

"Yeah, he looks like a blend. Is there more?"

"Of course. First, he speaks Japanese."

"His Japanese is Russian-accented. Not native."

"I'm quite certain Victor has no interest in being a native. Perhaps he once did, but if so, that hope was beaten out of him."

"What do you mean?"

"He was abandoned as a child, and raised by strangers. Bullied for being a half-breed. Not so hard to imagine he would be eager to separate himself from that trauma. To create a new, Russian self, and distance himself from the hated part of his heritage."

The word he used for half-breed was *ainoko*. He obviously intended it in a neutral sense, just quoting what the bullies would have called Victor. But even all these years later, I hated the sound of it. It's what they had always called me.

"How much do you know about his childhood?"

"If I am correct about who he is, he was left outside a Tokyo orphanage when he was five. He was holding a note. The orphanage still has it."

"What was the note?"

"A handwritten explanation, in Japanese, from an anguished mother who could no longer care for her child."

"She just . . . left him there?"

"Apparently so. The boy claimed she was coming right back, that she had told him to wait there with the note while she went to the store to buy food. He continued to believe this until he was a teenager. That something must have happened to his mother—she had gotten lost or waylaid, but would come back for him. The head of the orphanage is quite old and has long since retired, but I spoke with her. She told me the boy would stare out the window at the street where his mother left him. Every day. Whenever he was unsupervised, he would go to the window, press his hands against the glass, and stare out."

I remembered my eight-year-old self, sobbing night after night for months, drowning in an ocean of pain and confusion and grief after my father had died.

"That's . . . terrible," I said.

"Indeed."

"The father?"

"Unknown. Victor claimed he was a Russian general, who he also fervently believed would come to the orphanage and claim him."

"A Russian general? Does that make any sense?"

"No. If he is who I think he is, Victor was born around 1940. Relations between Imperial Japan and the Soviet Union were hostile in that period. We had fought an undeclared border war in Manchuria just a few years earlier—a war in which Japan was decisively beaten back. There were no Soviet generals in Japan."

"Could the mother have gone abroad?"

He shrugged. "I think the chances that a Japanese woman, so destitute that she had to give up her own child, had traveled to the Soviet Union, become pregnant by a Soviet general, and returned to Japan are so unlikely that they're barely worth considering."

"What, then? Just a story she told him? He's got Slavic in his face, that's for sure."

He leaned forward. "What is he like? Your personal assessment."

I blew out a long breath. "He's . . . a bit of a force of nature." I told him about Kobayashi.

By the time I was done, his expression had grown dark. "Recently, a body was recovered from the Sumida River. The face was traumatized beyond recognition, and there were multiple stab wounds."

"That sounds like Kobayashi."

"Masahiru Kobayashi is a foot soldier with the Gokumatsu-gumi. You're telling me he was working for Victor?"

"Victor said there was some kind of fuckup with the Gokumatsu-gumi, and Victor was giving him another chance. You make anything of that?"

"This is the first I've heard of it."

That wasn't exactly responsive to my question, but we were both being careful about what we revealed.

"Well," I said, "if you have dental records for Kobayashi, I'm guessing you can get a positive ID on that body you fished out of the river. Victor's work."

"I imagine it would be useless to ask you to testify as an eyewitness in a homicide? The Keisatsuchō could protect you, and—"

I shook my head. "Not going to happen, Tatsu. We need another plan."

He nodded. "All right. I had to try, of course."

"Of course."

We were quiet again for a moment. I said, "Go back. He's got Slavic in his face. Or something, anyway. You think the thing about a Russian general was just a fantasy?"

He sipped his beer. "It could have been. But my guess is, it was based on something his mother told him."

"That his father was a great general."

"Yes. To give him something to be proud of. Rather than the awful truth."

"That his father was a nobody?"

"Perhaps. But why a Russian general? Why not a doctor, a scientist, a musician? Any one of those, or many other vocations, would be enough to give the child some pride in his paternal lineage. And all would have been more plausible than what the boy was given to believe."

I tried to follow, but couldn't. "So what's your theory?"

He gave me one of his trademark *Why do I need to spell out every last aspect* looks. "Sometimes people fabricate. But more often, they exaggerate. They take pieces of truth and construct lies on top of them."

"So . . . a Russian soldier, but not a general?"

"Perhaps."

"But you said there were no Russian soldiers in Japan back then."

"I said no Russian *generals*."

"There were Russian soldiers? During World War Two?"

"As it turns out, there were."

I leaned back in my seat, impressed as always. "You've looked into this."

"Of course. There were several significant battles on the Manchurian border in 1938 and 1939. Our Imperial forces captured numerous Russian soldiers. Some of these prisoners were taken back to the home islands. Most of them did not survive the journey. Several did. One of them escaped."

There was a pause. I said, "Victor's father?"

"I believe so. Many records were destroyed during the war. But there is a record of a captured Soviet infantryman, Alexei Gavrikov, taken to Japan and then unaccounted for."

"'Unaccounted for'?"

"A euphemism, I believe, for 'escaped.'"

"And he meets Victor's mother, and . . . ?"

"And rapes her."

"Damn. But . . . I don't know, Tatsu. The guy escapes, okay, but then he's going to have a hell of a time staying that way, don't you think? A white guy, running around wartime Japan? Where does he hide? What does he eat?"

"The camp he was sent to was in Aichi Prefecture. In the vicinity of many small farms. Gavrikov escaped in the summer, when the weather was favorable. With a little luck, moving only at night, he might have managed to stay hidden. And found enough to eat."

I tried to picture it. "He sneaks into an outlying building on a farm. Or something. And while he's in there, looking for food, or a place to bunk down for the night . . ."

"Is startled by a farm girl. Grabs her. Perhaps thinks to kill her, but sees she's too petrified to sound any alarm. And so forces himself on her instead. Men do such things in war. And worse."

"Not just in war."

"Indeed. Perhaps she tells her parents right away. Perhaps not. Either way, she learns she is pregnant. For whatever reason, she is unable or unwilling to terminate the pregnancy. Her parents don't believe her story. They turn her out. She might have made her way to Tokyo, doing whatever work she could to survive and feed her infant son."

"Prostitution?"

"A farm girl in wartime Tokyo? It's hard to imagine what other options she would have."

"Still. It's a lot of speculation."

"As I said. Some I've been able to support. But yes, much of it happened sufficiently long ago, and in such turbulent times, that it can't be corroborated."

"Well, what else have you corroborated?"

"The note the child was holding when the orphanage found him said his name was Hikaru Yamada. There are archived immigration records of a person of that name leaving Japan for Russia at eighteen. No evidence of a return trip. I believe Victor traveled there looking for his father, the Soviet general. A foolish fantasy, but one burned deeply into his traumatized psyche. I doubt he would have had much to go on. I doubt his actual father even survived the war."

"And then?"

"He joined the Soviet Army, of course."

"Following in his father's footsteps."

"And perhaps fantasizing, consciously or unconsciously, that his father would learn of his exploits and claim him. Of course, this never happened. But Victor did distinguish himself, it seems, probably in covert conflicts in Africa and Southeast Asia. I suppose it's not impossible we crossed paths with him in Vietnam."

"Small world."

"Indeed. Whatever his exploits, they were sufficient for Victor to be one of the men picked to spearhead the Soviet invasion of Afghanistan in 1979. And two years later, he arrived here."

"You're really concerned about this guy."

"Aren't you? After what you saw him do to Kobayashi?"

"Yes. But it's more than that, isn't it?"

He nodded. "As you noted, his intel is superb. That's a problem because it's made him so effective, of course. But it also tells me he has powerful allies, likely within the government. And I've been unable to discover who, or how, or why."

"You want my help with that."

"Of course."

"Honestly, Tatsu, I'm more interested in eliminating this guy than in interrogating him."

"I understand that. But the one might lead to the other."

That was true. And he could have been pressing a lot harder. It wouldn't have been right not to give a little ground of my own.

"All right," I said. "I might have a lead or two. I'll try to learn more. Can you help me with Oleg?"

There was a pause, presumably while he weighed what I was asking him to enable.

"I can help," he said. "But you have to act only with great care, do you understand? This is about removing a cancer. Without harming any surrounding tissue."

I finished my beer and set down the mug. "You just tell me where to find the tumor," I said. "And I'll cut it out."

chapter
nine

I checked in with Oleg the next morning. Again, no leads on Sugihara. Again, I was relieved at the news. Because now the lead I was really waiting for was about Oleg himself.

I left the Ikebukuro hotel and found another one in Shibuya. I wasn't unduly concerned about Victor tracking me, but it's generally better to stay mobile than to present a fixed target. And it wasn't as though changing hotels was terribly difficult. I didn't have much luggage. Just a single bag, in fact.

I imagined meeting Maria that evening at Miyamoto's *biishiki* bar. And I thought about her teasing me about my rented tuxedo, and Kurosawa's obvious concerns about my attire as he looked me up and down in his office. Maybe a drink at a fancy bar would be a good occasion to do better. I decided to do some clothes shopping.

I took the subway to Mitsukoshi in Ginza, Tokyo's oldest and most prestigious department store. The interior was intimidating. Everything on display looked a lot finer than anything I'd ever considered buying before, and the customers browsing the expensive-looking merchandise were wearing similarly fine clothes—certainly finer than mine. I felt people glancing at me as I walked by them, judging my wrinkled shirt and faded jeans and scuffed boots, and for a moment, I felt like leaving. But then I saw a sign for the Men's Department on the sixth floor, thought *The hell with it,* and headed up the escalator.

The sixth floor was cavernous, and mercifully empty compared to the ground level. I started looking around, feeling weirdly stupid and helpless.

A guy in a pin-striped suit with a small badge identifying him as Employee Ito must have sensed my distress, because he came over and asked with great politeness, "Honored customer, perhaps I can be of service in some way?"

"Yes," I said. "Thank you." But I didn't know what to add after that.

"Are you . . . looking for something in particular?"

"Well," I said, scratching my head. What the hell was I looking for? "I'm meeting someone tonight. A woman. In a nice bar. And I thought . . ."

"Something appropriate for the occasion?"

It sounded so straightforward when he said it. "Yes. That's right."

"Do you have in mind something formal? Or more casual?"

Formal didn't mean a tuxedo, did it? Because the wedding had been formal, and everyone there was in a tuxedo. But in this context, the term must have just meant a suit and tie. Would that be too much? Probably. But what were the rules on casual? Was it something equally straightforward?

Again, he must have sensed I was struggling because he offered a translation. "A suit and tie? Or are you instead envisioning, for example, slacks and a nice shirt?"

"Right. Of course. I think probably . . . slacks. And a nice shirt." And in a burst of inspiration, I added, "She's Italian. I think she likes Italian fashion."

He laughed at that, not unkindly. "Everyone likes Italian fashion. Italian would certainly present a good choice."

An hour later, I left the store wearing a pair of charcoal gabardine trousers, a light-gray silk-and-cashmere V-neck sweater, a brown suede belt, and a pair of brown split-toe suede shoes, with moderate welting that was the right balance for the trousers and sweater. The terminology was courtesy of Employee Ito; the clothes, of Brunello Cucinelli, a new

Italian designer Ito assured me was the toast of Milan and would soon be taking over the world. Thinking it was best to get used to the new look, I'd asked Employee Ito to put my regular clothes in a store bag, which I carried as I headed out to the street. I noticed people looking at me in a way they hadn't when I came in, and it made me uncomfortable. Did I look good? Or like a fake?

I decided I probably just looked good. The average person wouldn't be able to sense that I was faking it, even if I was, right? The new clothes would be a worthwhile experiment, if nothing else. In the jungle, we had used different camo patterns and different camouflage face paint, depending on the background we were trying to blend into. If you couldn't blend in the jungle, you might as well have just painted yourself with a big orange target. But wasn't the city the same? I'd gone to that wedding thinking all I'd needed for cover was a tuxedo, and Maria had seen right through it. Next time, it might be someone less friendly. That meant I had a lot to learn.

So for the next few hours, I went in and out of jewelry stores and antique dealers and art boutiques. I played a game—pretending I had grown up rich and spoiled in Shirokanedai, a wealthy enclave in central Tokyo, the only son of parents descended from samurai and heir to a fortune made in the kimono trade. I led a life of leisure, and today was out shopping for baubles. I tried not just to imagine it, but to really *feel* it, the way McGraw had taught me.

And damn if it didn't work. People who never would have taken me seriously were suddenly fawning as though they really believed I was going to cart off a million-yen brooch or an antique lacquered chest. I believed it, and it made them believe it, too. Of course, the Brunello Cucinelli didn't hurt. The key, it seemed, was to both look *and* feel the part. And to recognize that look and feel weren't entirely separate categories. Rather, they seemed to reinforce each other.

By the time I got back to the hotel, the sun was low in the sky, and I was feeling more confident about my new look. I showered, changed back into the new clothes, and walked to Minami Aoyama. The evening was cool and breezy, and the thought of meeting Maria at a bar was causing my heart to kick surprisingly hard.

Halfway there, I realized I hadn't checked in with Oleg. All right, no problem, it wasn't much past five. I found a payphone and called him.

"You're late," he said by way of greeting.

"You have anything for me?"

"Did you go to hardware store?"

"Don't worry about what stores I've been to. That's my end. Information is yours."

"I have information, asshole. So I hope for your sake, you went to store."

Shit. "What information?"

"Man meets with people tonight. Fancy hostess club in Ginza. You have pencil?"

Shit, I thought again. "I don't need one. Where? When? What are the particulars?"

"Club is called Moonglow Ginza. Perfect place. Fifth floor. Many hostesses. Different rooms. Man goes there with many important people. You go, you chat with pretty hostess, you wait, man goes for piss, you come up behind, finish, leave by stairs. Easy job. Can't miss."

"When will he be there?"

"Seven o'clock."

Of course. When I would be at the bar with Maria.

"I don't think I'll be able to get there quite at seven, but—"

"Don't be stupid guy. You can't do in front of pretty hostess. You do in bathroom. And who knows when man goes to bathroom? You need to be in club for that."

I was really beginning to develop an antipathy to this guy.

"I understand that. I'll get there as soon as I can."

"What in fuck are you doing? You have date or something?"

For a second, I froze. Then I realized he was just probing.

"Yeah, I've got a hot date and that's why I'm taking the night off. Are you serious?"

"This is lead you wanted. You said you needed. Don't fuck up, stupid guy. By end of night, man better be taken care of. Or someone takes care of you."

He hung up.

I stood there for a moment, trying to figure out what the hell to do.

Maria would have already left the museum. I had no way to reach her. So, what, just forget her on the chance I might be able to drop her husband at this hostess bar? What if I went to Moonglow, but there was no opportunity? I would have blown the better long-term play—developing Maria as a source. The chance to tease out more about her husband. His schedule. Where he stayed when he visited constituents in Yamanashi.

But shit, that was all just rationalization. The real problem was the thought of her sitting in a bar while I was out stalking, and maybe killing, her husband. I imagined her waiting an hour, finally giving up, going home, wondering where he was . . . and then a couple of police knocking on her door past midnight to deliver the grim news.

I couldn't do it. I didn't want to do it. And I wasn't going to.

But what *was* I going to do?

You're being stupid. Don't get emotionally involved. You think you've never killed anyone with a wife before? This is no different. Just shut that shit down, go to Moonglow, and take care of business.

I struggled with that, without success. It seemed I couldn't shut that shit down.

You have to. You can't do this work and also indulge feelings.

Yeah, well. Maybe that was the point.

The hell with it. I'd go to the damn bar and enjoy my evening with her. That shouldn't be hard. And I'd call in tomorrow morning and tell Oleg it just didn't work out. That I went to Moonglow, but Sugihara had security with him, even in the bathroom. I didn't have an opening. What could he say to that?

They have someone who saw you at the wedding. What if the same guy is at Moonglow, and says you never showed?

So what? Maybe I was disguised. Maybe their guy didn't see me. You can't prove a negative.

He's going to say Victor wants to see you. That you need to come in.

Yeah, that was possible. But it wasn't going to happen. The next time I saw any of them, I'd be moving in from behind.

What about Miyamoto?

Shit, that was a good point. I wasn't just taking risks with myself. I was putting him in jeopardy, too.

But the best way to protect Miyamoto wasn't to propitiate Victor. It was to eliminate him. And quickly.

I called Tatsu and managed to reach him at the office.

"Nothing firm yet," he told me. "But . . . some potentially useful details. I have good people working to confirm. With luck, I'll have something for you tomorrow."

"I could really use whatever you've got. I'm feeling a little pressure at the moment."

"Understood. And you? Have any of those leads worked out?"

"I'm following up on one right now. I should know more tomorrow. I'll check in with you then." I hung up.

I walked to Zenkō-ji Temple in Omotesando, a sliver of old Japan holding its own against the encroaching morass of modernity. A waxing gibbous moon was just cresting the curved roof, the cold light glinting off the tiles. I stood before the censer and closed my eyes for a moment, the lingering notes of incense calming me a little.

I thought of my mother, who had tried to raise me Catholic and who had succeeded only in implanting a vestigial sense of guilt I probably would have been better off without. What would she have made of me now? She had wanted me to be a diplomat, or a senator, and was able to make her peace with my decision to join the army only by convincing herself it would be a stepping stone to something better. And yet I'd never gotten past what I'd started with. I never went on to anything else. I left the army, but kept on killing.

It's all right. It's normal to be drawn to the things you're good at. To enjoy them. You're no different from anyone else.

I didn't believe that. But neither did I know what to do about it.

Crazy Jake loved war. Loved killing. And he had no trouble accepting there was no coming back from it. I remembered him telling me, *There's no home for us, John-John. Not after what we've done.*

He was probably right. Maybe my problem wasn't that I was a killer. It was that I refused to accept the consequences of it. That I wanted to have it both ways, one foot in the shadows, the other in the light.

What happened with Sayaka should have proven to me how impossible that straddle really was. And yet here I was, about to meet a woman I liked, a woman I was attracted to, when if my mind were right I would probably be heading to Ginza right that moment to take out her husband.

But maybe that's why I was going to see her. Because I knew if I did, it would make killing Sugihara even harder.

That was it. That's what was messing me up. The thought of repaying her kindness and mild flirtation by greasing her husband, the father of her dead child, and shattering what was left of her family, her peace of mind, her whole world, felt impossibly wrong. My own father had been murdered when I was eight. I wasn't going to be the agent of some equivalent tragedy for her. I wouldn't do it.

I wasn't going to kill Sugihara. I was going to kill Oleg, and then Victor. Miyamoto would pay me for doing it. After that, I'd figure things out. Tonight, I was just going to meet a woman I was interested in. And see if I could get a better idea of the nature of her interest in me.

She's married, you know.

That made me laugh. Maybe the one advantage of having wrestled with killing her husband was that the notion of an affair seemed morally pure by comparison.

You're being stupid. You can't not see that.

I decided I didn't care. Which is of course both a symptom and a cause of stupidity itself.

I walked back out to Aoyama-dori and cut across to the other side, to Minami Aoyama. After a few minutes searching, I found the block I was looking for—a dim, mostly residential street. Fifty yards down on the left was an old, narrow house, its portico supported by two rough-hewn wooden pillars and illuminated by a pair of glowing sconces. A small sign on the latticed glass of the door discreetly announced "Radio." It was just past six o'clock, and I wondered if Maria might already be there. The thought gave my heart a little giddy-up. I adjusted the sweater and went inside.

The first thing that struck me was how quiet it was. Not silent, exactly—more hushed, as though the quiet was more a presence than an absence. Blending with the hush, and accentuating it, was some piano jazz I didn't recognize drifting from unseen speakers.

Before me and to my left was a long, quietly gleaming wooden bar. Behind it stood a trim man about my age in a tuxedo shirt, striped tie, and navy vest. *"Irasshaimase,"* he said with a bow.

I looked around. The place was gorgeous. Immaculate. Behind the man was a wall of polished wooden shelves, filled with bottles and decanters and elegant glasses. The walls and ceiling were painted indigo, and interspersed with wooden beams. The lighting, I noticed, was all indirect—a series of small lamps in the shelving and on the bar itself. The effect was to produce a feeling of privacy, even sanctuary.

"Konban wa," I said, returning the man's bow. "Is it all right if I sit?" It must have been strange to ask, I realized, but the place was so beautiful it felt wrong not to.

The man smiled. "Wherever you like. I opened only a few minutes ago, so you're the first one here."

There were several tables, but it felt strangely rude to walk off to one of them. So I took a seat at the far end of the bar. "I . . . have a friend coming," I said.

"Of course. Can I offer you something in the meantime?"

I looked around again. Without really meaning to, I said, "It's beautiful."

It would have been a trifle rude for him to thank me, as doing so would have implied too much agreement, perhaps the equivalent of saying, "Yes, I know" in response to a compliment in America. Instead, he simply bowed.

"I'm Fujiwara," I said, using my Japanese name, because it seemed I ought to introduce myself.

He bowed again. "Ozaki."

"This is your place, Ozaki-*masutaa*?"

"Yes. We celebrate our tenth anniversary this year."

He must have been older than he looked. Or else he'd started out at an unusually young age.

"A friend of mine suggested I come here. He told me you created a place characterized by *biishiki*. I see he wasn't exaggerating."

He bowed. "And your friend is . . . ?"

I hesitated for a moment, but then decided there was probably no harm. "Miyamoto."

"Ah yes, Miyamoto-san. A regular since we opened. And a particular aficionado of the gimlet."

Great, Miyamoto was a regular. I hoped he wouldn't wind up dropping in tonight. If he did, I'd have a little explaining to do. And likewise if Ozaki ever mentioned to him that he'd met a guy named Fujiwara who came for a drink with a stunning Italian woman. I supposed I could just tell him I was using Maria to get close to her husband, but I hoped it wouldn't come to that. For whatever reason, the thought wasn't a comfortable one. Maybe because I wouldn't want Miyamoto to see me as capable of something so cold-blooded. It wasn't something I wanted to see in myself.

"The gimlet?" I said. I didn't want to pretend, and probably couldn't have gotten away with it regardless, so I added, "I don't know much about cocktails. A little about Scotch is all."

"Well, there's not much to it, really. Cocktails are like Go. The rules are simple. Mastery is hard. The gimlet, for example, is no more than fresh lime juice and dry gin."

I wasn't sure when Maria was coming. Or, suddenly, whether she would be coming at all. She was only a few minutes late, so maybe she'd gotten tied up. But maybe she'd changed her mind. She'd seemed a little uncertain when I'd asked her.

Well, if she was late, I doubted she'd mind me ordering a drink while I waited. And if she'd changed her mind, I'd at least get to drown my sorrows.

"It sounds perfect," I said. "I'd love one."

He bowed, and for the next few minutes I watched him engage in what was obviously a carefully conceived and well-practiced ritual. First, he wrapped a lime wedge in a small white cloth and squeezed it into a shaker. Then he poured in a careful measure of gin and added several squares of clear ice. Finally, he held the shaker with his fingertips and shook it only with his wrists, keeping his elbows close to his body. In his careful movements, I saw the influence of *sadō*, as Miyamoto had said.

When he was done, he poured the translucent mixture, topped with a fine foam from the shaking, into a delicately etched cocktail glass. He placed the glass on a coaster, then eased it confidently forward until it came to rest under one of the counter lights, which illuminated it as though it was a little work of art.

I thought of Miyamoto and *nen*, and made sure to take a moment to appreciate the aesthetic appeal of Ozaki's creation. Then I carefully lifted it, held it under my nose for a moment, and took a sip.

It was delicious: cold and crisp, and while of course tasting of the lime and gin that had gone into it, imbued too with some additional flavor Ozaki seemed to have conjured by alchemy. Not wanting to make him turn away another compliment, I merely bowed my head for a long moment in appreciation. He returned the bow and said, "Please, enjoy," then moved off and began cutting some fruit at the other end of the bar. It made me think of Victor and his persimmon, but I pushed the image away without too much difficulty. Maybe the gimlet, already at work.

Two more people arrived—slightly older men in suits. Ozaki greeted them by name—more regulars, it seemed. They looked important, and I tried to puzzle out why. Their suits seemed high quality, but in what way? How they fit, or the material, or something. They carried no briefcases—suggesting they had minions who attended to the sorts of mundane matters that would necessitate a bag. And there was an unconscious confidence in the way they took their seats at the bar, as though they occupied a certain place in the world naturally, by privilege, by right.

I realized I was a little buzzed. It was all right. It felt good. I decided I needed to start breaking down what I could tell about people from the way they dressed, and walked, and talked, and carried themselves, reverse engineering who they were on the inside from what they showed on the outside. Not just so I could understand the subtle indicators, but so I could articulate them—and then imitate them, as necessary, to camouflage myself whenever and wherever I needed to.

Ten minutes later and one gimlet vanquished, I heard the door again. I looked up. This time, it was Maria, looking like a movie star in a black skirt and blouse. Her hair was up. Was that to signal to me that we were here for business, not the kind of more casual get-together loose hair would have implied?

Or maybe she just liked to wear her hair up. Maybe who the hell knew. I wished I could stop overthinking everything about her. I stood and gave her a little wave.

She smiled and walked over. When she reached me, she kissed my cheeks and said, *"Che eleganza!"*

I caught an intoxicating whiff of perfume. She had put on perfume . . . did that mean something?

I pushed away the overthinking again and tried to concentrate. "I know," I said. "I really need to thank my friend for the recommendation."

She laughed. "It's a lovely bar, but I was talking about you! I don't think I would have recognized you."

I felt myself blushing like an idiot. "I did a little shopping. I'm glad you like it."

"I do. Look at you. *Sei un figurino.* Didn't I tell you, Italian fashion is the best? If you dress like this at the museum, all the women will swoon for you."

I was half-pleased, and half-intrigued. "You can tell it's Italian? How?"

"Ah, the cloth, the cut, the quality. Not that Americans don't make some acceptable clothing. But they cut to hide the figure, not show it off. Same with the British. And the French overdo in the other direction because they try to imitate Italians. You see? With Italian, you look, mmm, confident. Like you're enjoying life, but not trying to make a statement. So? Was this my influence?"

I could feel myself blushing again. Really, it was pathetic.

"Maybe a little. After what you told me about the tuxedo."

"Ah, I was being too hard on you."

"No, not at all. I like learning things like that." And that was the truth, though I didn't expect she'd understand quite why.

We sat and she glanced at my empty glass. "What's that you were drinking?"

"A gimlet," I said, as I though I was an expert.

"Hmm. Usually I enjoy a negroni, but would you recommend the gimlet?"

I smiled. "Best I've ever had."

Ozaki must have had a nice sense of timing, because he chose just that moment to come over. "A gimlet, please," Maria said in Japanese. "My friend just suggested it."

I wanted to order another, but thought I should keep trying to expand my horizons. *"Omakase,"* I said. Whatever you recommend.

Ozaki bowed and repeated the ritual I'd witnessed a short while earlier. Maria watched, obviously enthralled. "Ah, *utsukusii ugoki,*" she whispered to me, using a Japanese term that literally means "beautiful movement," but that as a concept is more like the physical elegance associated with things like ballet. "And the bar—gorgeous. *Biishiki.*"

"That's what my friend said. The one who told me about the place." I felt in Miyamoto's debt already.

A few minutes later, Ozaki presented us with our drinks. Mine was called a bee's knees—gin, lemon juice, and honey syrup. We toasted and each took a sip.

"Ah," Maria said, bowing her head to Ozaki. *"Oishii desu."* Delicious.

I bowed my head as well. Ozaki smiled. "Please, enjoy," he said, and moved discreetly off.

For a while, we made small talk about fashion. She told me that Employee Ito from Mitsukoshi had given me great advice, because most men would be afraid to mix brown shoes and charcoal pants, but to her it was one of the best combinations possible. She also explained that if you want to tell if a man is really well dressed, look down—because most men, no matter what else they might get right, don't know shoes. And that ties should always have a dimple. And that a handkerchief in the jacket pocket should never, ever match the tie. And that British men wore their clothes like a barrier; American men, like an afterthought; Japanese men, like a uniform; and Italian men, like a come-on. She had an easy laugh, and seemed to take a lot of pleasure in sharing her information and insights.

As the evening went on, the bar began to fill up. At one point, a white guy came in and looked around. Mid-twenties, clean cut, in a suit, the tie loosened, and I guessed he was American, maybe a banker or lawyer on an expat package. But when he saw there were no open tables, he left. There was room for one at the bar, so maybe he was meeting a group. For a moment, I thought of Victor, but the guy didn't look Russian and, anyway, he didn't have that vibe.

Maria was on her second gimlet, and I on my second bee's knees, when I said, "I'm glad you came. Your husband doesn't mind?"

I wasn't entirely sure why I was asking. My plan had been to pretend Sugihara didn't even exist.

She took a sip of her gimlet. A moment later, she said, "Well, tonight he and his colleagues have to entertain a visiting delegation of businessmen. They'll be talking about boring topics like the trade imbalance in semiconductors, and opening up the Japanese market to California rice. So I had the evening free."

I had the feeling she hadn't told him, but that she didn't want to acknowledge it. The thought produced a small burst of warmth in my gut.

"Does he do that kind of entertaining often?" I said. Again, I wasn't entirely sure why I was asking. To propitiate the part of myself that continued to hope tonight was somehow operational? Or because I was hoping to learn that she viewed tonight as somehow . . . illicit?

She glanced at me. "And why are you so interested in my husband?"

I shrugged. "Just some of the things you said before. At the museum."

I hoped it was a smooth enough recovery, and apparently it was, because after a moment she said, "Well, yes, politics is a strange profession. The more senior you become, it seems, the more time you need to spend on it."

"I'm sorry."

"Why do you say that?"

"I just . . . it didn't sound like something you're happy about."

We were quiet for a moment. Just as at the museum, I had the sense that she was deciding whether to advance or retreat.

She sighed. "It's a hard topic to discuss without getting into areas that are . . . that I don't like to think about. That I don't like to feel."

"I'm sorry. I shouldn't have said anything."

"No. I'm not sorry you did. It's just . . ."

She paused and looked around for a moment. More people had trickled in since she arrived, and the bar was suffused with the purr of a dozen hushed conversations.

"I really love this place," she said. "I'm so glad you suggested it."

"So am I."

She glanced at me and smiled. "You're very, mmm, earnest, do you know that?"

I didn't know how to respond. "Is that bad?"

"No. It's actually quite appealing. I like that you blush so easily."

I could feel myself instantly blushing at that.

She laughed. "You see? Don't worry. Women like men who blush. It shows you appreciate us."

We were quiet again. Then she said, "You know, I think everyone struggles with some sort of regret. But we have to, mmm, play the hand we're dealt, is that not true?"

I nodded, afraid if I said anything it might impede her. After a moment, she said, "Have you ever been in love, John?"

I nodded again. "Yes."

"What happened?"

"I ask myself that every day."

She smiled. "Are there answers?"

"Not satisfying ones. We lived in different worlds. It couldn't work."

"Because you have two souls?"

"No. It wasn't like that. I got involved in some things after the war she wouldn't have been able to understand."

"What kind of things?"

"That's a story for another time."

By *another time*, I of course meant *never*.

"Was she Japanese?"

"Yes. Well, ethnic Korean, but yes."

"Where is she now?"

"In America, I think."

"You haven't tried to contact her?"

"I think it's better if I don't."

There was a deep sympathy in her eyes. "That's a sad story."

"Well, like you said. We all have them."

"Yes."

"What about you? Have you ever been in love?"

She looked at me. "That's a bold question to ask a married woman."

I returned the look, fortified by Ozaki's delicious elixirs. "I know."

"Well, the answer is yes. I was twenty years old and a third-year student at Sapienza when my husband came to lecture there. And here was this older man, charming and knowledgeable and so incredibly passionate about art. And so exotic for me, too, you know, having grown up in Italy."

She took a sip of her gimlet. "I think you can imagine the rest. I got pregnant. He couldn't extend his time in Italy. I almost didn't care. I was in love. So I came back with him. But my parents . . . they grew up in a small village, and they were from an earlier generation. For them, it was a horrifying scandal. They cut me off. Shunned me. So, when I left Italy, it was a one-way trip."

"They wouldn't be in touch with you? Even after you gave them a grandson?"

She clamped her jaw for a moment, as though bracing for something painful, and stared at her glass. "I think my mother wanted to reach out. But my father was very, mmm, domineering. And I think my mother was afraid to cross him. I think she and I would have reconciled.

I wished we could have. I never hated them for what they did. But my mother died before that happened. And when . . . my son died, I got a letter from my father. Telling me it was God's punishment for what I did to my parents."

"I'm so sorry, Maria."

She nodded. "I don't want to hate him for that. I've worked hard not to. But I can never forgive it. To say such a thing. To go *out of his way* to say such a thing. Whatever delicate threads there might still have been between us, with that he cut them forever."

She blew out a long breath. "I think I need another drink. You?"

"If you'd like one. Sure."

She looked up, and Ozaki appeared as though by magic. *"Masutaa,"* she said. "Two martinis, please. With a twist."

I wasn't sure why, but I liked that she ordered for both of us. Maybe because it showed how comfortable she was with me.

She looked around. "I love it," she said again. "What a magical little place this man has created."

We were quiet again for a moment while Ozaki began preparing our drinks. "So this is the answer to your question," she said. "I was in love with my husband. And we had a good life in Kyoto with our little boy. We called him Dante, for the poet, of course, and also because the name is easy to pronounce in Japanese."

Her voice caught, and she paused to collect herself. Ozaki set down our drinks, bowed, and moved off.

She raised her glass. *"Salute,"* she said, and took a big swallow. *"Mamma mia,* that man is a magician. The government should designate him a Living National Treasure."

I took a swallow, too, but I barely tasted it. I was too intent on her.

"Anyway," she said, "as I told you at the museum, we moved to Tokyo for my husband's new life as a politician. I was still happy— Dante made me happy no matter what. But then there was an accident. A very stupid accident with a revolving door in a building. After that,

I spent three years barely leaving the house. I must say, my mother-in-law was very good to me. Better than my own mother, as you see. And Director Kurosawa offering me a position . . . well, as I told you, it really did save my life."

A beat went by. I said, "Did you ever think about . . . other children?"

"Ah, that was one of fate's little ironies. I couldn't have more children. Only one accidental pregnancy. Maybe my father was right."

"No. That was a sick, horrible thing he said because he wanted to hurt you. God had nothing to do with any of it."

"How can you be so sure?"

I struggled for a moment because I didn't want to say too much. *Fuck it.*

"I told you. I've seen awful things. The worst things. And done them. Please don't ask me what. Nobody who comes back from that shit wants to talk about it. But I've seen more evil than anyone in his right mind would even want to know exists. And for all that, I've never seen punishments or rewards distributed other than at random. If there were a God, he would have struck me down a long time ago."

Even as it came out, I thought I probably shouldn't have said it. But I hated that she would believe she could be to blame for any of her misfortune. And maybe her doubts had tapped into something else, as well. I didn't believe in God. But sometimes not believing was a struggle. Maybe my remarks were directed as much at myself as at her.

I'd been buzzed after the first drink. And suddenly, I realized *buzzed* was an exit I'd passed quite a few miles back.

She took my hand and squeezed it, briefly but hard. Then she let it go and took a sip of her drink.

"Anyway," she said. "For too many reasons to go into, losing Dante became like a wall between my husband and me. He copes with his pain by burying himself in his work."

"How do you cope with yours?"

"Oh, by trying to see the beauty in the world. And, I suppose, to curate it for the sake of others. And by telling myself one day I'll be with my little boy again. I have to believe that, or life would be unbearable."

I said nothing, not knowing any words that would have adequately conveyed what I felt. She looked at me, and though her eyes were wet, she laughed. "You see? Earnest, even in your silence."

She lifted her glass in a toast, then finished the little bit still in it. Mine was already gone.

"Do you want to take a walk?" I said, because we'd been sitting for a while. And because I wanted to be alone with her.

She glanced at me. "Where did you have in mind?"

"I don't know. I stopped at Zenkō-ji on the way over. The temple in Omotesando. It's nice at night. Peaceful."

"That sounds lovely. I could use a little air. I don't remember the last time I had three cocktails."

"I don't remember the last time I had four."

She laughed. "Okay, we for sure should take a walk."

I paid the bill, and we said goodnight to Ozaki and headed out. I took a thorough look around as we went through the door, but didn't see anything that set off any alarms. The guy in the suit must have been nothing. I was glad. I didn't want to have to worry about anything but enjoying my time with Maria.

As we strolled along the narrow street, she took my arm the way she had outside the museum. Was it just an Italian thing? Did it mean something more? I decided I didn't care. I liked it. That was enough.

A few minutes later, we were at the temple. We walked up the stone path, and gradually the sounds of the street faded behind us. The moon was higher now, and the grounds were bathed in alternating pools of light and shadows.

"Ah, I love the little temples and shrines," she said, arching her neck and stretching her arms as though she could feel the place and not just see it. "I hope they never go away, no matter how big the city grows."

I didn't say anything, content just to look at her and listen.

She drifted over to the *chōzuya*, the water-basin pavilion at which visitors purify themselves by washing their hands and mouths before approaching the temple itself. She leaned back on one of the posts and looked at me. "Do you want to hear something funny?"

I walked over and leaned against the opposite post. "Sure."

"When I saw you at the wedding, I thought you were CIA."

That caught me by surprise. "What?"

"You were looking around the room so intently. And I thought there was something other than just Japanese in your face, something maybe American. So I decided to have some fun. But then I thought, no, no one so awkward and obvious could be a secret agent."

So that's why she had come over. Curiosity more than attraction. But for once, I didn't overthink it. We were here, weren't we?

"Hey, thanks a lot."

She laughed, then said, "You're not, are you?" Despite the laugh, her tone was serious.

"No."

"But I suppose you would have to say that, right?"

"I wouldn't know."

"I didn't think you were. But then . . . you were in the American army. And you mentioned being in a world the woman you loved couldn't be part of. And you seemed interested in my husband."

I looked at her. "The only person I'm interested in is you."

She smiled. "That's nice."

"It's true."

We were quiet again. She was hauntingly beautiful in the moonlight: her hair shimmering black, her skin pale white, her eyes hidden in shadow.

After a moment, she said, "What are you thinking?"

"You don't want to know."

"If I didn't want to know, I wouldn't have asked."

"That you are the most beautiful woman I've ever seen."

She laughed. "That's sweet. I used to hear it a lot twenty years ago, I don't deny. But not in a long time."

"I can't imagine there was a time you were more beautiful than you are right now."

She laughed again. "Ah, maybe the awkwardness at the wedding was all an act. Maybe you're a little smoother than I was giving you credit for."

I thought about making a joke about how maybe the clothes really did make the man. Something like that. But I didn't. I didn't want to joke. Or even talk anymore. All I could think about was touching her.

I walked over, my shoes crunching quietly on the gravel. She was facing me, but I couldn't see her eyes until I was very close. I reached out and brushed the back of my fingers against her cheek.

She looked down. "Ah, John," she said. "I don't know."

This time, I did make a joke. "Because you might be my boss at the museum?"

She laughed and took my hand. But she didn't move it from her cheek.

"I don't want to hurt anyone," she said softly.

"Who would we hurt?"

She laughed again. "Besides each other? My husband. In his position . . . a scandal would be so terrible."

I reached out and touched her other cheek. Somehow, without being aware of it, I had moved closer. We were standing so near each other I thought I could feel the heat from her body, some electrical current. "I'm not going to tell him," I whispered. "Are you?"

She was still looking down, but her hands went to my shoulders. "No," she said, shaking her head. "Of course not. But . . ."

Her voice dropped off. She squeezed my shoulders, and then my arms, and then she took my hands in her fingers. I thought she was going to gently disengage, but she didn't. She just held my hands, squeezing them tightly, still looking down.

Then her head came up and she looked at me, her eyes bright in the moonlight. "I'm a married woman," she whispered. "And my husband's work . . . I have to be respectable. I have to."

Her mouth was open and I could feel her breath on my face, warm and urgent and perfumed with gin. I wanted to kiss her so much, but the feeling of *almost* kissing her, of standing on the vanishing edge of whatever precipice we were on, was so delicious and so ephemeral I didn't want to let it go.

"I have to," she whispered again, her breath coming faster. "I have to." And then she gave a little whimper, and one of her hands slipped behind my head and pulled me in, and we were kissing, and the precipice was gone and I was falling, flying, intoxicated by the taste of her mouth and the feel of her tongue and the smell of her perfume. I pushed into her and she pushed back, and I ran my hands over her breasts, her hips, her body, and she held my face and moaned into my mouth, and I wanted her so much I forgot everything else, how I'd met her, who she was, where we were, everything. Without thinking, I swept up her skirt and pulled her into me, and then I slipped my hands inside her panties and the feel of her naked ass, her body against me, her tongue in my mouth, obliterated thought, and all I wanted, everything I needed, was to be inside her.

I started to slide her panties down, but she broke the kiss. "No," she said, panting. "Not here. Take me somewhere. Your place. A hotel. Anywhere."

I had to fight for a moment to understand what she was saying, and to formulate some sort of coherent response. "I'm staying in a love hotel in Shibuya."

She laughed, still panting. "A love hotel? You must have been pretty confident."

Even in the heated moment, I could feel myself blushing. "No, it wasn't that. They're just cheap and convenient. I mean, if I'd been confident, I would have stayed someplace fancier. But this one's okay. Basic. Not one of the themed types. Just a clean room with a bed and a shower and a bath."

She kissed me again, deeply. "Take me there, then. Hurry."

We adjusted our clothes and staggered back to the street. A moment later, we were in a cab. The ride took less than five minutes, but it seemed excruciatingly slow. We kept a discreet distance from each other in back, but everyone knew the top of Dogenzaka in Shibuya was a warren of love hotels, so between that and the electrical current I felt radiating from both of us, the driver must have had a pretty good idea of what was going on. It probably didn't help matters that Maria had her hand on my thigh, the slight pressure of which just inches from an erection that felt the size of Tokyo was making it a challenge to control my breathing.

To maintain a modicum of decorum and deniability, I had the cab stop on the main thoroughfare—Dogenzaka, for which the neighborhood was named. From there, we walked up a narrow, sloped street, with others like it snaking off in all directions, an area called Hyakkendana, meaning one hundred stores, many of which were love hotels. There were plenty of regular establishments, of course, including some excellent restaurants specializing in basic Japanese fare, and in fact I knew the area primarily for a unique coffee shop called Lion, which McGraw had liked to use for dead drops. But Hyakkendana was also famous, or infamous, depending on your view of such things, for the hotels, along with a startling variety of sex shops.

"I can't believe it," Maria said as we walked arm in arm. "You really stay here?"

"Well, most people use these hotels for 'rests,' not 'stays,' but yeah. You've never been to one?"

She laughed. "Why would I?"

"Don't worry, I told you, this isn't one of the crazy ones. It's called Hotel Elegant, which is maybe a bit of an exaggeration, but inside it's pretty normal."

"Oh, now I think I might be disappointed. I've always envisioned these places as so, mmm, extravagant. I heard they're like theme parks."

"Well, we could find one like that, if you like."

She laughed again and squeezed my arm. "Maybe next time."

We got to the hotel and hurried inside, past the receptionist window, the curtain behind it concealing all but the counter where money and room keys changed hands. We took the stairs to the second floor and, a moment later, were inside the small, plain room, kissing, the door locked, Maria's back pressed against it and my hips pressed against hers. I put my palms on the door above her head because I was afraid if my hands were free I'd go too fast, but maybe I needn't have worried because she took advantage of the position to slide my sweater up past my head and over my arms. I tossed it aside and put my palms back on the door, and she ran her hands over my ribs and chest and stomach.

"Oh mio dio," she said, looking at my naked torso. "And I thought the bar was beautiful."

"Is it okay?" I said. "I mean . . . this. Doing this."

She shook her head. "No. It's terrible. But I don't care. I want to. I think I wanted to when I saw you at the reception. But I convinced myself it was something else."

I looked down at her body, then began to undo her blouse, taking my time, hyperaware of the sound and feel of each button moving through each buttonhole, marveling as more of her cleavage, then the black lace of her bra, then the skin of her belly slowly revealed themselves to me. There were buttons at the wrists, too, and I undid those, then eased the blouse off her shoulders and ran my palms down her bare arms until the blouse slipped over her hands and onto the floor. I wanted so badly to have her naked. But, as at Zenkō-ji a short while earlier, I was aware of the feeling of being on the edge of a precipice, an ephemeral moment that was the threshold of something even better but that itself could never be recaptured, and I wanted to draw that moment out, savor it, treasure it, torture myself with it. If this was *nen*, I would never be able to repay Miyamoto for teaching me the concept.

"Turn down the lights," she said.

"I want to look at you."

"And I want to look at you. Just a little."

I dimmed the lights, then came back and scooped her up in my arms. "You're crazy, don't," she said, laughing and punching me in the shoulder. "You make me feel ridiculous."

I didn't answer. I just kissed her, and after a moment her arm snaked around my neck and she forgot her protests. I carried her to the low bed and eased her down, then lay next to her. I tried to keep going slowly, but the more our clothes came off, the more difficult that became.

Finally, we were naked. Her skin was wonderfully smooth and her body insanely voluptuous, and when I touched her, my fingers slipped easily inside. "Wait," she breathed. "Not like that. Not so fast. Here, I'll show you."

She took my hand and showed me how she liked to be touched. "Oh, yes," she said, breathing deeply. "*Oddio*, yes, like that. You see? Not so much so fast. You should, mmm, tease before you attack, you know?"

I smiled and did as she wanted. After a few moments, she was panting and her hand felt more like an afterthought than a guide.

"You really like teaching me," I whispered.

She laughed. "Yes, I think you're right. I'm going to teach you everything, everything I know, everything I like. Everything I've missed. Is that all right?"

It was about the most all right thing I could imagine. I kissed her and said, "Yes."

And she did teach me. She was wonderfully uninhibited about everything she wanted me to do—with my hands, my mouth, the positions she most enjoyed. And she needed no instruction at all in her corresponding explorations of my body, though once I had to warn her I was getting too close, to which she laughed and told me, "Ah, good, it's good you should wait for me, I'm glad I don't have to teach you everything."

I don't know how long it went on. An hour, at least. Long enough so that my balls actually started to ache. I didn't care, though. It was another precipice, another fleeting moment I wanted to make linger for as long as I could.

I was on top of her, looking into her eyes, moving in and out of her so slowly it was almost unbearable, when she breathed, "*Ancora. Ancora.* More. Now, give me *more.*"

I quickened my movements. But she said *Ancora* again, and again, and then a long furious string of Italian I couldn't make out, and she began thrusting back into me as though enraged, enraged because what I was giving her wasn't enough. I was afraid I might hurt her, but the *Ancora, ancora, ancora* was like a chant, a drumbeat accompaniment to the fury in her eyes and her voice, and it all pushed me over the edge of control and I started fucking her harder, deeper, but even that wasn't enough, and I wanted, needed, even more, and I dropped my arms around her legs and swept them forward, pinning her knees to her shoulders, and I gripped the sheets in my fists and looked into her eyes and fucked her faster, harder, as deeply as I could, and I didn't care if it was too much, nothing else mattered but being all the way in, all the way inside her, and her face contorted and she cried out, "*Sì, dai, così, sì!*" the last dissolving into a long, drawn-out inarticulate cry, and I felt her coming and then I was coming, too, and she grabbed my hair and pressed her mouth over mine and cried out again and again in time to our fervent rhythm.

Finally, it subsided. I released her legs and put my elbows on the bed to take some of my weight. I looked in her eyes, catching my breath, feeling mildly in shock, and she shook her head as though in disbelief and cooed something in Italian.

"What?" I said.

She shook her head again. "It's much too filthy to translate."

"Oh, please."

She smiled. "I just . . . haven't made love in so long. I tried to tell myself I didn't miss it. I didn't know I'm such a liar."

I laughed and eased myself onto my side next to her. She looked away as though in thought, and for a moment I just watched her, flushed, naked, her breasts rising and falling as she slowly caught her breath.

Then I realized—she was crying.

"Hey," I said, stroking her hair. "Hey. What is it?"

"It's nothing."

"Was it something I did?"

She wiped her eyes and looked at me. "Not you. I have a guilty conscience."

"Your husband?"

"My son. Those three years I couldn't leave the house . . . every day, I considered suicide to be with him. I was a coward not to, and I'm a coward still. What if he needed me? What if he needs me now?"

I looked at her for a long moment, moved by her sadness, and by the trust she must have felt to share it with me.

"You know how I feel about God and all that," I said. "But I think if there is any kind of afterlife, it has to be eternal, right?"

"I suppose so."

"Then what seems like years to you, from your son's perspective, would be barely an instant. It would seem like you're not even apart. And even if it did, I'm sure he'd be okay. I'm sure he'd want you to enjoy whatever fleeting time you had in this life before you joined him in the next one."

She smiled. "Ah, I thought you were a spy, but now I see you're a philosopher."

I stroked her cheek. "I don't want you to be sad."

"The strange thing is, I'm used to it. I've gotten good at covering it over, or distracting myself with work, but of course it's always there. But I accept that. I don't even mind, exactly. Sadness is my connection to Dante. And I wouldn't give up that connection for anything. But . . . the truth is, just for a moment tonight, a moment ago . . . I did forget."

A tear ran down her cheek and I brushed it away. "It was only a moment," I said. "I think it's okay to forget for a moment."

"I just . . . didn't expect it."

We were quiet again. Then I said, "I was afraid I hurt you. I mean, I was trying not to, but then . . ."

She stroked my cheek. "You're very considerate, John. But you know, it's possible to be too considerate."

"I'm sorry."

She laughed. "It's okay. You made up for it. Besides, we don't know each other so well yet. If you don't know a woman, you should err on the side of considerate. If she likes you to be less so, it won't be long before you learn."

"Can I ask you something?"

"Of course."

"Why do you like teaching me?"

"Ah, is it too much?"

"Not at all. Most of the important things I know, I learned the hard way. This is better."

She laughed again. "I don't know why, exactly." She paused, then went on. "But I think maybe . . . because we will only know each other for a short while. And I'm, mmm, egotistical enough to want you to remember me. No, not just remember. I think I want . . . part of me to stay with you. To shape you, and become part of you. To stay inside your soul, the way you've now been inside my body."

"Are we really only going to know each other for a short while?"

"Yes."

"Why?"

"Because something like this can never last. You're young, but not too young to know that."

I stroked her belly. "But you have so much to teach me."

She laughed. "For that, I think we have time. But not tonight. I have to get home."

"I wish you could stay."

"You know I can't."

I did know. But I was hoping she would at least say she wanted to.

She used the bathroom and got dressed again. I did the same. When she saw me pulling on my clothes, she said, "What, are you going out again?"

"I'll just walk you."

"Maybe it's better if I go alone."

"This part of Shibuya's a little dodgy at night. Can I walk you to the street and make sure you're okay? I promise not to make puppy-dog eyes or anything. I'll just see you to a cab and bow goodnight."

"Ah, I told you you're considerate."

"Will I see you again?"

There was a pause. Then she said, "We shouldn't. But . . . yes."

"How?"

"You can reach me at the museum."

"All right. I'm going to kiss you goodnight here. Outside, we'll be perfectly proper."

It was a tender kiss, but behind it I sensed sadness and some ambivalence. I wanted to say something, but didn't know what.

We took the stairs down and headed out. The hotel was at the corner of an L-shaped street. Straight would have meant more alleyways and hotels; left was the way back to the main thoroughfare. From a little ways off, I could hear the sounds of restaurant-goers and revelers. It was cooler now, the moon higher overhead.

Straight ahead, about fifty feet down in the shadows, was another banker-looking white guy, leaning against a telephone pole, having a smoke.

I didn't like it. Foreigners were relatively rare in Hyakkendana, and the street leading away from the hotel was a particularly empty one. I didn't know what he was doing there. I did know his position offered a great view of the hotel entrance.

I gave no sign that I'd particularly noticed him. We turned left and headed toward Dogenzaka Street. We passed a few couples, obviously in the area for trysts, and of course the touts in front of the sex shops. The street was quiet, but grew more lively as we walked, the sounds of boisterous restaurant and bar conversation louder, the crowds more substantial. This time, Maria didn't take my arm. There was some irony to that, because we probably looked less guilty when she was unconsciously taking my arm than we did now, walking conspicuously and silently apart surrounded by a dozen love hotels.

Assume the guy you saw in the bar was part of a team. Two men, maybe more. A safe bet you'll head to the main street after leaving the hotel, so the second man would be somewhere ahead. But where exactly?

I glanced casually left and right as we walked. Not many places to wait while keeping a view of the street. I assumed I was up against only foreigners. If there had been a Japanese guy on the team, he would have been the less conspicuous choice to position by the hotel. That they'd used a white guy showed they didn't have anything better.

We passed a convenience store on our left. Bam, there he was, the guy I'd seen in the bar, leafing through a magazine and standing with a perfect view of the street. I let my eyes go right past him, registering nothing. My heart started thudding hard and I felt a warm hit of adrenaline snake out through my torso.

I pushed aside thoughts regarding why. And self-recrimination for having idiotically failed to spot the ambush sooner. There would be time for all that later. If there wasn't, it wouldn't matter. It would mean I was dead.

Two-man team. Maybe more, but beyond three would be overkill.

Right. If there had been a third man, they would have rotated the one from the bar to the back, or taken him off me entirely. That they'd risked my spotting him in two places and thereby making him as surveillance meant very likely just the two.

They didn't follow you. They followed her *to you. That's why the first one poked his head in at the bar. To confirm she was with you. After that, they hung back, which is why you didn't spot them outside the bar or at the temple.*

But why? Why hang back? What did that mean for what was happening now?

They don't want her involved. They're waiting for you to be alone.

Tactically, that felt right. Still, I was acutely aware of Oleg's advice about hardware stores and rat poison and knives. There were people around, sure, but it wouldn't be so difficult to hit someone from behind and move off before anyone got a good look or understood what had happened.

Dogenzaka Street was just ahead, choked with pedestrians. I didn't know if the crowds would inhibit an attack, or invite one. A lot of potential witnesses, on the one hand. A lot of concealment, confusion, and movement, on the other.

But the main thing was, the moment Maria was in the cab, the leash would be off whoever was following me. Meaning, in all likelihood, I had maybe a minute left to live.

Or to kill my pursuers in less than that.

chapter
ten

The instant we got to the sidewalk, I turned right and raised my hand for a cab. The turn was natural, but also gave me a peripheral view of what was behind us. The bar guy had the point now, but he was hanging back. They didn't know I'd spotted them. They thought they had time to move in at their leisure. That was good.

A cab pulled over and the automatic door opened. Maria got in.

"I'll see you at work," I said, with a polite wave.

She smiled. *"Grazie."* The door closed, and the cab pulled away.

I might have turned left, or right. Or cut across the busy street. I might have run, and hoped to live to fight another day.

Instead, I turned and walked back the way we had come.

It was a reflex, honed by hard training and lethal experience. An ambush is planned around anticipation that, once you realize you're in it, you'll run away. So if you run, you're following the ambusher's script, and in doing so probably heading into something even worse. It follows that if you're ambushed, running is almost always a mistake. Your best chance of survival is instead to attack the ambush.

This isn't to say that attacking an ambush is a good thing. You've been ambushed, after all. Meaning you're already at a huge disadvantage. It's just that within the universe of crappy possibilities remaining to you following your galactic fuckup of not spotting the ambush before it happened, attacking back tends to be the least crappy alternative. Whether they realized I had spotted them or not, therefore, it was critical now that I not do the expected thing, the thing they would have anticipated and planned for.

So I nodded to myself and kept a slightly dopey grin on my face, as though still drunk on gin and the afterglow of lovemaking. In fact, whatever trace of either had been lingering in my system was now gone, eclipsed by an icy clarity. But they wouldn't know that. What they "knew" was that we'd been in a bar, and then a love hotel. They'd see my expression, and it would slot right into what they already believed. Comfort them. Lull them. Just like the doormen checking invitations at the wedding reception, and like the shopkeepers reacting to my fancy new clothes, they would see what they already expected to see. With a little assist from me, of course.

In my peripheral vision, I saw Bar Guy duck back into the convenience store. Farther up the street, I saw Hotel Guy ghost behind a lamppost. Yeah, they hadn't been expecting me to come back this way. Probably they didn't realize I was staying at the hotel. They thought Maria and I had gone there only for a "rest." My sense that they had followed her to me deepened, to be examined later. What mattered now was that I already had them reacting. They wanted to be behind me, not in front. I couldn't blame them. I wanted to be behind them just as much. And I had an idea about how to make it happen.

I knew the area reasonably well from having scoped it out when McGraw was using the Lion coffee shop operationally. And from having reacquainted myself earlier that day, when I was looking for a new hotel. Still, I should have known it better. I should have known every inch of the terrain, so that I could make maximum use of it for my own advantage. I'd been lazy. Complacent. Well, one way or the other, I knew I would never make that mistake again.

There was an alley on the left side of the street, across from the convenience store—probably for trash and storage for the restaurants that fronted on the street running parallel to it. If it was like most alleys in Tokyo, I thought I might be able to use it.

I cut over and went in. Immediately, the light and sound from the street faded. On my left, visible in the moonlight, was a rusted metal fence, half-covered in weeds, clots of garbage all along its base. To my right were the graffiti-covered backs of buildings, all of them lined with trash containers and broken furniture and abandoned appliances. Power lines ran rampant overhead.

I wondered if they'd follow me in. The alley was sufficiently dark, dirty, and off the beaten track to make them sense something might be questionable about my detour. On the other hand, someone unfamiliar with Tokyo might have guessed the alley could make sense as some sort of shortcut. Of course, if they were eager enough, they might not care either way.

Up ahead, I saw a cat dart out from between two buildings and run up the alley away from me. Good. That's what I was looking for—spaces between the structures.

I moved at a moderate pace—not so slowly that they could have easily overtaken me, not so fast that they would have thought I was onto them and trying to escape. I glanced around as I moved, and confirmed that there were narrow spaces between a few of the buildings to my right. Some were choked with refuse, and others were deliberately blocked off. But not all.

In less than a half minute, I reached the end of the alley and made a right onto a walkway that was only slightly less dim and decrepit. To my right was a construction site—nothing huge, but there were tarps, with bricks weighting down the edges. I snatched one up, liking the weight of it in my hand, the solidity, then sprinted ahead and immediately turned right again, moving parallel to the alley.

I stopped at the first navigable passage I came to, and stuck my head just past the edge to watch. A moment later, I saw Bar Guy pass my position. Having lost sight of me, he was walking faster, doubtless afraid he would lose me. I ducked into the passage, which was so narrow I had to move sideways. The ground was soft—dirt and moss and muck—and noiseless. In a few seconds, I had almost reached the alley again. I squatted, controlling my breathing, silent and still, waiting.

A few seconds later, Hotel Guy moved past my position. He was fixated on what was in front of him and didn't even glance in my direction—though it was so dark in the passage I doubted he would have seen me regardless. But I saw him, along with the knife he was holding in his right hand close to his thigh. I'd already assumed that, whoever they were, they hadn't tracked me just to offer their warm felicitations. Now I knew for sure.

I eased out silently behind him, walking the way I had learned in the jungles of Vietnam, where stepping on a branch could bring an NVA battalion down on your head, and where failing to spot a tripwire could cost you your legs or balls or both. The trash and dead leaves strewn here and there didn't even register for me consciously. I took it all in, avoided it, and moved quickly forward on the soles of my fancy new Italian shoes.

When we were ten feet from the end of the alley, I traded stealth for speed, wanting to close the gap before he turned the corner. But moving more quickly, I stepped on something I'd missed—a wrapper, a leaf, something like that. His arms came up and his head turtled in and he started to turn, some primitive part of his mind registering that the footfall he'd heard behind him was the sound of mortal danger. But it was too late. I raised the brick high, gripping it around the middle, and smashed a corner down into the top of his skull, caving it into his brain and possibly fracturing his neck, as well. His legs buckled and he pitched forward onto his face, his arms splayed at his sides, the knife clattering to the ground.

I had hoped he would die noiselessly, but absent a perfect headshot or transected throat, there are no guarantees in these matters. So it was just bad luck that, as he hit the ground, some weird final sound emanated from his dying throat, a sort of gurgling bark. It wasn't loud, but along with the clattering knife, I knew it was loud enough.

I searched desperately for the blade. He'd been holding it in his right hand, his arms were at his sides when he pitched forward—

Bar Guy came tearing around the corner, stopping not eight feet away when he saw the tableau in the moonlight. I checked his hands, afraid I'd see a gun, and instead saw another knife. If he'd charged me right then, his chances would have been excellent. A brick against a blade isn't usually an equal fight.

But he hesitated, needing an instant to process what he was seeing—along with how did I get behind them, how did I drop his partner, what did all this mean. Psychologists call this mental state "cognitive dissonance," as the brain, confronted with an uncomfortable or unexplainable fact pattern, struggles to make sense of it. And in that moment of hesitation, I saw and swept up his partner's knife.

The smarter thing for me to do, the safer thing, would have been to run. But I was still young, and not quite as governed by cold rationality as I liked to think. Plus, I'd been suppressing a lot of animosity dealing with Oleg and Victor, and my patience had started to wear thin. There was a beast inside me, a beast that had saved me many times in the war, a beast that was always looking for a reason and that I controlled only with difficulty. Being hunted, and having just stalked and killed one of the people hunting me, had unleashed that beast. Freed from my grasp, it wasn't much in the beast's nature to run. Its nature was to kill.

"I don't know what they're paying you," I said in a near growl. "But come at me, and I guarantee you won't collect. Ask your partner. I'm standing in his brains."

I saw it in his eyes then. Fear. The realization that I was telling the truth. That he'd just treed an animal with teeth and tusks. Along with the ability—hell, the longing—to use them.

I knew he was going to turn and run even before he did. So I was already switching the knife to my left hand and the brick to my right before he'd completed his pivot. And drawing back my arm before he'd planted his foot. And launching the brick like a mortar round before he'd gotten off his first step.

It caught him in the back of the head with a beautiful, bass-note *bumpf*. He went sprawling forward, his legs churning spastically, the limbs still receiving a truncated *Run!* message from his brain but unable to properly carry it out. He landed facedown, but managed to hold on to the knife.

Receiving a brick to the back of the head is never a welcome development, but I knew the damage was likely to be much less severe than what I'd inflicted on his partner. When your body has room to move with the impact, it makes all the difference—like being punched in the face when you're freestanding, as opposed to being punched the same way when your head is against a wall. This is just a principle of physics. The fact that he'd held on to the knife was a demonstration.

It didn't matter, though. His circuits would still be scrambled for at least a couple seconds, and it took me less than that to reach him, raise my foot, and stomp his knife hand with the pleasingly unforgiving heel of a new Italian split-toe brown suede shoe.

There are twenty-seven bones in the human hand. I didn't know how many I shattered with that adrenaline-fueled stomp, but in my strictly nonmedical judgment, the answer was undoubtedly "plenty." He shrieked and jerked his arm in reaction to the pain, abandoning the knife. I doubted he could have gripped it at that point no matter what, but still I kicked it away. Then I dropped a knee onto his spine, took a fistful of hair, jerked his head back hard, swept the blade under his chin, and pressed the edge against his neck just below the jaw.

"I haven't cut a man's throat in over ten years," I said, breathing like a locomotive. "You want me to keep that streak, or end it?"

"Keep it," he rasped.

I swiveled my head to check my flanks. All clear.

"Who the fuck are you?"

"Nobody. I'm nobody."

"Answer my questions or you'll be a dead nobody. Why were you following me?"

He groaned and tried to move his head away from the knife, but I already had his neck stretched so hard there was nowhere for him to go. His hair was slick, and I realized his scalp was bleeding from where the brick had landed. I tightened my grip.

"Don't," he said, panting. "Don't. You're making a huge fucking mistake."

"That's weird, from this angle, it looks like the one who made a huge fucking mistake is you."

He groaned again. "You do this, and you will be buried in a shit storm you can't even imagine."

"Yeah? Something worse than a couple of assholes trying to sneak up and knife me in the dark?"

"You tell me. You think you can take on the whole CIA?"

Just the mention was enough to make me do another visual sweep. But the alley was still quiet.

Maybe he was bluffing. A guy with a knife to his neck will say anything he thinks might get you to move it in a safe direction.

"You have a name?"

"Mike."

"Okay, Mike. What does the CIA want with me?"

"Look, man, I'm just like you. A contractor. Doing a job. You think they tell me why? Have they ever told you?"

"But they told you I'm a contractor."

"Ex-contractor, they said. Ex-military. Fifth Group. That was my unit, too."

Maybe it was. Maybe he was lying. Either way, he was obviously trying to build some rapport, to make it harder for me to kill him.

If so, whatever file they gave him must not have described me very well.

"How'd you know how to find me?"

"Look, I'll talk to you, all right? But will you show me some good-will? Soldier to soldier?"

"If you earn it."

"All we were told was to take you off the count. Not why, just who. And that the way to find you was to follow the woman."

"What about the woman?"

He groaned again. "Come on, man, I'm being straight with you. She's Italian. Works at a museum. We were given her particulars and followed her."

That tracked with what I'd pieced together myself. "Who told you? Who gave you her particulars? Who wants me dead?"

"I told you. The Agency."

"That's funny, maybe they mentioned I have a few acquaintances there. Who are we talking about specifically?"

"The seventh floor. You get it?"

The seventh floor was where the Langley top echelon had their offices. I tried to come up with a way to test whether he was telling me the truth, or was just bluffing to scare me. It was a delicate dance. Consciously or otherwise, this guy understood he was doing a version of Scheherazade, but with only a minute to hook me with his tale rather than a thousand and one nights.

"So you know the floor, but not the office?"

"Come on, you know the way things work. The guy who hires you doesn't say why or at whose orders, but you connect the dots."

"That's exactly what you need to do, if you want to survive this conversation."

"I'll give you a name, okay? A name. And you let me walk away. Just one soldier to another. I tell you something that'll save your life, you spare mine. A deal, okay?"

131

"It better be a good name."

"Wilson. Calloway Wilson. Goes by Cal."

I jerked him by the hair. "Never heard of him. Starting to be a really bad day for you, Mike."

"Easy. Easy. Listen to me. He's not with the Agency anymore. Not formally. He hasn't been for a while."

"You just told me the Agency is after me. Seventh floor, you said."

"It is. Wilson was thrown out by Turner and his people three years ago."

Turner would have been Stansfield Turner, Jimmy Carter's appointee for Director of Central Intelligence. Taking the job shortly after the Church and Pike Committees revealed that the CIA had been running amok—conducting assassinations, domestic spying, and unwitting human experimentation—Turner had purged over eight hundred operators in what became known inside the Agency as the Halloween Massacre.

"First you said the Agency wants me dead. Now you're saying it's a guy who got shit-canned three years ago."

"Listen. Wilson goes all the way back to the OSS. And who's Reagan's DCI?"

The OSS was the Office of Strategic Services—the World War II precursor to the CIA.

"William Casey," I said.

"Bingo. And Casey's former OSS, too. He's brought guys in from the cold. Buddies of his, from back in the day. Wilson's one of them."

"Why?"

"To do deniable shit, isn't that obvious?"

If it was a fabrication, it was smoothly delivered. It sounded like either the truth, or cover-for-action the guy had rehearsed carefully in advance. But in advance of what? The possibility that he might have someone kneeling on his back and demanding answers with a knife to his throat? And what would the fabrication even get him? If he'd invented something in advance as a bargaining chip, presumably he would have created something with a little more value.

"What's your connection to Wilson?" I asked.

"Same as his connection to Casey. I was out, and Wilson got me work."

He was sounding a little calmer now. A little more confident. He thought he'd established some rapport, that he'd improved his odds of talking his way out of this. That was good.

"How old are you, Mike?"

"Twenty-six."

"That's pretty young to be out."

"Let's just say I was asked to leave."

"Dishonorable?"

"It was bullshit. I did an informant in El Salvador. They said it was murder. You know what I'm talking about. You guys went through the same thing in Vietnam. Project Gamma, right? Terminate with extreme prejudice? What are we supposed to do, let some turncoat fuck compromise our mission? Get our guys killed?"

He was talking about something that had been reported in the press as "the Green Beret Affair," where US Special Forces had killed a suspected South Vietnamese double agent and tried to cover it up. The resulting trial introduced into the public lexicon the phrase "termination with extreme prejudice," but accomplished little else. The CIA, naturally citing national security concerns, refused to make its personnel available for the defense, and the judge dismissed the case.

"What about your friend? The one whose brains are leaking through the hole in his skull on the ground back there."

"He wasn't my friend. Just another guy Wilson hired. I barely knew him. I got no beef with you."

"How do I get to Wilson?"

"I don't know."

"Where is he?"

"I don't know."

"Where did he hire you?"

"At a 7-Eleven in Paterson, New Jersey, which is about the only job I could get after the army fucked me over."

Something else occurred to me. A lot of ex-military are obviously just that—buzz cuts, tactical watches, loud ties that are an overreaction to years of olive drab. But these two were a lot smoother than that.

"I saw you," I said, "but I didn't spot you. Some of that was my fault. But you knew what you were doing. Tell me how."

"Urban-ops course. Taught by the Agency. Wilson made sure I went through it."

I was intrigued. "What did they teach you?"

"It was like acting school. You know, a lot of fieldwork examining what we could tell about people from how they dressed and walked and what they carried. A lot of roleplaying, blending, that kind of thing."

It sounded like what I'd been doing on my own. I wouldn't have minded taking the course, though—it seemed to have benefited these guys.

"What else?"

"That's it, man. Are we cool?"

I pulled his head back a fraction. "I was really hoping you could do better than this, Mike."

"Easy, easy! Look, I'm telling you what I know. Why wouldn't I? Wilson's nothing to me. He's a paycheck. That's it. I got no loyalty to him."

"I doubt he has any for you, either."

"Exactly. He's just an old ex-spook. But this is different. I'm asking you, man. Soldier to soldier. Please. Don't do me. You don't have to. Don't."

"I'm not a soldier anymore," I said, and cut his throat.

The wound was so massive that the blood didn't spurt. Instead it flooded out of him, as though his neck was an overturned bucket. I leaped back, managing to avoid getting it on anything more than my hand.

He didn't make a sound—he couldn't. But he did somehow get to his knees, one hand on the tarmac, the other pressed uselessly over the gash in his throat. He planted a wobbling foot as though to rise, but then his brain, oxygenated blood plummeting out of it, went dark, and he collapsed and lay still.

I stood there for a moment, looking down at him, as detached as someone in the back row of a theater watching the credits roll on a movie. A knife is about the most horribly intimate way there is to kill a man, and if I'd allowed myself to feel anything at all, I wouldn't have been able to do it.

Of course, later would be a different story. But I'd deal with that when I had to. The way I always had before.

I kneeled and checked his pockets. Nothing but a map of Tokyo. Then I backed up, just ahead of a growing pool of blood, and did the same for his partner. Again nothing. It was worth checking, but I hadn't really been expecting they'd be carrying ID while operational.

I skirted wide of the blood and headed out of the alley. Around the corner, I wiped my hand as best I could on the weeds growing through a chain-link fence. The sleeve of my sweater was moist and stank of blood. I'd have to get rid of it.

I headed straight to the hotel, scanning my surroundings constantly. I saw no problems. Back at the room, I pulled the plastic liner out of a trashcan, jammed the sweater into it, cleaned the knife, wrapped it in a towel, washed up, changed into my more familiar clothes, threw the wrapped knife, the sweater, and my gear into my bag, and headed out. This time, I used an employee entrance around the side, unlocking the door from the inside and heading down an alley, again scanning as I moved. Nothing. So it seemed it had been just "Mike" and his partner. Whoever was behind them, their team was now down by two.

Good news, as far as these things go. But I didn't know how deep their bench was.

chapter
eleven

I kept to backstreets and headed west. In a neighborhood park, I tied the sweater around a rock and tossed it into a muddy pond. It might be found eventually, but by then there would be no sign of blood, and no way of connecting it to me regardless. The plastic bag went into a dumpster behind a convenience store, the towel into another dumpster. I was reluctant to part with the knife, but decided on balance I'd be better off not carrying around a murder weapon, and got rid of it in a sewer drain. I could pick up a clean one later.

Just after I finished dumping the incriminating articles, I got the shakes. It was okay. The aftermath of an adrenaline dump and the impact of realizing how close I'd come to dying. It wasn't the first time, and it wouldn't be the last. I kept walking, waiting it out.

You're okay. You fucked up and it was a close call. But you handled it. You're okay now. You're safe. Now you need to think. Think.

Yes. In the military, we called it an after-action report. What did we do well, what could we have done better, what can we learn to improve the odds next time.

So what had I done wrong?

I breathed deeply in and out for a minute, clearing my mind, calming myself. I reminded myself of one of McGraw's dictates: *First, tell me what you know. Then tell me what you don't know. Now tell me what you think.*

Okay. I started working it through.

You assumed that if you were clean, you were safe. You didn't account for the possibility that someone you were meeting was herself under surveillance.

Yes. That was stupid. Sugihara was a target. In retrospect, it wasn't so inconceivable that someone would treat his wife as a nexus. I'd been so infatuated, I hadn't wanted to see it.

All true. But you're being too easy on yourself.

Yeah, it was worse than not wanting to see it. I'd wanted to *not* see it. Sure, the suit could have been a banker uniform, and the obvious fitness might have been the product of leisure time for the gym. And some of my mistake could be attributed to the trip to Ginza that very day, and my subsequent focus on what clothes could tell me about civilians. I'd started to develop a framework, but then that framework had limited me. I'd seen one kind of professional when I should have been open to the possibility of another.

But I hadn't just been fooled. I had also fooled myself. I'd wanted to believe Maria was separate from Sugihara, from the life I was in. Because I wanted whatever was between us to be separate from all that, too.

Exactly. You listened to your heart and ignored your brain. You wanted to be a romantic in a business where only cynics survive.

I could feel myself resisting the idea even as it presented itself to me. Which was part of how I knew it was the truth.

I wouldn't make the same mistake again. And even if I couldn't control my heart, I could damn sure do a better job of watching my back. And of knowing that no matter how well I protected myself, anytime I met someone else, that person would automatically be the weak link in the chain of my own security. An ugly, selfish way to put it, maybe, but this wasn't about sentiment. It was about survival.

All right. Maria was a danger. But was she *in* danger?

No. If they'd wanted to take her out, they could have hit the two of us anytime. The temple would have been ideal—dark, quiet, and we were distracted and then some. But they didn't.

Almost. But then why not do just you *at the temple? Her back was to that post, remember? Your back was to the street. They could have approached from behind, hit you a half dozen times in the liver and kidneys, and been gone in five seconds. In the fear and confusion and the dark, she'd never be able to identify who did it. A couple white guys, if that.*

That made sense. So it wasn't just that they didn't want to kill her. They didn't want her involved in my death in any way at all. They didn't even want her to be around when it happened.

I thought about Sugihara. Could he have put them on me?

It made a certain amount of sense. He was a powerful man. If he was jealous, if he was having her watched, if he wanted her lover killed . . . presumably, he wouldn't want it to be done in her presence. Any detective worth a damn would zero in on the likely motive, and Sugihara would instantly be a suspect.

Okay, a certain amount of sense. But does it feel right to you?

No, it didn't. Not really. If those guys had been under orders from Sugihara, he would have had to be almost unimaginably jealous. Nothing had happened between Maria and me before that night. In fact, I'd seen her only twice. At the wedding, there had been a little flirtation, but overall she'd treated me professionally. Even if he'd known about the job offer or whatever it was at the museum, if he were so jealous of her that he'd use his connections to hire a couple of CIA contractors to take me out on no more than what had happened before tonight, she never would have talked to me the way she did at the wedding. She would have been afraid to. I supposed it was possible he kept his mad jealousy hidden from her or something like that, but the scenario just didn't feel right to me. And besides, wouldn't it have been easier for him, and probably more effective, to reach out to the yakuza for a hit than to the CIA?

But if he had reached out to the yakuza, they'd have to funnel it through Victor. Those are the rules now, remember? Victor has a monopoly on contract killings. And if you violate his monopoly, a contract goes out on you.

I chewed on that. Not impossible, I supposed, but still far-fetched. It required an insanely jealous Sugihara. Who reaches out to the yakuza. Who funnel the job through Victor. Who outsources it to the CIA. Or at least an insanely jealous Sugihara who reaches out directly to the CIA through some contact there.

No. It didn't add up. Parsimony suggested my problem wasn't with Sugihara.

Or not directly with him.

Right. After all, someone knew they could find me through Sugihara's wife. But why? Who had I offended?

Victor.

So back to Victor and the CIA.

Assume there's a connection there.

I tried, but it was hard to imagine what it would be. Why would Victor have decided to have me killed? As far as he knew, I was over at Moonglow in Ginza right this minute, trying to get to Sugihara. Could he have . . . what, changed his mind? Decided I was a liability for some reason? Why? And even if he had, and even if he had some kind of access to the CIA, why would he deploy a couple of white guys in Tokyo to do the hit? He had plenty of locals under him; I'd seen that. Why wouldn't he have used his own people, who could have gotten closer so much more easily? After all, this was someone who had killed his way to the top of the Japanese-crime food chain.

How do you know it was his people doing the killing?

I considered that. And realized I didn't know. I was assuming—describing not what I knew, but what I thought. McGraw would have chewed me out for it, and rightly so.

But a Victor-CIA connection?

That would explain the intel behind his rise, wouldn't it? You wondered yourself, when you first met Miyamoto for tea at Hamarikyu: How could Victor's intel about the LDP be so superb? There's your explanation.

Well, one possible explanation, anyway. Though I couldn't see why. I could see what the CIA could offer Victor—what maybe they *had* offered him. But what would be in it for them?

I tried to imagine it. Local muscle? For what? And why a guy like Victor? Information was valuable currency. The CIA could have used it to buy whatever local muscle they needed. And yakuza, who were so insidiously integrated into Japanese politics, would have been far more useful than a half-Russian psychopath from the other side of the world.

There's your answer, then.

The other side of the world? An outsider?

Sure. Doesn't it sound familiar?

I considered again. Okay, the CIA wanted an outsider for . . . what, jobs that couldn't leave Japanese fingerprints? The concept made sense, but I had no idea what the specifics might be.

And what about the knives? The Agency could bring a damn arsenal into Japan in the diplomatic pouch if it wanted to. So why did Mike and his partner not have guns?

If this was an off-the-books operation, they might not have been able to get guns. Or even if they could, a gun homicide in Japan would be like a bombing anywhere else. A ton of publicity. A massive investigation. A suggestion of outside influence. Maybe they didn't want any of that.

Intermediaries. Outsiders. And fresh, wholesome, locally sourced weapons. All of it felt like someone's attempt at keeping a low profile. But who? Why? And how the fuck was I mixed up in it?

I spent a few frustrating minutes trying to puzzle my way past the impasse, and couldn't.

That's okay. Back up. Start with what you know. Victor.

It was hard to imagine that, if I hadn't gotten mixed up with Victor, tonight would have happened. I accept a job from a psychopath, and a few days later a couple CIA contractors try to take me out? That would be one hell of a coincidence.

Maybe I was looking at it backward, though. Could Mike and his partner have been hired to *protect* Sugihara?

It didn't make sense. If the CIA knew I'd been hired to kill Sugihara, they would have known who'd done the hiring. Why try to block a bullet, when you could just disarm the guy holding the gun?

I was stuck again.

Call Victor, then.

And say what? "Hey, asshole, did you hire two guys to kill me tonight?"

Just report in. You were supposed to do Sugihara tonight, weren't you? Play dumb. Call in, see how he reacts. Or Oleg, whoever. Read between the lines.

I thought about that. It made sense. I could see how they reacted. And then . . . Tatsu. For information about this ex-spook Wilson. For all I knew, Mike, or whatever his name had actually been, had made the whole thing up.

Yeah, first Tatsu. And then Miyamoto, who might be able to help connect the dots, too.

Three different avenues for intel. A decent chance at least one of them would pan out.

I didn't want to think about what I'd be facing if it didn't.

chapter twelve

I took the train to Sugamo and found another love hotel. After a scalding bath, I fell asleep instantly—the postcombat parasympathetic backlash to adrenaline—then woke with a start only an hour later, my mind racing. Too much had happened that night. First, everything I had hoped for, and more, with Maria. And then the shit with the contractors, or whatever they were. Either one by itself would have been enough to keep me tossing and turning. Having the two in juxtaposition was overloading my brain. It was getting light outside when I finally managed a little more sleep.

I set out from the hotel at a little before nine, checking my surroundings carefully. Nothing remarkable—just a humid, rainy morning. I picked up an umbrella at the station, and called Oleg from a payphone. Rivers of salarymen and office ladies streamed past me, cogs in the vast machine of Japanese commerce, oblivious to the little drama being played out in their midst.

"What happened?" he said as soon as he heard my voice.

It sounded more an accusation than a question. Did he know Sugihara was unharmed? If so, how? Did they have people watching him? The same insider they had reporting from the wedding reception?

And if so, what the hell did they need me for?

That's a key question. Come back to it.

"I couldn't get to him."

"Why not?"

ZERO SUM

"No opportunity."

"What does this mean, 'no opportunity'? Man is at club for four hours. Goes for piss three times. Golden opportunity. Where were you?"

Yeah. An insider. I decided it was time to press.

"Hey, Oleg. How do you know how many times Sugihara pissed?"

"You don't worry how I know. You worry what happens when you are fuckup guy."

He knew how many times Sugihara got up to take a leak. And "Where were you?" suggested he knew I wasn't there. But did he know? Or was he fishing? I needed to find out.

"Every time it happened," I said, "there were other people in the bathroom. Witnesses. Not what I call a 'golden opportunity.'"

"I told you how. Fast, from behind, and run. You want, what, for guy to wait for you in dark alley all alone? Maybe with face to wall? This is what you need to do simple job?"

He didn't know I wasn't there. Otherwise he would have challenged the lie. But he knew about Sugihara's bathroom breaks. Which meant . . . what? If it was the same inside man they had at the wedding, that he hadn't seen me at Moonglow? Yes, maybe that. And if so, I was lucky. Maybe the club was big enough, crowded enough, or laid out in such a way that the inside guy could only report, *The man from the wedding? No, I didn't see him. But it was dark. There were a lot of people. I can't be sure.*

I almost said something like, *If it's so simple, asshole, why don't you do it yourself?*

You know why. Now test it.

"You want me to take that kind of risk with witnesses," I said, "the price just doubled. Tell Victor."

"Price is price."

"No, price is too low. Risk is too high. This is your idea of intel? 'Do him in front of three witnesses in the bathroom, then get past

143

twenty more on your way out of the club'? What kind of outfit are you running?"

There was a pause. Which way he played it would tell me what I needed to know.

He laughed. "Victor's right. You've got some balls. Okay, balls guy. We give you more money."

That confirmed it. But I had to play along. Keep him complacent. "Not just more. Double."

"Okay, double. And we give you one more lead. And you get one more chance. And you know how we pay you if you blow next lead?"

I said nothing.

"We pay by cutting hole in belly. Not big hole. Just enough for hand. My hand. And I reach inside and pull out intestines. Three feet, five, maybe ten feet I pull. Then wrap around neck. This is how we pay. So. Do job, you get double. Fuck up, I fucking strangle with intestines. We have good understanding now, yes?"

Oh, yeah, asshole. You're not going to believe how well I understand.

"Just get me the lead," I said, and hung up. Then I shouldered my bag and started walking.

I wandered in the direction of Komagome, not looking for anything in particular, just trying to process what I'd learned on the phone. I came to Somei Reien, one of the city's cemeteries and a popular spot for cherry-blossom viewing. It was empty this morning, presumably because of the weather, a small splotch of green in the midst of the insensate gray sprawl around it.

I found a bench on a grassy slope overlooking the markers and sat. The only sound was the quiet drumbeat of the rain. The solitude, and the feeling of communing with the dead, some of whom had undoubtedly once sat here as I now did, was soothing. I supposed some people might find cemeteries conducive to contemplation of life's great questions—who are we, why are we here, what does it all mean. For me, the contemplation was typically more tactical—who are they, why are they after me, what did I do to antagonize the wrong people. For whatever reason, I found I did some of my best thinking among the dead, and reflecting on this made me feel for McGraw, who'd been a connoisseur of Tokyo cemeteries, something strangely akin to affection.

Why? Why had Victor hired me?

You know why. To be a patsy. And if you don't see that by now, you deserve the role.

Yeah. If I'd learned anything from McGraw, it was what it meant to be set up to take a fall.

Victor's information on Sugihara was solid. He had a man inside the damn club on top of it. And he had capable personnel. So what the hell did he need me for? Why was he so intent not just that Sugihara die, but that I be the one to kill him?

What had he said about Kobayashi? That he'd been a soldier with the Gokumatsu-gumi, one of the yakuza clans, and that Victor had given him a second chance after the Gokumatsu-gumi had expelled him.

Sound familiar?

Yeah, it did. It sounded like what "Mike" had said about how he'd gotten back in the game on the other side of the pond—Wilson giving him a new role after a dishonorable discharge.

What's the common element?

Deniability, obviously. Victor wanted to put distance between himself and Sugihara's death. If Kobayashi had killed Sugihara, the trail would have led to the Gokumatsu-gumi. If I killed Sugihara, the trail would lead nowhere.

You sure about that last one?

I was reasonably sure. Who was I, after all? I'd been off the grid for a decade. Even if anyone were to look into it, all they'd find would be a mercenary who'd spent the last ten years in the Philippines. A guy who'd sign up for anyone's cause—if the price were right.

A guy who's former US military. Who, before the Philippines, was a bagman for the CIA.

But Victor had known about the military connection—he'd tried to bait me about it at our first meeting. Miyamoto wouldn't have mentioned the bagman work, which came later, but even if he had, it wouldn't have mattered. The point was, Victor knew about my previous connections with the US government. Meaning those connections weren't a problem for him. The main thing from his perspective, I supposed, was that I wasn't connected to him.

What does all that tell you?

That this whole thing was about insulation. A circuit breaker. A cutout between Victor and Sugihara.

Yeah. It seemed a lot of people were looking to conceal their role in some nefarious goings-on. Why, though? What was the game?

I thought about Victor's man in the club. And the fact that he knew in advance Sugihara was going to be there. It sounded like Victor had a mole in the LDP. But how many people would have known Sugihara's plans that night? It could have been ten. It could have been a hundred.

But no, maybe not that many. Someone told Oleg how many times Sugihara had pissed that night. The mole had been there. That meant the field of suspects was, what, five? Ten?

Still a lot of people, though. I'd tell Miyamoto, but how the hell was he going to narrow down the list?

By cross-referencing it with another list.

Holy shit, that was it. I should have seen it earlier.

They were following Maria. Yet they clearly didn't want to hurt her, or even involve her. Her only function would have been as a conduit to me. And how had Victor known I'd met her? We'd been making "sexy eyes" at the wedding. The inside guy again.

I paused for a moment, suddenly feeling doubtful. Because if Victor had an inside guy, why hadn't he told me about the wedding in advance? It would have been an opportunity to get to Sugihara.

You already know the answer. They don't want the wife involved. They didn't tell you about the wedding reception because they didn't want the hit to go down there.

In which case, what, Victor had just been giving me a hard time afterward about not killing Sugihara there?

Maybe. Or maybe the inside man doesn't report directly to Victor. And there are divergent agendas in play.

That seemed possible, and I filed it away for later consideration. For now, it felt like I was getting the broad contours right, even if I still didn't have the details. The main thing was, there was some kind of inside man. And maybe the list of possible suspects wouldn't be so unmanageably large after all. We'd be talking about someone who had been at the wedding, and also at Moonglow. Probably someone close to Sugihara. And definitely someone with a sharp eye for the way people connected, because whoever it was, he'd realized that putting a tail on Maria might be a way to get to me.

I still didn't know why. But I was getting closer to who.

And maybe I'd never learn why. But if I could learn who, and then where, I'd have enough to shut this shit down. And walk away from it clean.

Yeah. I still believed something like that was possible.

chapter
thirteen

I called Tatsu. The person who answered told me he was out. No, I didn't want to leave a message, but when could I reach him? Oh, wait, I was in luck—he was just coming in.

A moment later, I heard his voice. *"Hai."*

"Hey. It's me."

"I haven't had a chance to check on the status of the information we discussed. It's been a busy morning."

"Double homicide? That kind of thing?"

There was a pause. "Indeed. Quite a messy one. Two foreigners in Shibuya. The Keisatsuchō hasn't yet identified the bodies. What do you know about this?"

"Just a lucky guess. But if you want to learn more, you might look into an American named Calloway Wilson. Goes by Cal. Former CIA, apparently, all the way back to the OSS, purged by Turner, apparently reactivated in some capacity by Casey. Wilson might be involved with Victor. Maybe feeding him intel. For what in return, I don't know. Could be a wild-goose chase, but . . . I have a feeling there's something there."

"I will refrain from asking you how you came by this information."

"I think that would be best for everyone concerned. I have a favor to ask in exchange."

"Another?"

"Hey, what about what I just gave you?"

"The value of any of that remains to be seen."

"Fair enough. But look, if there's anything there, I need to know who this guy is. Where he is. Why he might have a beef with me. If I can't figure all that out, there's a good chance the next homicide you investigate will be mine."

There was a pause while he digested that. "Call me this afternoon. I assume I won't be able to reach you?"

"Yeah. I need to keep moving for a while."

"That's probably wise. I'll do what I can."

"I know you will, old friend. Thank you."

I hung up, found another payphone, and called Miyamoto. I didn't want to meet him—if someone had known to watch Maria to get to me, they'd know to watch Miyamoto, too. But I didn't want to tell him about an LDP mole on an LDP office line.

Which was cause for inspiration.

"Listen," I said when he picked up. "I have something for you. It's important and I can't discuss it over the phone. If we meet, though, you need to be damn sure you're alone. I had a little problem in that regard just recently."

"What do you have in mind?"

"Remember where you used to leave the money ten years ago?" The place was under one of the seats on the platform of Gaienmae Station.

"Of course."

"You never told anyone about that, right? No way anyone else could know?"

"Of course not."

"Okay. Meet me there in an hour. Assume you're being followed."

There was a pause. "Am I?"

"I don't know. But you have to act as though you are. Use elevators and make sure you're the only one who gets on. Use the subway, get out, and wait on the platform to make sure everyone else has gone before you get on a train going in the other direction. Have a taxi take you through neighborhoods where there's no traffic and it would be easy to spot a tail. Remember, think like the opposition. Can you do that? You have to be sure."

"Of course."

"Okay, good. I'll see you in an hour."

I hoped it would be enough. Countersurveillance is as much art as it is science, and though I knew Miyamoto had been working on it, this would be the equivalent of taking a few swings in batting practice and then stepping into a big-league game.

I wanted to get to the station early, so I took a cab. Halfway there, I realized I still hadn't picked up a knife. Victor with his paring blade, Oleg with the rat poison, the two guys in Shibuya . . . Tokyo suddenly seemed to have a surfeit of people who liked sharp pointy things, and, in the absence of a gun, carrying a knife seemed like not a bad idea. But I didn't have time to create some sort of light disguise so I wouldn't be remembered, then find a store, and still get to Gaienmae ahead of Miyamoto. I decided the knife could wait. I doubted I'd have a problem so soon after Shibuya.

Twenty minutes later, I was standing midway down the platform at Gaienmae Station. I waited and watched while successive trains arrived and departed, sucking in and disgorging passengers. No one failed to board an incoming train. No one got off a train and waited. No one set off my radar. But the real problem was less that someone could anticipate Miyamoto, and more that someone would follow him.

Just ahead of schedule, I spotted him, walking onto the platform from the northwest entrance, struggling with a dripping umbrella. He was sporting a tie as wide as the Sumida River and as bright as a seventeen-year-old's kimono. He might as well have been wearing a damn beacon. I gave him a discreet nod and kept my focus on whatever was coming in behind him.

A cluster of middle-aged men in interchangeable suits, one of them working his teeth with a toothpick. Salarymen, probably on their way back from lunch break. Not a hard-looking guy among them. A mother pushing a stroller. Two elderly women carrying groceries in *furoshiki*—traditional cloths for wrapping and carrying packages, gradually going out of style as plastic bags took their place. That was all. It looked like Miyamoto was clean—

A burly black guy rolled onto the platform. Shaved head, jeans, button-down shirt with the tails out, and a dark sport coat. Nice, easy gait. Athletic. Casual. And just the right distance from Miyamoto, and with enough people between them, to keep eyes on the target without being made. His clothes were dry, I noted, though he wasn't carrying an umbrella. Maybe he'd held one low to obscure his face outside, and ditched it when he saw who was on the platform.

Maybe because he wanted his hands free.

My heart started thudding hard. I gave Miyamoto a friendly wave and started walking toward him—exactly the kind of acknowledgment I wouldn't have given him if I'd known he was being followed.

He waved back, his expression a little hesitant. I'd already given him the subtle nod. He rightly found it odd that I'd offer such an open greeting under the circumstances.

It's not for you, amigo. It's for your audience. Don't want him to realize I've made him.

I kept the black guy in my peripheral vision. He was drifting smoothly forward, his hands open, his arms swinging, not overtaking anyone in front of him, trying to maintain the screen of pedestrians. He was doing a pretty good job of imitating a tourist taking in the sights around him—his head moving left and right, his expression open and interested. The problem was, he was looking at everything but me. It's uncomfortable to make eye contact with a surveillance target, and takes a lot of practice to do it right—to do it without projecting anything that can tip the target off. And absent that practice, most operators default to the next-best thing, which is making no eye contact at all. That's good enough most of the time. But when it feels like not just absence, but avoidance, it can also give you away.

As I walked, I drifted to my right, away from the tracks, closer to the wall. Miyamoto naturally mirrored my trajectory. When we were several feet apart and had slowed to the point of stopping, I took a step left. I wanted to be facing the black guy but with Miyamoto off to the side so he wouldn't be in my way. My heart was pounding combat hard now. I focused on my breathing, on projecting calm and unconcern.

"Were you followed?" I said, pleased that my voice sounded normal. From far down the tunnel, I heard a train approaching.

"No. I did what you told me."

There was no question about his truthfulness. If Miyamoto had wanted to set me up, he would have had people waiting at the station. He wouldn't have hired a foreigner to follow him onto the tracks while I watched. He was just new and clueless. Not his fault. Not his world.

"Okay, good." I didn't want to tell him about our problem. He'd probably look, or tense up, or otherwise signal to our friend that I was onto him.

"So . . . where should we go?" He seemed a little less certain than usual. Probably all the cloak-and-dagger had unnerved him.

"Here's what you need to look into," I said. "Listen carefully because we only have a few seconds. Someone in your organization knew Sugihara was going to be at a Ginza hostess club called Moonglow last night. I'm pretty sure the same person was there. And I'm pretty sure the same person was at the wedding reception, too. You need to cross-reference those three things. Can you do that?"

The salarymen walked past us.

Miyamoto waited until they were out of earshot, then said, "You think this person—"

"Is feeding information to Victor, yes. And maybe to the CIA."

"What?"

The mother with the stroller passed us.

"Listen. We only have a few more seconds. Whatever you find, don't do anything about it. Don't tell anyone. For now, this is just between you and me. Do you understand? That is very important."

"I understand."

The old women passed us. The train was louder now, and I had to raise my voice over the sound of its approach.

"Good. I need to meet you tonight. Can you do that?"

"Yes. But why tonight? What about now?"

"Just listen carefully. You once told me about a bar. A place with *biishiki*. Bar Radio. You know it, right?"

"Of course. I've been going there since Ozaki-*masutaa* opened it."

"Be there tonight when it opens. Outside—don't go in. I don't care how you get to Jingumae, but I want you to walk to the bar from the corner of Omotesando-dori and Aoyama-dori."

"What? Why?"

"You'll understand soon, I promise. Now, one more thing. In a few seconds, something crazy is going to happen. As soon as it does, walk away. Keep your head down. Don't try to help me. Don't look back. Just walk away quickly and smoothly. And button that jacket. Your ties are way too memorable."

"What?"

The black guy was twenty feet away now. Fifteen.

It was an effort to keep my tone even, my posture open and relaxed. "You heard what I just said, right? That's all that matters."

He shook his head, plainly bewildered. "Yes, meet you tonight, walk from the corner, and something crazy. But . . . I just don't understand."

I shrugged and raised my hands palms-up in a *whatever* gesture. I wanted my new friend to see my empty hands. And to be comforted by them.

Eight feet.

"I don't want you to think about it. Just do it."

Four feet.

"All right, but . . . what is this crazy thing you're talking about?"

"Trust me," I said, smiling as though enjoying some harmless joke. "You'll know it when you see it."

The black guy was just about beyond the range of my peripheral vision now. I forced myself to wait, not to turn too soon, to make sure he thought he'd gotten behind me. At the limit of my view, I saw his right hand floating toward a back pocket.

A civilian would have waited. Maybe he was reaching for his wallet. A map. A tissue. *You couldn't have known,* a civilian would argue. *You couldn't be sure.*

The problem with all that is the civilian would have died collecting his proof.

I braced with my right foot, spun, and shot in, left foot forward, watching him turning, turning in my adrenalized slow-motion vision, his right foot planted, his left leg coming around counterclockwise, the right hand on the verge of accessing whatever was in his pocket. I drew back my left hand and drove it forward, slamming the heel of my palm into his skull just behind the ear. His body jolted from the impact, but he was still turning, still in the game, and I grabbed his right sleeve in my right hand and jerked him violently toward me, dragging the arm high, far from his pocket.

We struggled like that for a moment, his jacket sleeve wrapped in my fist. He was bigger than I was, and strong, and twice tried to jerk his arm free. But a judoka who couldn't keep a sleeve grip wouldn't be worthy of the name, and I would have had to be dead to let his arm go and give him another chance to access a weapon.

He tried to hit me with a left hook, but I danced clockwise away from the blow, bringing my left hand in and grabbing his right hand with it, yanking him in short convulsive jerks, keeping him from regaining a good base or balance. I wanted to slip behind him, but he was reacting to my attempts to drag his arm past by pulling the opposite way.

So I reversed direction, jamming his hand in toward his chest as though I was looking for some sort of wristlock. He might not have understood my feint, but by instinct he tried to obstruct it—by pushing into me.

The instant he did so, I shot in, spinning counterclockwise, stretching out the arm and coming in low under it, rotating his hand thumb-out as I did so. He sensed his elbow's vulnerability and tried to pull back the arm, but it was already too late, and as the arm straightened and his palm turned fully up, I exploded upward, my shoulder catching him just above the elbow. Somehow he managed to lean forward and dilute the impact, but still I felt and heard a loud *pop!* from his elbow as it extended past its natural range of motion. He cried out and tried to yank his arm free, and I keyed on the sound of his yell and snapped my head back into his face with a satisfying thud. And again. I felt him straining back to avoid a third shot, and knew in that instant his concern had shifted from his injured arm to protecting his face. I dropped again, yanked the arm forward, and came up under it with everything I had. This time, the elbow didn't just pop. It snapped, the sound as loud as a log breaking even over the roar of the approaching train.

He howled and went up on his toes to take whatever pressure he could off his ruined elbow, and I dropped again, popped my hips back, and straightened, pulling the arm and throwing him in probably the ugliest *seoi-nage* ever attempted. He flew over me and slammed into the platform on his back.

At the last instant, I released my grip to ensure I didn't get tangled up with him. He managed to roll to his stomach and get his good arm under him, but he was shaking now, slow, and I had all the time in the world to step in and kick him soccer-style full in the face. His head snapped back and blood shot from his nose, and his arm went out from under him.

I looked up. The train was in the station now, slowing, not twenty feet away. Some more people had drifted onto the platform. I flash-checked them—civilians. Not backup.

He planted a hand on the ground and pushed himself up again. I gauged the distance, saw it would work.

I closed and kicked him in the face again. He spun away from the force of it, his head now facing the tracks, and before he could collect himself, I stepped to his right, grabbed him by the back of the collar with my right hand and the back of the belt with my left, and yanked him violently up and forward, sending him screaming and flailing over the edge of the platform and onto the tracks. A second later, the train rolled slowly over him, and his scream abruptly ended.

I dropped my head instantly and moved quickly along the platform. Miyamoto was on his own; all I could do was hope he'd had the presence of mind to do what I told him. I knew all the attention would be focused on me, with luck affording him a moment to slip away undetected, *undetected* in this case meaning no witnesses remembering his fucking tie. A description like that could have led the police right to him.

I could feel people looking at me, could hear voices crying out in distress. "Stop!" someone shouted. But I was already heading up and out. I hit the street, my head sweeping back and forth as I moved, looking for another attacker. I didn't see anyone, but how could I be sure?

I got off the main street and onto quieter ones, moving southeast, looking for a weapon of convenience. The best I could find was a loose curbstone. I swept it up and kept moving.

Idiot, you should have kept the knife from the guy in Shibuya. Or bought a new one. Idiot.

What difference did it make that what I'd taken in the alley had been a murder weapon? I should have been armed with something. A kitchen knife. A fucking corkscrew. Something.

As I got farther from the station, I let myself move faster. Actually, "let" wasn't quite the right word—I was so overloaded with adrenaline, I couldn't help it. I needed to do something to burn it off. I felt like running, sprinting, just to put distance between myself and the train station. But that would draw attention. So I managed to keep at about the pace of someone who was a little late for a meeting. Quick, but not markedly so.

I made a few aggressive moves and still detected no one behind me. *You're okay. You're okay. Slow it down. Relax. Relax.* Relax.

I ducked into a neighborhood shrine in Akasaka just as the shakes started—the effect not only of what had just happened, but of having fought so hard beforehand to stay calm, to project no awareness of what was coming. I breathed in and out deeply, trying to slow my heartbeat. After a few minutes, I started to feel a little steadier.

Damn, but it had been a close call. And that awkward sleeve grip. I resolved that if I survived whatever the hell this all was, I would train judo at least one day a week with nothing but unconventional grips. Positions you'd never expect to find yourself in. Until it actually happened and you almost died from it.

Yeah, it was close. But mission accomplished with Miyamoto. Plus, the other team is now down by three.

That was true. And not a bad feeling at all.

An image of Maria flashed into my mind—under me in the hotel room, my arms around her legs, gripping her, holding her, fucking her as hard as I could—and I was instantly, monumentally hard. Extreme horniness is a reaction to combat. Civilians don't like to talk about it because it seems sick—as though killing is some kind of turn-on. I didn't really care about the psychology. I just knew it was real. And it was so overwhelming that, for a second, I actually considered going to Ueno to see her.

No. Business first.

Right. I set aside the longer-term and started focusing on next steps. Miyamoto, of course. But that wasn't until tonight. What about Tatsu?

I thought about calling him, but decided to wait. Probably he was already out, examining a body on a train platform. That was fine. The main thing was, it wasn't mine.

chapter
fourteen

I went to a love hotel in Akasaka and passed out for a couple hours. Parasympathetic backlash again.

Afterward, I called Tatsu from a payphone. "You wouldn't believe the day I've had," he told me. "Or maybe you would."

"Another homicide?"

"If you keep this up, I'm going to think you're clairvoyant. Or arrest you, one or the other."

I chuckled. "You have anything for me?"

"Yes. And you?"

I appreciated that he answered without asking me to go first. He was a tough negotiator, but also a good friend, and he knew I was in a tight spot.

"I'm not sure," I said. "Was the information I gave you earlier useful?"

"It was interesting. Though so far, inconclusive."

"Can you meet tonight?"

"I think we should, don't you?"

"Yeah. Same place as last time? Say, eight o'clock?"

"I'll look forward to it."

"Listen, one more thing. There are people trying to get to me. And they seem to be doing it through people I know. It's hard for me to imagine they've infiltrated the Keisatsuchō, but . . ."

"I'll be certain not to bring any company."

That was reassuring. Miyamoto had a good heart, but his tradecraft was practically nonexistent. Tatsu was another story altogether. If he said he'd be there alone, he'd be there alone.

"Okay. Good. I'll see you at eight."

I had a little time to kill, it seemed. I badly wanted to call Maria. And not just because the thought of meeting her at a love hotel was overwhelmingly appealing. I felt like I should warn her. But warn her of what? And how?

I wandered along Akasaka's backstreets until I reached Hikawa Jinja, a small shrine I liked. I sat on a bench in the corner of the mossy grounds, listening to the birds in the trees, finding the quiet and solitude calming.

I considered what it was that had tipped me off about the guy in the train station. Whatever it was, I wanted to be sure I never made a similar mistake.

Well, he was a foreigner, of course. That's an instant disadvantage in Tokyo.

But that only made you notice him. It wasn't what made you decide.

That was true. But what was it, then? The rigid posture, the athletic gait. And that his clothes were dry, but he didn't have an umbrella, as though he'd tossed one away to be ready for action.

All those things. But something else, too, underlying all of it. The essential element. The thing that made you decide.

Intent, I realized. That's what it was. I could feel his intent. He had been aware of me, intensely aware. So aware that the best he could manage was to pretend not to be aware. But pretending not to be aware is at best a simulacrum. For someone with the right sensitivities, the pretense can be distinguished from the real thing.

Okay. But weren't you doing something similar in reverse, pretending you hadn't noticed him?

Yeah. That was true, too. Maybe I was just a slightly better actor. Or he was a more gullible audience. Or both. Regardless, it wasn't enough.

I needed something better. I needed to find a way to wall off my awareness so it wouldn't be visible. Not just to hide my intent, not just to create an *absence* of intent, but to create the *presence* of some other thing. I had to know down deep what was happening, while simultaneously feeling something completely different on the surface.

It sounded difficult, but how hard could it really be? Wasn't it just an exceptionally high-pressure version of what actors did every time they performed? "Mike" himself had described the Agency's urban-ops course as being like acting school. As I thought about it, I realized that acting was exactly what I'd already been doing. I just needed to practice and get better at it.

No, not just better—the best. So I could fool the best. And spot the best, before they fooled me.

I thought of Maria again. It was killing me not to call her. Maybe she could slip away. An hour. Just an hour.

What part of you is going to help you survive this? Your brain, or your dick?

I sighed. Not much arguing with that framework.

At a little before six, I made my way back to Zenkō-ji Temple in Omotesando, where I'd been so overcome by ardor with Maria that I hadn't realized a couple of guys were lurking nearby, refraining from killing me only because, for whatever reason, they wanted to leave her out of it. This time, I waited in the shadows near the street, watching the corner where I had told Miyamoto to go before he walked to Bar Radio.

He showed up right on time, getting out of a cab on the south side of Aoyama-dori and walking northeast before making a right on the tiny, nameless street that led to the bar. I waited in the shadows, watching, for ten minutes. No one followed in his wake. Okay. This time, it seemed he was clean.

I crossed the street and headed straight to the bar. Miyamoto was waiting outside, as I'd directed.

"Are you all right?" he said, walking toward me as I approached, his hands open in supplication or relief. "I wanted to help at the train station, but you'd told me not to. And honestly, I'm afraid I was never very capable in such matters, not even when I was a soldier. But I was worried."

He was talking unusually fast, and I realized the thing on the train platform had shaken him. "I'm fine," I said, patting him on the shoulder. "You did exactly the right thing. Let's keep moving, though, just in case. I'm pretty sure you weren't followed, but let's make certain."

We started walking southeast toward Nishi Azabu. These were quiet streets, ideal for spotting surveillance. I kept a brisk pace to make it a little more difficult for anyone who might have fallen in behind us. It was only a precaution, but it didn't cost anything, either.

"My sincere apologies," he said, struggling to keep up. "I thought I had been so careful before. I did everything you said to do."

"I'm sure you did. Don't worry about it. It turned out okay. But tell me, did you see any foreigners behind you before you reached the train station?"

"No. None that I noticed."

I considered that. "They might have had locals on you. If they had enough to rotate, they'd be hard to spot. And maybe they brought the foreigner in at the end."

My theory was possible, of course, but I judged it unlikely. The black guy had been reasonably smooth. With an umbrella to obscure his features, and Miyamoto's lack of experience, he probably could have done the job without a local team. But there was little to be gained in making Miyamoto feel worse than he already did.

Ten minutes later, we were inside the gates of Chōkokuji, a Buddhist temple in Nishi Azabu, wandering among the markers of its small cemetery, the dim grounds within the walls still and silent.

"Were you able to cross-reference the information I gave you?" I asked.

"Indeed."

"And?"

"I'm saddened to report that the mole seems to be . . . my immediate superior."

I could see how it might be sad for Miyamoto. But I was nothing but excited at the possibility of turning the tables on whoever was coming after me.

"You're certain?"

"Positive."

"Tell me how you know." It wasn't that I doubted him, exactly. But given that my continued longevity was now likely a function of the quality of his information, I wanted him to show his work, not just his conclusions.

"There were five people attending both the wedding reception and the Moonglow outing. Four of them have nothing whatsoever to do with the sorts of activities I myself am involved in. That leaves only one."

"Five overlaps? I was hoping for fewer."

"As it happens, the Moonglow attendees were the subset of the wedding attendees. So we are fortunate in that only six LDP members, one of whom was Sugihara, were at Moonglow at all. Many of these events have much larger guest lists."

"Why was this one so small?"

"It was a corporate junket. A visiting American semiconductor trade group. Such meetings aren't secret, exactly, but they're not widely publicized, either, following the recent unfortunate revelations regarding Lockheed and the LDP. So they typically involve only senior members."

He was talking about a bribery scandal of a few years earlier, in which it was revealed that Lockheed had been paying top members of the LDP, all the way up to the prime minister, to ensure that the

Japanese defense forces and Japanese airlines bought Lockheed products. I knew all about the Lockheed money, of course. The bag I had once carried to Miyamoto from the CIA was filled with it.

The overlaps implicating Miyamoto's boss weren't quite the smoking gun I'd been hoping for. But something else occurred to me.

"Your superior," I said. "Is this the guy who replaced the previous guy, who Victor killed?"

"It is, yes."

"What's his name?"

"Yokoyama. Yoshinobu Yokoyama."

"Well, your old boss's murder was a promotion for Yokoyama, is that right? I mean, the fact that his predecessor was killed worked out well for him."

He looked at me, frowning slightly as though disturbed at the pattern he was newly seeing. "It did indeed work out well."

I shrugged. "Well, neither one of these things is proof. Not even the two of them together. But . . ."

I trailed off, thinking. I realized I might have a way to confirm. No, better than confirm.

"Just to be sure," I said. "You never said anything about me to Yokoyama? Or to anyone else, right?"

He looked at me, his distress that I would think so little of him scarcely concealed. "Of course not."

I nodded. "Okay, apologies for that. I don't doubt you, old friend. But for information this critical, it's best to double-check."

He smiled, more in appreciation for my effort at diplomacy, I thought, than in actual agreement. "I understand," he said. "But what do we do now?"

This was what I'd been thinking about—a way to both confirm the accuracy of Miyamoto's intel and, assuming the intel was indeed accurate, to turn his boss Yokoyama without Yokoyama or anyone else even knowing.

"We had a mole in the war," I said. "He caused a lot of damage. But when we finally identified him, we didn't expose him. Not right away, anyway. We fed him false coordinates. The ruse didn't last—it didn't take too many wild-goose chases for the NVA to figure out what was happening. But in the meantime, we were able to launch some devastating raids."

"And this is what you propose to do here?"

"Close enough."

"How?"

"Think about it. Someone who wants me dead is getting intel from your boss Yokoyama. 'Follow Miyamoto. Follow Sugihara's wife. They'll lead you to this guy Rain.' Okay, fine. But both attempts failed. Now I'm being much more careful because I know someone's after me. Plus I have an idea about where I was vulnerable—you and Sugihara's wife— and I'm taking steps to mitigate those vulnerabilities. All of which means they need a fresh lead. Of their two potential sources, they can't very well ask Sugihara's wife. Besides, she wouldn't even know where to find me. That leaves you."

"You think Yokoyama will ask me? Under what pretext?"

"Does it really matter? He's your boss, right? I mean, if he just straight-up said to you, 'I need to know how to find John Rain,' would he expect you to refuse? Retaliate? Or just cough it up?"

"I see your point."

"Right. But that said, my guess is, he'll try something like . . . 'Oh, we have a new matter, very sensitive. And this man you've used success- fully in the past, I understand he's in town again, and I need to meet him personally. Where can I find him?' Something like that, does that sound plausible?"

There was a pause, during which he nodded to himself as though imagining. Then he said, "Quite plausible."

"Okay, good. I'm pretty sure he's going to approach you, and sooner rather than later. When he does, I want you to tell him how we set up meetings."

"Which is how, exactly?"

"Just tell him the truth. When I want to reach you, I call your office. When you want to reach me, you call the answering service. The best lies are always as close as possible to the truth." Another pearl of wisdom courtesy of the late Sean McGraw.

"And then . . . you think he'll ask me to set up a meeting?"

"I think he'll tell you to. But listen—you need to be reluctant. Make him work for it. Make him drag it out of you. That'll make him feel like it's real. If you give in too easily, he'll suspect a setup. You understand?"

He smiled. "I've spent more than twenty years in this sewer. Do you not think I know a bit about how to get the rats to go down the proper tunnels?"

"You're right. It's just—"

"Please, no need to apologize. I understand your concern. And as you said, it's better to double-check. But yes, if, or when, he comes to me, I will display the proper level of discomfort and distress. Before reluctantly giving you up. Now, where and when is this meeting of ours?"

"I'll tell you that when you call me, same as always. I have a feeling your boss will instruct you to choose the meeting place. You just tell him I'm the one who always decides that, and that if you try to decide it instead, I'll know something's wrong. He'll back off."

"But what if it's not my boss, and I really need to meet you?"

"Yeah, that was the next thing I was going to say. If it happens the way I'm expecting, and Yokoyama has directed you to set up a meeting, start the conversation with some sort of small-talk reference to the weather."

"Why can't I just say to you, 'It's not Yokoyama' unless it is? Why the code?"

"What if he insists on being right there while we're on the phone?"

"Ah. That is a good point."

"And if it's not Yokoyama—if it's just you, same as always, and you want to meet—then, obviously, don't say anything at all about the weather. You'll be able to say anything you want, in fact, just not that."

He smiled gently. "Has anyone ever told you that you have a tendency to micromanage?"

"Not exactly, but if someone did, I'd have to admit he might have a point."

He laughed, but it quickly died away. "So you think . . . what? My boss will send someone to kill you?"

Not exactly, I thought. *Better than that.*

But all I said was, "What do you think?"

"I think . . . it's possible, yes. But how do you know?"

I smiled grimly. "I'm still learning about *nen*, my friend. And *biishiki*. And a lot of other important things. But if there's one thing I do well, it's putting myself in the shoes of the opposition. Asking, 'If I were trying to get to me, how would I do it?' So yeah, I don't know it like I know the sun is going to come up tomorrow, but I know it well enough to expect it. And to damn sure be ready when it happens."

chapter
fifteen

Later that evening, I was back at the Yūrakuchō *izakaya*. I was confident no one would be able to follow Tatsu without his knowledge, but still, I made sure to get there early and set up across the street so I could watch him arrive and see what might be trailing in his wake. Some years later, President Reagan would popularize the Russian proverb *Doveryai, no proveryai*: Trust, but verify. At the time, I might not have known the phrase, but I knew to live the concept.

Having detected no problems, I went inside and joined him at his table. "Ah, you're late," he said as I took the chair ninety degrees from him. This way, both of us had a view of the entrance and were close enough to talk without being overheard by the patrons around us, who in any event were sufficiently drunk and boisterous that being overheard probably wasn't a major concern. "Ordinarily, you're early."

There were two mugs of beer already on the table. We touched glasses and drank.

"You know me. Never want to get boring and predictable."

"Indeed. Did you know there was another homicide of a gaijin in Tokyo today?"

"Really? That's three, right?"

"Yes. Which, for Tokyo, constitutes an epidemic."

"Have you been able to learn anything about the deceased?"

"Not yet. None of them was carrying identification, and no one has stepped forward to claim the bodies."

"No ID? What do you make of that?"

He looked at me, and I couldn't tell whether he was enjoying the game, or tiring of it.

"The two in Shibuya might conceivably have been robbed. The one today, at Gaienmae Station, was thrown onto the tracks in front of an oncoming train after what witnesses described as a struggle."

"Well, you know better than I do, but with Tokyo's low crime rates and the overall circumstances, my bet is they were spooks of some sort, traveling sterile while operational."

He grunted. "Yes, I believe that is a sensible theory. In which case, it was their misfortune to encounter someone opposed to whatever it was they were doing."

"A connection with Wilson, you think?"

"Possibly."

He was going to make me ask directly, so I did. "You manage to learn anything about him?"

He nodded. "You were right in the particulars—former OSS, then CIA. He has operated all over the world and speaks a half dozen languages—English, of course, and also French, German, Italian, Spanish, and Russian."

"Russian sounds pertinent, under the circumstances."

"Perhaps. But let's first stick to what we know."

I smiled. He sounded like an avuncular version of McGraw.

"Please," I said. "Let's."

"Wilson parachuted behind enemy lines during World War Two to organize partisans against the Nazis. Perhaps ironically, he was then involved in Operation Paperclip—the recruitment, rehabilitation, and resettlement of top-ranking Nazis in the United States following the war in exchange for their scientific knowledge or intelligence value."

"'Paperclip'?"

"So named for the practice of clipping together intelligence files documenting actual atrocities and new, whitewashed identity documents for resettlement in the United States."

"Ah."

"Wilson was also part of Operation Gladio, involving 'stay-behind' militias intended to harass Soviet forces in the event of a Soviet takeover of Europe. Operation Mongoose in Cuba, including the use of the American mafia for assassination attempts on Fidel Castro. Operation Chaos, targeting various American media and dissident groups. Project FUBELT, which led to the ouster and killing of Salvador Allende in Chile. And most notoriously, the MKUltra program of mind control and human experimentation."

"Impressive that something in a list like that could distinguish itself on grounds of notoriety."

"Indeed."

"But Allende . . . I thought he committed suicide."

In response, he only looked at me.

"Right," I said. "Good point."

He took a sip of beer. "Following revelations of these activities, and others, by the Church and Pike Committees, men like Wilson were considered tainted. Part of a period the Agency wanted to consign to the past. When President Carter appointed Stansfield Turner as Director of Central Intelligence, Turner fired some eight hundred such operatives."

"Well, with eight hundred disaffected experts in sabotage, subversion, and assassination suddenly on the loose, what's the worst that could happen?"

"What happened was, many of them offered their expertise to foreign governments. Others, to criminal organizations. Wilson was one such. He has a reputation for gunrunning and money laundering. And for training the security services of various unsavory governments in Africa and Latin America."

"Unsavory enough to engage in sabotage, subversion, assassinations, and mind-control experiments? Those governments are the worst."

He tilted his head and peered at me as though studying the contours of some curious organism. "I won't pretend to understand your sense of humor," he said. "But I do know what it indicates."

"Yes?"

"Nervousness."

"Don't tell anyone. I'd prefer people to think I'm funny rather than nervous."

"Thank you for making my point."

I lifted my glass in salute. "You know, Tatsu, sometimes the quality of your information is almost scary."

"I'm glad you find it so. For me, it rarely feels like enough."

"What about the notion that Casey has somehow brought this guy in from the cold?"

"Plausible, but unproven. Certainly Casey has been at pains to rebuild the CIA's roster of practitioners of the dark arts. Bringing back former operatives would be an expedient way of doing so."

"While maybe keeping some of them at arm's length, for deniability."

"Also plausible, but unproven."

"All right, what do you think? A connection between Wilson and Victor?"

"Possibly. In favor of this proposition is the fact that Mr. Wilson is currently visiting Japan."

I smiled. "I told you. Almost scary. And might I inquire as to the location of Mr. Wilson's lodgings?"

"It seems he entered the country as Carl Woods. But no one by such a name is checked in to any of the major Tokyo hotels. My guess is that he uses a different name for air travel than he does for hotels. Standard operating procedure for a man like this."

"You can't dig a little deeper?"

"It's one thing for me to have a trusted man go through immigration and customs records," he said, a slight sharpness in his tone. "Laborious, but discreet. It's quite another to requisition resources sufficient to comb through the guest lists of a half dozen or more hotels—many of which are frequented by dignitaries, diplomats, and celebrities. At a minimum, I would have to explain myself to my superiors."

I held up my hands in apology. "Got it. Sorry for asking. Any way to know whether, or when, he's been here before?"

"My people already checked travel by Carl Woods. There's nothing earlier than the current trip."

"Meaning he hasn't been here before, or—"

"Or that he has been here, but under a variety of aliases. My sense is, the answer is the latter. But I have no evidence to support that sense."

It was frustrating—we had so many pieces, but I still couldn't see how to assemble them.

"Any idea what he's doing out here?"

"No. If not for the information you provided me, we wouldn't even have known of his presence. Unsurprisingly, given his credentials, he's adept at keeping a low profile."

I took a swallow of beer. "Well, you're welcome, then."

He leaned back and crossed his arms. "What you've told me has led to more questions than answers. What you're holding back about your own involvement with Victor is likely what I need."

I almost made a weak crack—something along the lines of *Holding back what?*

But I knew he was right. He'd held up his end. And given me a lot. It would have been unworthy not to respond in kind.

And worse than that, it would have been stupid.

"That job Victor hired me to do," I told him. "I'm not going to do it. You need to understand that before I go on."

"All right."

"The target is an LDP guy. Koji Sugihara."

He looked at me for a long moment, his face worryingly expressionless. Finally, he said, "Have you ever pondered this talent of yours for getting mixed up in things that are far above your pay grade?"

"I haven't had time to ponder. Too many people trying to kill me."

He shook his head in what for Tatsu passed for an ostentatious display of exasperation. "What did you think would happen if you were to kill a ranking member of the LDP?"

"I told you, I'm not going to do it."

"That you would even consider it is giving me great pause about your judgment."

"Look, I told Victor no right away, at which point he told me if I didn't, he'd kill my friend. All I've been trying to do since then is play for time—and a chance at Victor."

In response, he merely shook his head again.

I knew he was doing a lot, and that I was putting him in a difficult and possibly even dangerous position, and all at once I felt bad about pushing him. I wanted to tell him that, but thought it would all come out in some foolishly wordy American way. So I said nothing, hoping he would recognize some solicitude in my silence.

"Let's . . . back up," I said after a moment. "Who benefits if Sugihara dies?"

He shrugged. "When a politician dies, there are always beneficiaries. This is true of any cataclysmic event. The pieces on the board are rearranged, creating openings and opportunities where before there had been blockages and stagnation."

"Yes, but specifically."

"This is my point. When the benefit is so diffuse, it's difficult to work backward to infer causality."

"Is Sugihara known for anything in particular? Some . . . I don't know, trade-industry activities or something? My understanding is that recently he was out with some American semiconductor people."

"He is popular among Japanese farmers, whose domestic rice sales he protects with significant levies on imports. But he's hardly unique in that respect. His death would do nothing to pave the way for, say, a surge of imported rice."

I smiled. "When you put it like that, it does sound far-fetched."

He nodded, and I knew we were past the tension of a moment earlier.

"All right," I said. "I seriously doubt Victor wants Sugihara dead for his own reasons. So it's really a question of, who hired Victor to do it?"

"That is indeed the question."

"Wilson, maybe? Whoever it is, they want to keep their fingerprints off the job. You see that, right?"

"Of course. Why else would they hire you?"

That actually stung a little, just on the level of professional pride. But what was I going to do, argue with him that, no, my track record of killing for hire was actually pretty good? The whole conversation was already as close to the line as I'd ever come with Tatsu. So close I wasn't sure we were still on the right side of it.

"Not just me," I said. "Also Kobayashi. Think about it. If Kobayashi had killed Sugihara, they probably would have killed Kobayashi immediately after. And then you'd be wondering why the hell the Gokumatsu-gumi killed a Diet member. And if I'd done it . . ."

I had intended just to recite my previous thinking, about how I was deniable, too. But now something was nagging at me.

"What is it?"

"Victor knows about my background," I said slowly, trying to see it from a fresh perspective. "MACV-SOG. All that. And he wanted to hire me anyway. And I was thinking . . . it didn't matter to him. That the main thing from his perspective is that I'm not connected to him. So I drop Sugihara, his people drop me, and whoever I was, there's no way to connect me to Victor."

"That seems a reasonable inference."

"Yeah. But now I'm wondering—"

"Whether you were focusing too much on Victor, and not on who is behind Victor."

I looked at him. "Yes. That. Exactly."

Suddenly, I could see it. All at once. What I'd been missing before.

I leaned forward. "I mean, okay, picture this. Victor gets rid of Kobayashi because Kobayashi fucked up. He hires me to take his place as designated hitman/fall guy. Now someone, maybe Wilson, checks in. 'What's going on with Sugihara. He was supposed to be dead last week.' And Victor says, 'No problem. Have new guy. Very good. Highly recommended. Former American Special Forces. MACV-SOG. Vietnam combat veteran. And half-Japanese, so knows Tokyo and can get close to man.' You get it?"

He nodded quickly, which was about as visibly excited as Tatsu ever got. "And when the person who checks in hears the new contractor is former US military, he is unhappy. Because a connection to the US government is a problem."

"Exactly."

"But is this really so much of a connection? Former military. Discharged a decade ago."

"It was a little more than just military—MACV-SOG was into things the US government is still denying, as you know. I seriously doubt the government would welcome anyone shining a light on what we were doing there. And there's more than just the military connection. There's the work I was doing in Tokyo with the CIA ten years ago. Imagine I kill Sugihara and get picked up. It's a disaster for the Agency."

He nodded, clearly pleased, and I realized his protest about former military being not much of a connection was merely a probe—a test to ascertain whether I was seeing the larger picture. It was hard to say which gave Tatsu more satisfaction—when I kept up with him, or when he got to treat me like a barely educable student.

"You seeing it the same way I am?" I said.

"Yes. It's not difficult to imagine Wilson in that role."

I took another swallow of beer. "There's one thing that's not quite right, though. I can see why a guy like Wilson would want me taken off Sugihara—taken off the count entirely, because just from Victor trying to hire me, I already knew too much. But Victor hasn't tried to take me off. In fact, he's been feeding me fresh intel about Sugihara. That's how I knew about the meeting with the semiconductor people. Though I suppose that could all be at least in part a setup, to fix me in time and place."

"You're missing another possibility," he said dryly, and I realized he was getting both kinds of satisfaction tonight.

"Yeah? What's that?"

"That Wilson and Victor are at cross-purposes."

"You mean Wilson told him to take me off Sugihara, and Victor ignored him?"

"Why not? Did Victor strike you as especially amenable to close control by his handler?"

"No, that's not the first way I would describe him, now that you mention it."

"Or it could be that Wilson decided to let you keep going after Sugihara while he directed his own people to go after you. Why not? You already know too much, as you say, so that part of the damage is done. If you get lucky and kill Sugihara, and Wilson's men kill you immediately after, from Wilson's perspective that would be perfect. If his men get to you first, the damage is contained. Either way, by starting to track you right away, learning your haunts, your habits, zeroing in on how he can get to you, he's being efficient. Even if he can't make his move until later, he's able to make it more quickly when the time comes."

"Which do you think it is?"

He didn't hesitate. "The second one. A shrewd man, an experienced man, would do it that way. Mitigate the risk, preserve some possible upside. I doubt he would even have told Victor to stand you down. Why bother? From Wilson's perspective, the less Victor knows, the better."

That also made sense. And it explained what I had wondered about earlier—why Victor hadn't told me about the wedding reception. I'd been right: he didn't know. Wilson hadn't told him, because Wilson was more concerned about discretion than Victor was.

"So you're pretty sure my problem is with Wilson."

He shrugged. "What do the Americans say? 'If it walks like a duck, and has feathers like a duck, and quacks like a duck . . .'"

I smiled. It was rare for me to hear someone talk about foreigners as the out-group, implying that I, as Japanese, was part of the in-group. And while I didn't like to admit that I longed for that kind of acceptance, I guess on some level I did.

"I know I'm asking a lot," I said, giving in to my American urge to speak despite my earlier determination not to. "I'm sorry for that."

In response, he grunted, which from Tatsu was an exceptional display of sentiment.

"And I feel a little bad for pressing," I went on, "but I'll tell you, it would be really helpful if you could get me close to Oleg."

"I confess I'm ambivalent about doing so. Three homicides in as many days is already bad for Tokyo. Three *unsolved* homicides is bad for the Keisatsuchō."

"I can imagine. Still, no locals. No civilians. And it doesn't sound like those three gaijin were tourists. So hopefully, the kind of thing that might . . . blow over?"

"It might. If it doesn't get worse first."

"Are you saying you've changed your mind about Oleg retiring?"

"Where does it end?"

"You know where. With Victor."

"What about Wilson?"

I laughed. "You telling me you want me to? Or you don't?"

I thought that was at least a little amusing, as well as a good point. But he remained impassive.

"It's not easy to work with you," he said after a moment. "I try to make cases. What you make is bodies."

I looked at him. "Does that really bother you so much, Tatsu? If they're the right bodies?"

I hadn't meant to put it so plainly. It was the American in me—I lacked Tatsu's propensity for obliqueness. Especially when a former *Spetsnaz* psychopath was intent on killing me and I needed information to get to him first.

A moment went by. Then he sighed. "Oleg has a taste for Japanese girls, it seems."

He had something, and had decided to tell me. It was a concession, and I didn't want to embarrass him by acknowledging it.

"Well, then I guess he's come to the right country."

"Not really. The girls he likes are professionals. And most establishments purveying Japanese girls won't allow gaijin."

"Are you serious? What brothel doorman is going to turn away someone like Oleg?"

"Among other things, Oleg and Victor are businessmen. Forcing their way into establishments that don't want them would be an insult to the yakuza that control the sex trade. And while Oleg and Victor are obviously more than willing to incur enmity for substantive reasons, they seem smart enough not to do so merely for pleasures of the flesh. Besides, there are at least a dozen Yoshiwara *toruko* establishments more than willing to entertain gaijin. And Oleg finds the girls at several of them quite to his liking."

Yoshiwara was one of Tokyo's pleasure quarters, first designated as such by the Tokugawa shogunate in the early seventeenth century. *Toruko* was short for *toruko buro*, a phrase consisting of the Japanese words for *Turkish* and *bath*. But beyond the presence of soap and water, the establishments in question had little to do with Turkish baths, and in 1985, after sustained protests by the Turkish government, the association running the toruko held a contest for a new name. *Sōpurando*—soapland, the squeaky-clean euphemism that continues to this day—was the winner.

The information was intriguing. But I didn't see how it would be actionable. Unless . . .

"I don't want to intrude into your sources and methods," I said, "but are you getting this intel the way I think you are?"

He shrugged. "As I've said, the yakuza are happy to pass information to the Keisatsuchō if they think doing so could damage Victor. Once one of the gaijin-friendly establishments confirmed Oleg's visits, it wasn't difficult to get confirmation from others, too."

"I would have expected a guy like Oleg to be a little more security conscious."

"His behavior is less risky than you might think. There are several establishments he frequents, so a certain shell-game dynamic is in play. He doesn't make appointments. He always has a man waiting outside. And he doesn't stay long."

"The ladies must love him."

"I wouldn't know. But I doubt anyone he visits wishes he would spend more time."

"What does he have against Shinjuku? There are plenty of foreigner-friendly places there, no?"

"Shinjuku is a stronghold of the Gokumatsu-gumi. Oleg feels less safe there."

I considered that. Yeah, Yoshiwara was much less a gangster locus than Shinjuku. Apart from the sex trade, the neighborhood was quiet—so quiet that a visitor could pass through during the day and barely notice what really put it on the map. There would be local muscle, but no more than would be required to handle a belligerent drunk. I could see where Oleg would feel more secure there.

His mistake.

"So we're talking about a window of, what, an hour? With no warning beforehand?"

"That's correct."

I blew out a long breath. "Going to take some luck. How often does he visit?"

"That's the one bit of good news. Several nights a week, at least. Often more."

"Guess you weren't kidding when you said he likes Japanese girls."

"But you're correct, this will take more than a little luck. So much so that I hesitated to tell you. I had a feeling you would take the chance."

"No, it's better you told me. And it's not as bad as you think. I know what his men look like—they patted me down when I visited their headquarters."

"Then they know what you look like, too."

"If I do it right, they won't see me. At least not until it's too late."

"If."

"I appreciate your confidence."

"I think one of us should be realistic."

I thought for a moment. If I knew when, and where, I could do it. But all within an hour . . . that was going to be tough.

"Can you get me a police radio?" I said.

He nodded. "I had a feeling you would ask."

"How about a gun?"

"Impossible. A department head would have to sign it out from the armory."

"How about a rock or a stick?"

He shook his head. "The jokes. Not a good sign."

"Who's joking?"

He sighed. "Well, I suppose the good news is that if you weren't nervous, it would mean you were stupid."

I finished my beer and smiled grimly. "No. The good news is, you're going to get me Oleg."

chapter
sixteen

An hour later, I was wandering the dim and déclassé alleyways of the area now known officially as Senzoku, but in all other respects eternally Yoshiwara. Tatsu had given me the names and addresses of five *toruko* Oleg was known to favor, and I made a slow run past each of them, assessing the layout, trying to determine where Oleg's man would set up, imagining my approach, weighing the advantages and vulnerabilities.

Unlike Shinjuku, Akasaka, and the city's other, better-known pleasure districts, Yoshiwara had no real attractions other than the *mizu shōbai*, the so-called "water trade" famously depicted in Japanese woodblock prints known as *ukiyo-e*—literally, "pictures of the floating world"—and *shunga*—the explicit depictions of what the floating world offered. There were no corporate headquarters, no government ministries, no embassies, no department stores, no famous eateries, no cinemas or stages. During the Tokugawa shogunate, the area had been a virtual city within a city, enslaving, employing, and attracting thousands, and was still laid out in a grid characterized by old wooden houses and unremarkable concrete buildings, with even the newer structures at most a few stories high. The only restaurants were small affairs—scattered *ramenya* noodle boutiques and *kissaten* coffeehouses and the odd *izakaya*—and the only shops were mom-and-pop establishments and convenience stores. In Shibuya, love hotels were popular as after-dinner destinations for couples enjoying a night out, and on any given evening in Hyakkendana you might pass dozens of lovers strolling arm in arm, seeking almost as a kind of foreplay a hotel that struck their mutual fancy. Here, the hotels were used primarily by visiting clients ordering girls from one of the local purveyors, and the foot traffic was furtive and brief. As a result, despite its long history of *baishun*—"selling spring"—and dubious renown, Yoshiwara was moribund during the day and subdued even at night, like a secret shopping mall operated by a skeleton crew. There was neon, yes—the *toruko* entryways were nothing if not gaudy. And there were touts, calling to passersby like me. But there was little noise, no tumult, and mostly singletons rather than crowds. Yoshiwara had locals, and it had visitors making a brief pilgrimage to scratch a transitory itch, and that was about it.

Not a bad place, I decided, to hunt Oleg. Not a bad place at all.

I did what I could to avoid approaching too closely as I reconnoitered. I wasn't worried about touts remembering my face—they saw too many potential patrons, and the area was too poorly lit, for that to be a real concern. No, what was occupying me was the admittedly slim chance that Oleg would be enjoying himself at one of the local *toruko* this very night, and that I might stumble upon one of the men Tatsu had warned would be posted outside. If a bodyguard spotted me here, Oleg would know I hadn't come for a bath. He would take countermeasures, and I would have shown my hand without in the process degrading Victor's forces.

It was strange to wander Yoshiwara. For whatever reason, I was intently aware that Victor's mother might have wound up here. If Tatsu's theory was right, what other options would have been available to her? I tried to imagine a cast-out, pregnant farm girl in wartime Tokyo—how alone and terrified and desperate she would have felt, where she would have searched, how much she would have surrendered to survive and protect the child that had been forced on her before washing up onto Yoshiwara's unforgiving shores. I didn't need to have read Sun Tzu to understand the importance of knowing your enemy, and I told myself that imagining Victor's mother was one way of getting into his head. I even visited Jōkanji, a 350-year-old temple in the area where the souls of some twenty thousand courtesans were said to be interred. But if Victor's mother was among the antique markers, I felt no distinct sign of her, only the sad history of a place that had engraved on its own walls a kind of disclaimer to the generations of women drawn by the hope the gods might bestow some mercy: *Birth is pain, death is Jōkanji.* The Yoshiwara version of the warning in the *Inferno* found inscribed on the gates of hell: *Abandon all hope, ye who enter here.*

The next forty-eight hours were uneventful. I called Oleg twice a day from various payphones. He had no new leads on Sugihara. Tatsu gave me a police radio, which he would use to alert me the instant he got news of Oleg visiting a Yoshiwara brothel. And I finally broke down and called Maria. My heart was pounding as I dialed her office number, and I was irritated at myself for being so nervous, but I couldn't help it. How would she be feeling? Happy? Full of regret? Irritated that I hadn't called sooner? Irritated that I was calling her at all?

"Am I catching you at an okay time?" I asked when she picked up.

There was a slight pause. Then: "Yes."

"I mean, can you talk now?"

"Yes."

The short replies were making me nervous. "It's good to hear your voice, even if it's only one syllable at a time."

She laughed at that, and I felt an embarrassingly large measure of relief.

"If you wanted to hear my voice, you might have called a little sooner."

Damn, but that was a nice thing to hear. "I . . . would have. I wanted to. I just wasn't sure if you wanted me to."

"Ah, so little confidence?"

"No. Well, sort of, maybe. But more . . . I just didn't know how you would feel after. I thought you might regret what happened. Or feel guilty. Or even angry at me."

"Yes, all of those things, certainly. But not so much that I didn't want to hear from you."

"Does that mean you want to see me again?"

There was another pause. I gripped the phone hard, knowing it was a stupid thing to say, that I shouldn't be playing with any additional fire when I had so many conflagrations to attend to.

Then, her voice slightly husky, she said, "Very much."

"When?" I said with no hesitation at all, continuing an unbroken stupid streak.

"The next few days are difficult and I don't think I can get away."

"Oh, come on," I said, not faking my disappointment at all. "What could be that important?"

"The exhibit I curated—there's a private dinner and showing at the museum Friday night. I have a lot to do to get ready. But call me Friday. I might even be able to see you that night." She paused, then added, "And stay at a better hotel this time, all right?"

Amazing, how a simple command like that, said in the right tone and by the right person, could produce such an instantaneous hard-on. But there you have it.

"I will," I said, aware my mouth had gone slightly dry. And then, without thinking, added, "Wear something you won't mind getting torn off."

There was a sharp little exhalation. Then she said, "I have to go. Call me Friday or I'll be very angry."

She hung up, leaving me standing there in the grip of a paralyzing mix of excitement and self-recrimination.

Focus. You need to focus. You want to see Maria? You need to be alive for that.

ZERO SUM

I stayed at a business hotel just outside Yoshiwara. I thought about
using one of the local love hotels, but my paranoia—or call it survival
instinct—was on high alert, and it was too easy for me to imagine
Victor getting a call from someone who saw me in the area. Unlikely, I
knew, but there was little cost to avoiding the possibility entirely.

There were various advantages and disadvantages to the terrain
around the several *toruko* Oleg favored. But the one common denomi-
nator was that I wouldn't be able to reach any of them without being
spotted on the approach. If I'd known the exact place and time, I would
have posed as a customer, gone to the bordello in question just ahead
of Oleg, and hit him from inside, thereby avoiding his sentry entirely.
But with the kind of intel available, I'd inevitably be getting there after
the sentry was already in position. That meant I needed a way to get
past him without his recognizing me—or to get close before he could
do anything about it.

I thought about what Tatsu had said at the *izakaya*—that he could
tell when I was nervous because I made jokes. I sensed that was true,
and wondered what other tells might be giving me away. When I'd first
gone to see Victor, for example. How was I acting? How did I present
myself?

I realized I'd been nervous then, too, and had been compensat-
ing with a certain degree of cockiness. I'd gone in there feeling like a
MACV-SOG veteran and mercenary badass, wearing the attitude like
an amulet. I'd known guys in Vietnam who'd handled the fear in a
similar way—for example, by stenciling on their flak jackets mottos like
*Yea, though I walk through the valley of the shadow of death, I will fear no
evil, because I'm the meanest motherfucker in the valley.*

But it was one thing to stencil something like that on a flak jacket.
It was another to wear it in environments where stealth—where being
underestimated or, better yet, unnoticed—was a critical advantage. I
needed to work on setting aside badass and cultivating bland.

At the same time, I realized my mistake with Victor might have been fortuitous. He and his men knew me in a certain guise now. If I could conceal that guise—no, not conceal it, *replace* it—they might not see me coming until it was too late.

The first step was to go to a men's store in Ueno and outfit myself like a salaryman: gray suit, white shirt, cheap shoes and belt, boring tie. I made sure to choose a separate jacket and pants so I could get a jacket several sizes too big—I was planning on wearing more than just a shirt under it.

Next, I bought an attaché case, hair gel, and a pair of wire-rimmed eyeglasses, explaining to the saleswoman that I wanted the nonprescription display version, because they would make me look more intelligent for an upcoming interview. Finally, I stopped at a jewelry store for a gold band. If the guy wondered why I was getting a ring for myself, he didn't ask. Maybe he thought I'd lost mine and was afraid of having to explain the circumstances of its disappearance to my wife. It didn't matter. The point was, the details counted. Getting them right might not help. But getting them wrong could only hurt.

At a sporting-goods store, surrounded by aerobics outfits and waffle-soled running shoes, I picked out a pair of dumbbells and a few small plates, along with some athletic tape. Most of it was for appearances—buying a single dumbbell, or dumbbells with no plates, would have been strange, and therefore memorable—and a few blocks from the store I tossed what I didn't need into a sewer. What I kept was a single bar, a little over a foot long and about five pounds of solid iron, the length of which I wrapped in tape to improve the grip. Screwed tightly to one end of the bar was one of the iron collars. Swung even at half speed, it would be more than enough to break an arm or cave in a skull. And I wouldn't be swinging at half speed, or anywhere near it.

My next stop was a motocross store, where I picked up a state-of-the-art bodysuit—the chest, back, shoulders, and forearms all constructed with Kevlar—and an additional, extra-large Kevlar vest. Oleg's apparent obsession with knives and rat poison suggested I might want more over my skin than just a shirt and suit jacket when I ran into him. I knew Kevlar wouldn't stop all knife strikes—a powerful thrust with the right blade, for example, particularly if I were pinned against a wall or the ground, would likely penetrate—but it would offer some decent protection.

Back at the hotel, I removed all but the lower back plates from the vest, got out of my clothes, and pulled on the vest inside out and backward, adjusting the Velcro straps until the lower back plates were positioned over my stomach. Then I got into the bodysuit, again adjusting the Velcro straps until I had a proper fit. I shadowboxed in front of the mirror, and was pleased with how light it all was, and how much mobility I had.

The new clothes fit perfectly over the armor. The shirt was a little snug, but not unduly so, and the larger jacket was just right for my newfound girth. My face might have appeared a bit thin in comparison with my body, but I doubted anyone would notice the incongruity. To the extent anything registered with witnesses at all, and to the extent they might recall it, it would be an image of a man heavier than I was. And for purposes of lulling Oleg's sentry, adding thirty or so pounds to my appearance was a plus, as well.

And then I practiced. I slicked my hair and put on the glasses and donned the protective gear under the suit and went out. I threw the attaché case up against a wall a few times to make sure it didn't look too new, then filled it with magazines so even the weight would be right, and to make it more effective as a shield, if it came to that. And then I spent time riding trains and visiting coffee shops and interacting with various Tokyoites. I sensed I needed to do more than just get used to the costume. I needed to inhabit the role, make it a part of who I really was, and see that it worked so I would be confident in my own performance when it counted most.

Just before midnight on the second day, while I was lying in the hotel bed, staring at the ceiling, the radio crackled on the nightstand next to me. My heart started pounding. I grabbed the radio and keyed the mic.

"What time?" I said.

Tatsu's voice: "Four o'clock."

That was our prearranged code. He'd told me about five places. We'd numbered them accordingly. And agreed that we'd refer to whichever it was as one o'clock, two o'clock, etc. Not the world's greatest code, but the radio wasn't secure and it was better to be oblique. Number four was a place called Super Doll, almost at the geographical heart of Yoshiwara. And, by dictate of Murphy's law, of the five it had the most difficult approach.

I dropped the radio and rolled out of bed, already dressed and ready—hardly the first time I'd slept in combat gear. My fingertips and palms were covered with the athletic tape—as effective as gloves in preventing prints, but less noticeable. And the attaché case and dumbbell bar were already wiped down and sterile. All I needed to do was tighten the tie, pull on the shoes, slip on the jacket, and grab the attaché case, to the bottom of which I had taped the bar. I was out the door in less than two minutes.

The night air was cool, with little cones of mist spinning slowly under the streetlights I passed, and the streets were slumber-quiet. I pictured the club as I walked. It occupied a two-story building set on the corner of a couple of typically dim and narrow Yoshiwara streets, the entrance maximally far from the corner. Across from it was a small parking lot that created a sort of plaza surrounded by an eclectic combination of old wooden houses, some small apartment buildings, and several additional brothels. There were no hidden approaches: no nearby alleyways or cross streets, no good way to get close before revealing myself. The disguise would be my only concealment.

I did one last mental run-through of the approach I'd decided on. Then I buried all that deep inside my persona: a salaryman, leaving an office function late, and deciding on a nervous nightcap in Yoshiwara before going home and lying to my wife. I pictured the whole thing: a tiny apartment in nearby Nippori; a dutiful marriage; a baby on the way. An early-morning commute, crushed inside a subway car with a thousand other stoic workers. The pressure, the bills, the worries. And every now and then, a stolen night like this one. That's why I was here. That's who I was. There was nothing else.

I crossed into Yoshiwara, a few touts calling out to me from in front of places with names like Race Queen and Fantasy Land and Honey Pot, the pavement lit now only by the neon of the club signs and the glow of a few solitary vending machines. My heart rate was elevated, but no more so than that of the salaryman I was, nervous about this illicit foray, looking for a place that felt right to me.

Fifty feet ahead was the club, a skinny tout in a white shirt and dark tie loitering at the corner about thirty feet to the left of the entrance, where he could better engage passersby. He spotted me and called out, *"Irasshaimase."* To my right was the parking lot, about a third full. As I passed the parked cars, I got my first glimpse of the club's entrance. Alongside it was Oleg's man, one of the two who had patted me down on my visits to Victor's office, standing unobtrusively to the right of the doorway, but for his position in the shadows looking like nothing more than one of the area touts. I let my gaze move casually past him, then back to the tout. I had seen nothing in the sentry's expression or posture that would indicate he had recognized me. And why would he? The streets were dim and shadowy. I was still fairly far off. This was a different place, not a setting in which he would expect me. Most of all, I was a different person now.

The tout was twenty feet away now. *"Dōzo,"* he called out, gesturing toward the club entrance. *"Dōzo, okyakusama."* Feel free, honorable customer.

I slowed to let him know I might be interested, which increased his apparent ardor. *"Ii desu yo,"* he said, with a politician's smile. It's all good. *"Ii desu yo. Dōzo."*

I stopped when I was just to his left, positioning him between the sentry and me. *"Kirei desu ka?"* I said, my tone uncertain. Are they pretty?

"Mochiron," he said, taking my left arm and gently pulling me toward the entrance. *"Saikō desu yo."* Of course. The best.

I allowed him to guide me along, asking him hushed and nervous questions as we walked about how much, how long, what services were available, were the girls really pretty. All just excuses to keep my face down and toward him, and concealed from the sentry. With luck, I'd be escorted right past him without his giving it a second thought.

Ten feet to the sentry now. The tout continued his practiced enticements about how beautiful the girls were and how everything was available, whatever services I desired, his tone infused with the pleasure and goodwill of a man who senses he has already earned a commission for his services. I kept the sentry in my peripheral vision. He was watching our approach, but hadn't changed his posture.

Five feet. The sentry was looking at me more closely now. He glanced at my hands, but with one around the handle of the attaché case and the other open and palm-in, he couldn't see the tape. I kept my gaze off him and continued my babbling about what to expect inside the club.

We reached the glass doors and they opened from within. A doorman dressed the same as the tout stepped out, bowing obsequiously low and holding the door for me, purring, *"Dōzo, okyakusama, dōzo."*

Through the glass, I was aware of the sentry frowning as he stared at me. He sensed something was wrong, I could tell—he had seen this face before, in some other place or context he couldn't quite process. He wasn't yet sufficiently certain to act. But there was no doubt he was heading in that direction, and might get there any second.

Immediately I understood that plan A—ghosting right past him—had failed. I felt a hot hit of adrenaline in my gut and my heart kicked into overdrive as I realized it was time for plan B.

I switched the attaché case to my left hand and with the right ripped loose the dumbbell bar. Dropping the case, I leaped to my right, past the door and in front of the sentry, the warrior erupting through and shredding the meek salaryman persona. I brought my arm out and back as though I was about to slam home a tennis forehand, the heft of the iron bar and the screwed-on collar satisfying, deadly, in my fist. The sentry's mouth dropped open and he began to duck and turn away, his arms coming up to protect his head, everything happening in slow-motion now in my adrenalized vision.

I'd anticipated his flinch and compensated for it easily, leaning in to lengthen my reach and extending the bar farther as I whipped it forward, the weighted end sizzling in and smashing his right hand into the side of his face. He staggered with the force of the blow and I stepped in closer, letting the bar continue on its trajectory past him, then backhanded it into the opposite side of his head. The rigidity flowed out of his body and he sank to his knees, his arms falling away from his head, and I raised the bar and brought the weighted end down directly onto the top of his head, smashing it through his skull.

I spun back to the door. The doorman, his mouth open in a perfect O of shock and terror, had gripped the handle with both hands and was trying to pull it shut. I grabbed the edge of the door, and supercharged with adrenaline, flung it open. It rocketed past me and shattered against the concrete wall, glass spraying out over the concrete.

The tout turned and ran. The doorman backed away, his hands raised in fear and supplication. I swept up the attaché case and strode inside.

A third man was coming from around a desk. Whatever he saw of the tableau before him and of my expression, it made him stop. I charged directly into him, dropping the attaché case again en route. I grabbed him by the throat with my free hand, raised the bar, its end now mottled with blood and gristle, and slammed him into the wall behind him.

"The Russian," I growled in Japanese. "Oleg. What room is he in?"

His hands went uselessly to my grip on his throat and he glanced in terror at the dripping bar. "T-twelve," he stammered.

"If that's wrong," I said, gripping his throat tighter and looking into his eyes, "I'm coming back for you."

He shook his head frantically. "Twelve. I swear."

"Where?"

"Upstairs. End of the hallway."

I released his throat, grabbed the attaché case, and took the stairs three at a time. I passed half a dozen doors, all numbered, all closed. I hadn't meant to shatter the front door—an overreaction produced by fear and adrenaline—but it seemed it hadn't alarmed anyone on the second floor, at least not enough to induce them to come out and investigate.

The last room on the right was marked twelve. I stood outside it for a second, sucked in a deep breath, raised a leg, and blasted open the door with a kick. I forced myself to hesitate for an instant before charging inside, pausing just long enough outside the door for a visual sweep of the room, trading speed of entry for some intelligence about what I was about to run into.

The room was dark, and in the light spilling in from the corridor, I took in a naked girl cowering on the floor alongside a bath to the left. On some instinctive, nonverbal level, I understood instantly what this meant: Oleg had heard the door slam and shatter. Unlike the other patrons, he had paranoid combat reflexes that would always assume the worst, and cue him to act accordingly. He had leaped from the bath, threatened the girl into petrified silence, killed the lights, and positioned himself—

I felt him coming before I even saw him. I pivoted and instinctively brought up the attaché case just as a naked, dripping Oleg hove out of the darkness on my right, his teeth bared, his right arm retracted, a blade gleaming in the corridor light—

If I hadn't paused before entering, he might have had me. But my position just outside the door meant he couldn't attack in a straight line, that he had to adjust and turn in to me, and in the extra second that took him, I brought the attaché case around just enough to get it between the knife and my guts. Still, he stabbed with such ferocity that the blade plunged through both sides of the case and the magazines inside it, jamming the case back into me, where the tip was stopped by the Kevlar vest plates.

He reacted instantly, yanking back the knife, but instead of resisting, which might have allowed him to clear the blade, I twisted the case and pushed it into him, keeping the weapon stuck in place. He swore something in Russian and backed into the room, jerking at the knife, trying desperately to clear it, and as he did so, I raised the bar and whipped it down onto his wrist, breaking it. He howled and lost his grip, and his injured arm reflexively retracted to his chest.

Disarmed, facing an attacker with a weapon, and reduced to a single working arm, most men would have backpedaled. A few might have tried to engage and neutralize the weapon they were up against. Only the best would do what Oleg did—which was to attack back.

It was a version of how I'd turned the tables on the two men following me in Shibuya: low probability of success, but less bad than the alternatives. He leaped forward, his good hand shooting out, fingers splayed to rake my eyes. I released the attaché case and popped my left arm forward, catching his forearm with mine and deflecting it, at the same time dropping into a half crouch and spearing the end of the bar forward and up directly into his exposed testicles.

This time he didn't howl—his knees buckled and he folded forward and he squeaked like a deflating balloon. I slipped behind him, transferring the bar to my left hand and holding it in an icepick grip. He tried to turn with me, but his system was overloaded with shock and pain, and he no longer had nearly the necessary speed or mobility. I planted a knee against his back to stabilize him, jammed the bar across his throat from right to left, crossed my right hand over to the opposite side, took hold of the free end of the bar, and shoved my knee forward, at the same time dropping my elbows and pulling my arms back, the bar and the bones of my forearms crushing his neck from three simultaneous directions like a giant walnut cracker.

His good hand flew uselessly to his neck, and for a few seconds he scratched spasmodically at the bar. Then his torso twitched and the air suddenly reeked of feces—his body, in extremis, blowing the ballast and diverting all available energy to the fight. But it was useless. He scratched at the bar feebly for a moment more, and then I felt the crunch of his cricoid and thyroid cartilage breaking, and his arms slumped to his side, and he was deadweight in my arms, supported by nothing but the bar across his throat. I took a step back, away from the shit, released the bar, and dumped him. He collapsed to his back, his knees splayed and legs folded unnaturally at the knees, his face contorted and his tongue protruding.

I looked at the girl cowering by the bath. In the dim light and her own terror, I doubted she'd be able to describe me well. And, like the doorman, the tout, and the host, being part of the *mizu shōbai*, she'd have every reason to tell the police she'd seen little and could remember less.

I grabbed the attaché case and walked quickly back into the corridor, controlling my breathing, my heart still pounding wildly. A few doors were open now, prostitutes and patrons alike peeking out to see what had caused the sound of a second door crashing open. I kept my head down and moved to the stairs, where there was a metal roof-access door I had spotted on reconnaissance. If it had been locked, I would have gone out the front, but the less expected route was worth a try, and when I pressed the bar, it swung open easily. There was a walkway just beyond it, littered with cigarette butts. I glanced around to ensure no one was enjoying a tobacco break at that very moment, then proceeded to the fire escape, dropped to the alleyway behind the building, and drifted back into the Yoshiwara night.

I moved quickly along backstreets, staying in the shadows, and after a few minutes, I was far enough from Super Doll and Oleg's corpse to start to feel safe. I found a sewer, where I disposed of the dumbbell bar, then paused in a dark parking lot behind an apartment building and breathed steadily in and out, gradually slowing my heartbeat, getting back into character—just a salaryman, on his way home after a late night at the office or an evening out with colleagues, minding his own business, wanting nothing more than to get out of his suit and into his bed.

I glanced at the attaché case and saw Oleg's knife, still protruding from its side. For a second, I was horrified that I'd overlooked something so obvious and had been walking around with the handle jutting out for anyone to see. But okay, I'd gotten lucky. I extracted the knife and looked at it. I was half expecting some kind of fancy *Spetsnaz* weapon, but no, it was an ordinary Ka-Bar military knife—seven-inch serrated blade, worn wooden handle. I touched the edge, and was unsurprised to find that it was razor sharp. Since there was nothing too distinctive about it, I decided it was worth hanging on to. I'd clean it, then find an appropriate sheath at an outdoor store. I'd had about enough of people trying to stick me without having anything to stick back with.

I put the knife in the case and started walking again. *Okay, motherfucker,* I thought, smiling in grim satisfaction, *you wanted to talk, right? Well, we talked.*

I pushed aside the satisfaction, the exultation of having fought and survived, in favor of a more tactical focus on what the battle I had just won meant for the disposition of the forces still arrayed against me.

But that made me smile, too. Because as I'd discussed with Tatsu, Colonel Victor had just lost his best soldier. And now he would have to take the field himself. Where I'd be waiting for him.

chapter
seventeen

T he next morning, I called Victor's office from a payphone in Nippori. He picked up right away. "Yes."

"Oleg?" I said, playing dumb.

There was a pause. Then, "No. Victor."

"Where's Oleg?"

"Why do you ask this?"

"He's the one who always answers the phone."

"Oleg is sick today."

I didn't let myself smile. Or even feel what I wanted to feel. It might have come through in my tone.

"I'm sorry to hear that. I hope he gets well soon."

"You don't worry about Oleg's health. You worry about your health."

My effort not to smile faltered. I took a moment to get it under control, then said, "You have that lead you've been promising me? Or was that all bullshit?"

There was another pause. I sensed he was struggling to control himself. Good. When you're not in control of yourself, someone else is.

"Yes, asshole, I have lead. From eight o'clock Friday night, man will be at museum where wife works. Someone dies there. You want to know who?"

He must have been talking about the private dinner and showing Maria had mentioned—the one for her exhibit. Her husband would be there, of course, and probably mentioned it to Miyamoto's boss, Yokoyama, who fed it to Wilson, who in turn passed it along to Victor. I realized I should have made the connection on my own.

But I didn't like that whatever Victor had in mind would happen so close to Maria. Didn't like it at all.

"I'm sure you're going to tell me," I said.

"Either man dies. Or wife dies. And if wife dies? Your friend who introduced us also dies. And then you die, too. You want sexy time with wife again, you do your job and not be fuckup guy."

I considered his words without allowing myself any accompanying feelings. Why would he have thought he could use as leverage a woman I had merely flirted with at a reception? Plus, after the reception, it had been "sexy eyes," while now it was "sexy time," which sounded like more. So if he was using Maria as collateral, he must have known about the bar and the temple and the hotel. And he could only have known all that from the men I'd killed in Shibuya. Either he'd heard it from them directly, or, more likely, from Wilson, to whom presumably they had reported their findings before dying later on the evening in question. This was as close to proof of a link between Wilson and Victor as I was likely to get. Though what kind of link, I still didn't know.

"Well," I said, my tone deliberately mild, "when you put it that way, it seems like a fairly straightforward choice."

There was a long silence in response, and I imagined him seething. No more jokes about what a funny guy I was, I noted. Or clinical observations about how I wasn't afraid of him. I'd engaged his inner psycho, just as I had hoped. I was in his head now. And I was going to stay there until I put his fucking lights out forever.

"You know," he said, "I think your friend made mistake recommending you. But for sure we find out Friday night. Remember. Man dies. Or wife dies. And I don't think you will like how she dies. I don't think you will like at all."

He hung up.

I stood there for a moment, trying to keep my emotions at bay, forcing myself to think. Was Maria really at risk? They'd obviously been intent on not involving her so far. But that would have been for operational reasons, and before I'd pushed Victor to the point where the personal would be overriding the operational. So his threat to kill Maria felt real. In fact, it felt like more than just a threat. Even if he killed me first, I sensed, he would relish killing her afterward as some way of further exorcising me, posthumously punishing me, as well.

Which meant even killing Sugihara wouldn't be enough to protect Maria. Or Miyamoto. The only way to finish this was by killing Victor.

The good news was, I knew how to do that now. Or at least where. He'd be at the museum, Friday night. Waiting for me.

Just like I'd be waiting for him.

I called Tatsu, and we met again at the *izakaya* that evening. I watched him arrive like the last time, then walked in ten minutes later, after confirming that no one was rolling up behind him.

"It was only supposed to be Oleg," he said, the reproach in his tone so dry it almost crackled.

I lifted one of the mugs of beer he'd ordered, raised it in a toast, and drank. "I thought the deal was no civilians," I said, setting down the mug and belching.

"I confess I don't remember our exact words. We had drunk a fair amount."

"I think it was something about only cancer, no surrounding tissue, or something like that? I figure a bodyguard is more cancer than tissue. But I concede it's a bit of a gray area."

I sensed he was struggling not to smile. I knew he wouldn't lose the struggle, and was satisfied just that he had to engage in it.

"Are you all right?" he said after a moment. "No problems?"

"No. Your intel was rock solid. Any problems on your end?"

He shook his head. "Unsurprisingly, no one seems to have seen anything. Somehow, someone managed to shatter the front door, kick in an interior door, beat one person to death and strangle another, and escape leaving no witnesses."

"Maybe ninja," I said. "I hear they're deadly."

This time he actually did smile, albeit with a slight shake of his head. "I'm glad you're all right," he said. "But this isn't over yet. Victor is going to come at you hard."

"I know. I want him to. I've been goading him."

He looked at me closely. "You know, the Keisatsuchō works with several excellent psychiatrists. I could arrange for you to see one."

I smiled. "When I'm done with Victor, I'll see anyone you want me to."

"How will you get to him?"

I told him about the conversation from that morning.

"You know what this means," he said when I had finished. "The moment they think you've killed Sugihara, they plan to kill you."

"What do you mean by 'they'?"

"Some combination of Victor, Wilson, and whatever forces they can marshal between them."

"Maybe. But look at it this way. Victor knows I killed Oleg. His comrade-in-arms, his best soldier, his right-hand man. That alone would be more than enough to make this extremely personal for him. But on top of it? It's bugging the shit out of him that I seem to be immune to the fear he causes in everyone else."

"Are you?"

I considered for a moment. "I'm not sure. Maybe I'm just better at hiding it, even from myself. But I think it's more . . . he needs people to be afraid of him. It's everything he's about, and it's always the advantage he seeks. I understood that the second I first saw him. And

I'm just not going to give him that advantage. I'm going to take it and turn it on him."

"We have nothing to fear but fear itself?"

I took a sip of beer. "Something like that, I guess. All I know is, he hates that I'm not afraid of him. And worse, that I've been rubbing his face in it. Maybe you're right that I make jokes when I'm scared. But when I bust Victor's balls, it's not like that. It's straight-up contempt. And it's been preying on him, more and more. I'm in his head, and there's only one way he can get me out."

"He's not stupid. He'll know what you're doing. He'll put himself in your shoes the same way you've put yourself in his."

"That might affect his tactics, but it won't change his motivation. He needs to kill me himself. My whole existence threatens his self-conception."

"Which is?"

"He's the silverback. The alpha dog. The apex predator. There can't be two of those. Only one. He needs to know it's him, and the only way he'll be convinced of that is by killing me himself. Do you get it? In his mind, it's a zero-sum game. For him to win, I have to lose. If he doesn't kill me, he's not who he needs to believe he is."

"Then he's willing to die trying."

"Yes. And that's why I know he'll be at the museum himself. He went out of his way to try to scare me into being there. He threatened to kill Sugihara's wife that very night if I didn't take out her husband." I didn't mention the threat to Miyamoto—it wouldn't have added anything to the conversation, and Tatsu had already intuited more on the topic of my LDP contact than I liked.

He sipped his beer. "I can't help but ask why Victor would be under the impression that threatening Sugihara's wife would motivate you to try to protect her."

I didn't answer.

After a moment, he nodded. "When this is done," he said, "let's be sure to connect you with one of the psychiatrists I mentioned."

I smiled. "And there's one other reason I know Victor will be there."

"Yes?"

"Even if he wanted to send someone else—and he doesn't—who would it be? Oleg is dead. Oleg's bodyguard is dead. There are a couple of second stringers I saw in Victor's office, but he's an outsider, and I doubt he can recruit beyond that fast enough for it to matter. Anyway, this isn't something he'd be willing to outsource even if he could. He needs to do it himself."

"What about Wilson?"

"What about him? Whatever connection Victor has with Wilson, there's nothing to draw on now. Wilson doesn't have an army. His team is down by three, and if he'd had more than that, the extras would have been part of the surveillance he put on me. There's no junior varsity now. No one left on the bench. Just them. And me."

"If I didn't know better, I'd think you sounded happy about it."

"You're damned right I'm happy about it. By my count, Victor and Wilson are down six men since they first met me. My odds might not be great, but they're a hell of a lot better now than before."

"Yes. But that's not quite the source of the happiness I sense."

I didn't answer. Was he right? Did some sick part of me love this shit? I remembered the gangs who'd bullied me when my mother had first taken me to live in America at age eight. How I'd learned to evade them when they were together, and fight them when they were alone. I'd always thought that was all just a learning exercise, my first encounter with guerrilla warfare, my first recognition that I had a talent for it. But did I also relish it? Maybe somehow seek to replicate the experience again and again later in life?

"I don't know," I said. "Maybe you're right. But does it really matter? Love it or hate it, you know what I have to do."

He nodded, and for a few moments, we sipped our beers in silence.

I thought about Sugihara, and how badly Victor, or more likely Wilson acting through Victor, wanted him dead. What Sugihara represented to Wilson might have been academic at that point—if I could kill Victor, and Wilson, too, I'd be content to leave their motivations a mystery. But it couldn't hurt to know why this whole thing had been set in motion.

"Have you given any more thought to Sugihara?" I said.

"In what way?"

"Who benefits if he dies. Earlier, we were focusing on what his death alone might mean. But what if other people are also dying, and Sugihara's death is just a part of what whoever's behind this is trying to bring about as a result? I mean, we know Wilson's involved. Meaning probably the CIA itself, all the way up to Casey. If it's bigger than just Victor, it's probably bigger than just Sugihara, too, right?"

"That's reasonable. Unfortunately, other than the recent epidemic of deaths of which you are the vector, there have been no notable homicides of late."

"What about the guy Kobayashi killed by mistake?"

"An accountant. Once you informed me of what actually happened to him, I noted a superficial physical resemblance to Sugihara. An unfortunate case of the wrong man in the wrong place at the wrong time, coupled with an incompetent assassin."

"But there has to be something else. You're a cop. Don't you feel it?"

There was a pause. Then he said, "Yes. But I don't see it."

"Then widen the aperture. Forget about political assassinations. What about just, I don't know, political deaths?"

"The only high-profile political death in recent memory that wasn't of a retiree dying of old age was Masayoshi Ōhira, who died of a heart attack two years ago after a parliamentary vote of no confidence."

"Wait a minute. What do you mean, a heart attack?"

He looked at me. "Are you going to suggest someone caused Ōhira's heart attack?"

I happened to know with certainty that such a thing was possible, but I didn't see an advantage in confirming my firsthand knowledge. "Let's just assume it's possible," I said. "What happened?"

He looked at me for another moment, as though trying to decide whether to indulge me, or to bring up psychiatrists again. But he must have decided the former, because he said, "You don't know?"

"I haven't really been keeping up with the news."

"Ōhira was ousted as prime minister in a vote of no-confidence. But instead of resigning as expected, he called for new elections. After two weeks of frenetic campaigning, he was hospitalized for exhaustion. Twelve days after that, he died in the hospital of a massive heart attack."

I didn't say anything.

He frowned. "You don't really think—"

"Pretend for a moment he was killed. Just . . . humor me. They oust him with a vote of no confidence, but the guy doesn't do the expected thing and resign. Instead, he surprises them by campaigning. Did he have popular support?"

He frowned again. "In fact, he did."

"You see how this would look from the standpoint of the people who thought they'd be getting rid of him just with some cheap and easy parliamentary maneuver?"

"Maybe."

"Well, indulge me a little further. Why would someone want Ōhira dead? Who would benefit?"

His frown deepened—not because he was resisting anymore, I sensed, but because he was dramatically reconsidering his previous assumptions about the naturalness of Ōhira's death.

"Well, he was replaced by his deputy, Masayoshi Itō, but that was for all of a month."

"Okay. Who succeeded Itō?"

"The current prime minister, Zenkō Suzuki."

"Tell me about him."

"You don't even know who the prime minister is?"

"I know the name and I know he's LDP. That's about it."

"You really ought to read the newspaper."

"I'll put it on my to-do list, right after psychiatry."

He sighed. "In fairness, there's not much more to say about Suzuki than there is about Itō. He was elected in a landslide on a wave of popular sympathy for the LDP following Ōhira's death. He's been not much more than a caretaker, really. In fact, early on, he announced his desire not to stand in the current election."

I felt like we were getting close to something, and tried to control my excitement. "Well, who's going to succeed him?"

"Insiders seem to believe it will be Yasuhiro Nakasone."

I thought back to my conversation with Miyamoto at the Nakajima Teahouse. "Right," I said. "I heard the same thing from a source inside the LDP."

"The one who introduced you to Victor?"

Tatsu couldn't stop being a cop. But that didn't mean I needed to answer him.

"Does it matter?"

"I suppose not, if you're satisfied with the quality of the source's information."

"Well, my information seems to track with yours. Who's your source?"

He dipped his head in acknowledgment of how I'd turned the tables. "No source. Just talk. But from knowledgeable people."

"Well, my guy says Nakasone will get the nod because he wants a tighter military alliance with America."

"Yes, Nakasone is a rightist. He wants to abolish Article Nine of the constitution, which limits Japan's military."

"I know what Article Nine is."

"I thought you knew little of politics."

I couldn't tell if he was a friend needling me, or a cop reflexively probing what seemed an inconsistency. Maybe both.

"Little. Not nothing."

He grunted—his most enigmatic sound. "When Nakasone was head of the Defense Agency in 1970, he wanted to triple military spending from the traditional cap of one percent of GDP. He was also in favor of Japan having nuclear weapons."

I thought of Miyamoto, and his confidence that, no matter what, money always wins.

"So if Nakasone becomes prime minister," I said, "a lot of money's going to be made because of increased military spending, is that it?"

"Yes, but not only that. There are geopolitical implications, as well. Nakasone has said he wants Japan to be America's unsinkable aircraft carrier. An aircraft carrier permanently positioned alongside the eastern coast of the Soviet Union, China, and North Korea."

"Well, would Sugihara be able to stand in the way of that or something?"

He looked at me, and I could tell he was finally beginning to think I might really be onto something. "I don't know. I'm no expert on the inner workings of the LDP. What about your source?"

"I'll ask him. Anyone else? Any other deaths? Even by heart attack. Or not even a politician. Something's going on here, and we're not seeing it. And if we're not seeing it, it's because we're not looking in the right places."

He dipped his head and glanced away, his fingers drumming the table. Then he looked at me. "A journalist," he said. "Kazumi Yukimura. A year ago, he was stabbed to death by a rightist. Who then—"

"Hanged himself in police custody?"

He furrowed his brow. "Cut his own throat with a hidden razor, as it happens."

I looked at him, waiting for him to go on.

"Yukimura had written several articles critical of the Imperial household, and had received numerous death threats as a result. His killer was associated with various fringe rightist groups in Japan, and, other than the suicide, it was an open-and-shut case. But now . . ."

I waited while he processed it, knowing he was looking at everything he knew based on an entirely new theory.

"Yukimura had a significant following on the left," he said after a moment. "He eschewed government press pools, preferring to scrutinize official documents and find discrepancies. Many of the revelations in the Lockheed bribery scandal were his work. And—"

"Don't tell me. He was a pacifist. Treated Article Nine and the one-percent military-spending limit as sacrosanct."

"If I didn't know better, I'd say you know more of politics than you acknowledge," he said dryly.

"Not really. But now that we're putting our heads together and widening the aperture, I'm starting to see certain shapes. Aren't you?"

He nodded. "It's not inconceivable that the factions seeking to profit from increased military spending would have found Yukimura's continued muckraking . . . inconvenient."

"So they got some known rightist worked up, told him where and when he could find Yukimura, and then had some complicit cops cut his throat when they had him in custody."

He nodded slowly. "There's no proof, of course. This is just speculation. But . . . it fits."

"What about Wilson? The CIA? What's the connection with Victor?"

"You already know what it is. You said so the last time we talked."

"A cutout."

"Indeed. If you were the head of the CIA, or perhaps someone even higher in the US government, and you killed a Japanese prime minister to pave the way for someone more amenable to buying American armaments and offering the use of Japan as an unsinkable aircraft carrier, you would need more than deniability. You would need multiple circuit breakers. So no one could ever see the connection, much less prove it."

I thought about that for a moment. It explained why Victor was willing to have an LDP bureaucrat like Miyamoto's former boss beaten to death, while being so circumspect afterward. A Diet member like Sugihara, especially after the dead bureaucrat and a heart-attacked prime minister, would have created a possible pattern. Which had to be avoided at all costs.

I thought about Victor, how difficult he would be to control. Maybe he wasn't supposed to have killed Miyamoto's boss so ostentatiously. Maybe he just couldn't help doing things in a way calculated to make people afraid of him. Maybe afterward, Wilson had stepped in to try to impose some discipline and discretion. Maybe that's what was going on right now—cross-purposes, as Tatsu had said.

"So you agree with me about Prime Minister Ōhira's 'heart attack'?" I said.

He nodded. "It's a long game they've been playing, but not so long as to be unbelievable. The parliamentary maneuver fails. Somehow, they get to Ōhira in the hospital, and either cause a heart attack, if that's possible, or create the appearance of one—"

"And then Wilson gets activated, maybe by his former OSS buddy William Casey himself, and then works his global contacts until he identifies a half-Japanese, half-Russian former *Spetsnaz* soldier and current gangster, who speaks Japanese, knows his way around, and even carries a psychological grudge for the way he was treated as a child."

"Indeed. Who then returns to Japan and takes on the yakuza, using Wilson's intelligence."

"Just like the rightist they sent after the journalist. To the cops or anyone else who's looking, it all seems like it has a perfectly obvious explanation. Which obscures what's really going on."

He grimaced. "I should have seen this myself."

"No. You didn't have enough pieces to see the shape. And neither did I. Now we do."

I downed the rest of my beer. "I'll check in with my contact to find out how Sugihara might fit into all this. But I think we have most of it."

He polished off his beer as well, then wiped his mouth with the back of a hand. "You realize that anyone who knows that we know, or even just that we have most of it, will be exceptionally unhappy as a result."

"Well, you know how I hate to make people unhappy."

"I told you, I get concerned when you joke."

"Who's joking? In fact, if I've made Victor and Wilson unhappy, the least I can do is put them out of their misery."

chapter
eighteen

That night, Thursday, I took a room at the Imperial Hotel, one of Tokyo's finest. Maria had said she might be free the following evening. So if I stayed for two nights, and if things went more or less as I planned at the museum, she'd get the nicer hotel she wanted. And indeed, the room was far larger and more opulent than anything I was remotely accustomed to. For a while, I wandered around, picturing all the places we could make love—the sumptuous bed, the overstuffed couch, the plush carpeted floor, the enormous bath, up against the paneled walls—and the thought that she might be there in less than twenty-four hours was producing a constant adrenaline trickle.

I knew it was dumb to divert so much of my focus to pleasure when I still hadn't taken care of business. But I also knew if I didn't finish Victor at the museum the following evening, it wouldn't be just me who'd be dead. It might be Maria, too. Focusing on what it would be like with her in the hotel room was a way of denying all that.

I slept poorly. The next morning, after showering and fueling up with breakfast, I checked with the answering service. Miyamoto had left a message. I called him back right away.

"It's me," I said.

There was a pause, and I knew instantly I'd been right about his boss. I could just feel it—no need for a code.

Still, a moment later, he said, "I have some information for you. It would be useful for us to meet."

His delivery felt a little stiff to me. If Yokoyama was right there, and I assumed he was, I hoped he wouldn't pick up on it.

"Sure. When did you have in mind?"

"Well, if you want an outdoor venue like last time, it would be good to do it soon, before the rain starts up again. Perhaps tonight."

There it was. And there was indeed more rain in the forecast, so the reference was congruent enough. Still, I wondered how sharp his boss's antennae were. No way to know for sure. I'd just have to account for the possibility in my tactics.

But shit, tonight was Victor. And Maria. I almost said no, we needed another night.

And then I realized. I knew Victor was trying to set me up at the museum—so why was Yokoyama trying to set me up separately?

Because they're not coordinating. Tatsu was right. Miyamoto's boss reports to Wilson. So does Victor. But they're not directly in touch with each other. And now they're at cross-purposes.

Without hesitating any further, I said, "That's a good point. All right, I can do tonight, but it would have to be late. Can you be there after midnight? In fact, let's say two in the morning. Okay?"

"Yes, that would be fine. And where would be convenient for you?"

I'd already decided the place. "You know Zenkō-ji Temple in Omotesando?"

"Yes, of course."

"I'll see you there. And be careful—you don't want anyone following you."

"Of course."

I hung up, nodding in satisfaction. Maybe it was a little weird that I'd chosen the place where Maria and I had first been intimate—where Wilson's men probably could have killed me, if they hadn't had reasons for leaving her out of it. But having been there twice recently, I was freshly acquainted with the terrain. Along with how to use it. Best of all, at two in the morning, Zenkō-ji would be utterly deserted. No civilians for an ambusher to hide among, meaning anyone I saw who looked the least bit suspicious would be fair game. A Tokyo free-fire zone.

I walked to nearby Hibiya Park. The ground was soft and damp from the recent rain, and I strolled among the park benches, some occupied by pensioners in shirtsleeves, others by younger people in even more casual garb, probably part-time convenience-store workers and other members of a growing tribe of underemployed that a few years later would be recognized as *furiitaa*—a portmanteau consisting of the English word *free* or *freelance*, and the German word *arbeiter*, or laborer—by a society bemused and disturbed at the willingness of young people to subsist on marginal, low-paying jobs, rather than sacrifice themselves to the corporate needs of the wider society.

I cleared my mind and started thinking about how to get to Victor. Which is to say, I started thinking about how Victor would try to get to me.

He was experienced. And he knew I was experienced. He wouldn't do anything obvious, nor would he expect me to.

The focal point was the museum. There was only one visitor entrance to the main building. So wherever he set up, it would have to be a place that had a clear view of that choke point.

Which meant he didn't have a lot of options. There was the fountain on the plaza, with two stands of trees to either side of it, but that would be too far off to ensure a clear view and quick access. There were additional wings to the left and right of the main building, each with some decorative trees in front, but not enough to provide decent concealment.

I wasn't seeing it. I started to get frustrated.

Back up. You're too focused.

Yes, that felt right. But on what?

Concealment. Concealment is a tool. It's not an end in itself.

Yeah, but he still has to conceal himself. If he doesn't, I'll see him.

Are you sure?

I thought about how I'd gotten close to the bodyguard outside Super Doll—not by concealing my appearance, but by changing it.

I felt my heart kick harder as I realized the way he would play it. Of course. What had Tatsu said about how Victor and his men had gotten inside the palace in Kabul and killed the Afghan president and his entire guard? By dressing as Afghan soldiers. They'd camouflaged themselves as something the enemy wouldn't notice because the enemy would have previously classified it as harmless. Harmless because it was common, routine, an everyday sight.

Victor probably knew I'd been to the museum, or at least suspected. And even if he didn't, he'd know I was familiar with Ueno Park.

Right. And what are you accustomed to seeing in the park and around the museum?

I closed my eyes for a moment and imagined what I'd encountered on the way to the museum that day to see Maria. Schoolkids, of course, but I didn't see Victor squeezing into a school uniform anytime soon. Mothers with strollers, likewise not terribly likely.

There were a lot of homeless people in the park. But none on the museum grounds.

Then what did you see on the grounds?

The gardeners.

Holy shit, that was it. It felt exactly right. The baggy *monpe* pants and *hanten* coats to conceal the build. And with a hat pulled low across his face, and his head down to attend to his leaf sweeping or grass clipping or whatever, he'd rightly expect me to completely overlook him. If any of the other gardeners questioned him, he'd probably mumble a few words about having just been hired, and go on with whatever he was doing. As Maria had said, no one was expecting a heist; if a strange man wanted to do a bit of the gardening, how likely was it anyone would be suspicious enough to do anything about it?

And besides, he wouldn't need to be there long. He'd told me Sugihara would arrive at eight. But he also knew that I knew that he was going to be there, waiting for me. Meaning I'd get there early. Meaning Victor would be earlier still.

I didn't like the dynamic, with each of us trying to out-think and out-anticipate the other. What I needed was an out-of-the-box approach. The kind of thing he wouldn't anticipate.

And the right weapon. Not a knife—they all had knives. Something better.

I went to a medical-supply store and bought a long black leg brace—the kind with huge Velcro straps from ankle to thigh that people wear after knee surgery or other trauma. It came in a black canvas case, which would be perfect. I also picked out a cane, which would complete the picture. And at a surplus store, I found a leather sheath suitable for the late Oleg's knife.

I'd dumped the outfit I wore the night I killed Oleg because it had gotten sprayed with the bodyguard's blood and brains, so my next stop was a men's store, where I bought a new suit, along with a shirt, tie, belt, and shoes. It was pretty ordinary stuff—good for blending, but not, I realized, nearly as fine as what Employee Ito had helped me select in Ginza. I had to admit I liked the Ginza clothes better. I was glad I was increasingly able to spot a distinction I'd once been blind to, but I could also see where good clothes could become an expensive habit, one I couldn't afford right now, and didn't need anyway.

Back at the Imperial, I changed into the new outfit and fitted the brace onto my right leg, adjusting the angle until it was not quite straight. Using the cane, I hobbled around the room for a few minutes. This time, there was nothing to practice or imitate—my leg was immobilized exactly like that of someone who'd just had knee surgery, and I had no choice but to move awkwardly and with a pronounced limp.

Next, I taped Oleg's sheathed knife to the inside of my left forearm, where I could quickly access it with my right hand. I didn't expect to encounter Victor until that night—he might be expecting me early, but not this early—but if I was wrong, I wanted a weapon I could instantly access. Satisfied, I slipped on the jacket, pocketed the lock-picking tools I'd learned to use ten years earlier from a slightly illicit old Korean handyman in Shin-Ōkubo, checked myself in the full-length mirror, and, seeing nothing out of place, headed out.

I caught a cab in front of Hibiya Park, and had the driver take me straight to the museum. As we got close, I told him to circle the grounds—I was early, I said, and with the braced leg, now resting across the seat, the cab was the most comfortable place to sit. He did as I asked, and, as we drove, I refreshed my recollection of the terrain. The grounds themselves were spacious and parklike—long, grassy slopes and clusters of trees spread like a carpet of green around a half dozen gray buildings clustered in the interior. The perimeter was entirely encircled by iron-barred fences, the highest of which was the northwestern; the lowest of which, and the only one not topped with spikes, was the southwestern, which was also the one with the visitors' gate. I supposed the spikes were intended to be more decorative than functional. From a security standpoint, making one wall formidable while leaving another vulnerable didn't make a lot of sense.

If Victor expected me to come hunting for him, and I assumed he did, he might anticipate that I'd avoid the visitors' gate, choosing instead a less-obvious route. And the most obvious less-obvious route would be over that low, nonspiked southwestern wall. Which is why I rejected it.

On the second trip around, I decided I liked the southeastern side. The spiked fence was about seven feet high there, but there was a metal access door in the middle with no spikes on top that I could get over in seconds. Again, a pretty glaring weakness from a security perspective, but as Maria had pointed out, there weren't a lot of museum robberies in Japan.

Still. That's just where Victor would expect you.

Shit. Was I being paranoid? He couldn't risk an ambush site that didn't give him a view of the museum entrance, could he? Because if he chose wrong, he'd miss me entirely. The entrance was the choke point. He needed eyes on that.

Still, I decided the metal door was just a bit too obvious a vulnerability. I'd do better to choose a spot slightly less tempting.

On the third trip around, I asked the driver to slow down. There, on the northwest corner, the fence disappeared behind a small copse of trees. It was still high and spiked and not at all inviting, but the trees would provide some concealment. I'd noticed a few other spots like it, too, so even if Victor were anticipating my thinking, it would still be a coin toss as to which such spot I'd choose to breach the fence. He'd have no choice but to default to somewhere that gave him a view of the museum entrance. Meaning I'd be fine on the entry. Whatever happened was going to happen after that.

I thanked the driver for circling and had him take me to the entrance, looking left and right as we pulled up. It was only early afternoon, and I couldn't imagine Victor would set up this early—it might be a long wait, meaning a long time to be exposed. But I wasn't taking anything for granted. I saw nothing that set off any alarms—no gardeners, no homeless, no loitering people at all, just a few clusters of ordinary-looking visitors.

I paid the driver, then hobbled up the stairs, checking potential hotspots as I moved. All clear. Inside, I scoped the lobby. Again, all clear. And no sign of Maria, either, or of Director Kurosawa. If I ran into them, I had a story prepared about visiting the museum to learn more before my interviews, despite a leg injury incurred during judo, a story I would deliver as though abashed at having my ardor for museum work discovered—concealing the commission of a greater crime by the apparent confession of a lesser one. But I had a feeling Maria would be busy with final touches on her exhibit. As for Kurosawa, I sensed he spent most of his time in his cave of an office, surrounded by treasured artifacts.

There was a guard to my left. I waved and made my way over, leaning heavily on the cane and grimacing slightly as though from pain or effort.

"Pardon me," I said. "Can you tell me where to find the elevator? The stairs in front were hard enough."

He glanced quickly at the leg brace and the cane—anything longer would have been rude—and nodded sympathetically, not seeming the least bit suspicious. And why would he be? I wasn't trying to conceal anything. I'd openly approached him with a question completely congruent with my own obvious discomfiture. And thereby established the leg brace in his mind as . . . nothing more than a leg brace. The way a hammer can be established as nothing more than a hammer.

"Of course," he said. "Around the corner to the right of the stairs."

I gave him a slight bow and hobbled ostentatiously away. I stopped in a restroom, where in a stall I loosened all but one of the Velcro straps around the brace. The black case the brace had come in was already alongside my leg, indistinguishable from the brace itself. Then I headed out to the elevator.

Two minutes later, I was standing outside the basement storage room, my heart beating hard. Maria had confirmed that security was low, but that didn't mean Murphy's law was in abeyance. If someone came along, my only plan was to pull off the last strip of Velcro, lose the brace, and run. But inside a minute, courtesy of the lockpicks, the excellent tutelage of my erstwhile teacher, and my own ardent practice, I had defeated the lock and was inside. I closed the door behind me, flipped on the lights, and then jammed the handle of the cane up under the doorknob, kicking the rubber-capped bottom along the floor until I was certain the door was firmly stuck. If someone happened to come by, hopefully he would assume something was wrong with the door and go to get maintenance or other help, giving me time to slip away. Plus, this way, I couldn't forget the cane.

I headed straight to the swords. I lifted the one I had handled the other day, my favorite, and then, as though checking a pistol for a chambered round, pulled back the wood *tsuka* hilt just enough to visually confirm the blade was indeed inside the *shirasaya* scabbard. I eased the blade back in place, then slipped the closed scabbard into the black case alongside my outer leg. I secured the Velcro straps, tightening the package against my leg, hobbled to the door, kicked loose the cane, killed the lights, and cracked the door to check the corridor. All clear. It looked like Mr. Murphy wasn't going to show up today. At least not yet.

Back at the elevator, I was in luck again—it was still on the basement level, so I didn't have to wait or risk it arriving with a museum employee inside. I got on, and pressed the button for the second floor. But it stopped on the ground level. I concentrated on breathing naturally, forcing away the knowledge that I had just stolen a priceless samurai sword, and focusing instead on who I was—just a salaryman, probably newly unemployed and therefore ashamed, hiding from the world with a visit to the museum.

The doors opened and, despite my efforts, for an instant I imagined I saw Maria—but it was only a group of elderly museumgoers. They filed on around me, several of them glancing at the cane sympathetically, and then the doors closed, and we continued to the second floor. None of them could have been less than twice my age, but still they made a show of letting me hobble off before them. I supposed doing so made them feel hale in comparison. As for me, I was glad the brace and the cane were attracting the proper attention.

I badly wanted to get the hell out of the museum in case anyone noticed the sword was missing and sounded some kind of alarm. But I didn't want the guard to see me leaving too quickly, which would have seemed odd, and I didn't want to kill the time in an exhibit, either, where there was a chance, however small, that I would run into Maria or Director Kurosawa. So I ducked into a restroom and slipped inside one of the stalls. I closed my eyes and breathed steadily in and out, my heart rate slightly elevated.

I realized what I had just done was foolish. There were other swords available in Tokyo, including quality imitations, that would have served well enough. Why did I want this one? Why take that risk?

I wasn't sure. It had just felt so right that time with Maria, when I'd held it in my hands. Like the sword was an extension of me—or I an extension of it. It was something bound up in my childhood in Japan, and, at the same time, something I'd connected with again so recently, after so much time and circumstance. Of course, all that had been no more than coincidence. But somehow . . . it felt like more.

Yeah. Maybe my thinking had been talismanic, but I didn't want to be holding just any sword when I faced Victor.

I wanted it to be this one.

I spent the next forty minutes focusing on my breathing, not thinking about what I had just done, not thinking of what I had to do next, just waiting, and focusing on that.

When I judged I'd been there long enough, I flushed the toilet and eased out of the stall. I had almost made it to the door when it opened. And Director Kurosawa shuffled in.

He squinted and looked right at me. There was nowhere to go. I couldn't even turn away. I prepared to deliver my rehearsed story.

I had opened my mouth, the words on the verge of tumbling out, when I realized—he was going right past me. I stifled the urge to speak and just kept hobbling along. Had the cane and the brace thrown him off? Maybe. That, and the fact that his eyes were probably as weak as his ears.

I'd meant to pause at the door and check the corridor before leaving, but that would have seemed odd. So I left without looking, started to turn right—and saw Maria heading straight toward me, a pair of young Japanese men, who I took to be museum staff, alongside her.

Fuck. I pivoted and hobbled the other way, hunching over the cane, doing all I reasonably could to change my posture and persona. As soon as I rounded the corner, I headed into the *Fashion of the Edo Period* exhibit and moved more quickly, trying to put more distance between us. A few visitors glanced at me, the echoes of my oddly cadenced footfalls and the squeak of the rubber end of the cane catching their attention, probably wondering why the man in the leg brace seemed to be in such a hurry. But I was less concerned about attention from strangers than I was about seeing Maria, and kept to my brisk pace. By the time I was through the exhibit and had rounded the next corner, Maria and her small entourage were nowhere behind me. I headed down the main stairs, gripping the bannister and hopping on my "good" leg.

Naturally, the guard was standing in front of the entrance, and got to watch my entire laborious approach. By the time I reached the bottom, I was sweating profusely. He looked at me, frowning as though perplexed.

"It's up the stairs that's hard," I said, the words belied by the sheen of moisture I could feel on my forehead. "Down is actually kind of fun."

He nodded wordlessly, doubtless thinking he had better things to do than engage with hobbled lunatics, and I limped past him and out of the museum. I paused to do a visual sweep—all clear—and then cut left and got the hell out of there.

I'd been wrong about Murphy taking the day off. He'd merely been late. But hopefully that would be his only appearance. Because getting the sword had been the easy part. Successfully deploying it was apt to be a bit more challenging.

chapter nineteen

I took another taxi back to the Imperial, where I removed the brace and eased the sword from the scabbard. Even bereft of its combat *tsukaito* hilt, the grip was secure, the steel somehow both effortlessly light and lethally substantial in my hand.

I replaced the blade in the scabbard, carefully placed it under the mattress, hung the "Do Not Disturb" sign on the door, and headed out for another shopping expedition. It was a relief to be able to move normally again, and I realized I'd been suppressing a lot of fear that I might encounter Victor while I was half immobilized by the leg brace. I'd been armed with Oleg's knife, of course, but still, now that the brace was gone, I realized just how badly it would have impeded me. I wondered again at what had impelled me to take so many risks to acquire this particular sword. Again, I couldn't say for sure. But I certainly felt stronger, surer, now that I was armed with it.

I made two stops: first, a men's store for another suit jacket and shirt—this time overlarge ones—and a pair of deerskin gloves. Then a used photography shop, where I equipped myself with a cheap SLR camera, and a folding tripod in a long nylon case.

Back in the room, I carefully wiped down Oleg's knife and the hilt and scabbard of the sword, placing the sheathed sword in the tripod case when I was satisfied I had erased any possible fingerprints. Then I geared up in my modified armor—the Kevlar motocross bodysuit and vest. I slipped on the new shirt, secured Oleg's knife to my forearm again, and then donned the jacket. I slicked back my hair, put on the glasses, and examined myself in the mirror. Staring back at me was a salaryman, thirty pounds overweight, in fashion-challenged eyeglasses and an ill-fitting afterthought of a suit. *Good.* I slipped the camera lanyard over my neck and hefted the tripod case. Now I looked like one of the scores of Tokyo's amateur photographers, off work a little early and out to indulge his hobby. It wouldn't fool Victor, if he saw me before I saw him, but it wouldn't get a second glance from passing civilians the way, say, a man carrying two and a half feet of samurai sword in a *shirasaya* might. A long nylon case by itself might contain anything. Alongside a camera, the case must contain photography equipment. It was like a magician forcing a card, except that the card I wanted to force was all about perception.

I considered taking the train, but imagined Victor waiting somewhere outside Ueno Station. I knew I was getting excessively paranoid, but decided there was no harm in getting another cab. I had the driver drop me off at Kaneiji, a Buddhist temple behind the northwestern corner of the museum grounds and, with its famous pagoda, a suitable-enough spot for a man with a camera and tripod case.

I waited for the cab to depart, then pulled on the gloves and wandered out to the street. It was twilight now, the air autumn-cool. Early, considering that Victor had told me Sugihara wouldn't arrive until eight o'clock. But about on schedule, I thought, if Victor were hoping to anticipate me.

There weren't many pedestrians about, and when I saw an opening, I ducked behind the trees and stepped close to the fence. I paused to look and listen, but the museum grounds on the other side, similarly thick with trees, were still and silent.

I took the camera from around my neck and tossed it over the fence, then placed one end of the tripod case on the ground, and wedged the other end partway between two of the iron fence posts.

And then, apologizing to the distant gods of Japanese swordsmithing, I planted a foot on the top of the case, gripped the metal bars, and pulled myself up.

With the case, bolstered by the wooden scabbard inside it, under me, half my body was already above the fence. Using exceptional care, I eased my stomach down onto the spikes, reached over with my right hand, and slowly rotated my legs over. The Kevlar prevented me from being skewered, but still, I could feel the pressure my body was exerting, and sensed what would happen if any of the spikes slipped past my armor.

But they didn't. I got my legs to the inside of the fence, pushed up with my arms, and then kicked off, landing in an *ukemi* breakfall on the other side. I sprang instantly to my feet, facing the interior of the grounds, my right hand gripping the handle of Oleg's knife. Nothing happened. No movement, no surprises. Wherever Victor might be, it wasn't here.

I went back to the fence, reached through the bars, and worked the tripod case upward until it had cleared the spikes and I could take hold of it and bring it over. Then I picked up the camera, hurried over to a cluster of trees, and unzipped one end of the case. I reached inside and took hold of the hilt of the sword. To deploy it, I'd just drop the camera, grip the case with my free hand, and free the sword with my other. Out of weapons-check habit, I tested the draw, and then, satisfied with its smoothness and speed, moved out from the trees and toward the interior.

It was still light enough to see, but dark enough to obscure details. And just past six o'clock—about how early Victor might expect me to arrive. I felt his malevolent presence. But where?

Somewhere by the entrance to the main building, I reminded myself. It was his only choke point.

But he's running the same play you are. Anticipating you anticipating him.

Right.

I moved west behind the main building, keeping to the trees and shadows, my eyes sweeping the area, my ears alert for the telltale crunch of a leaf or snap of a twig. My heart rate was slightly elevated, but overall I felt calm and focused, the way I once had in the jungle. I saw no one. The museum was still open, I knew, but at this hour, visitors would have little reason to be strolling back here.

I circled wide of the building until I was even with the front west corner. Several gardeners were out, I was satisfied to see, sweeping and raking leaves in the gray light, the path lamps now offering more illumination than the remains of the fading day. None took any notice of me. None had any kind of a suspicious vibe. None was built like Victor.

I headed back the way I had come. My heart was kicking harder now. Reconnaissance was nearly done. If the enemy was here, I was about to encounter him. I gripped the sword hilt more tightly and slowed my pace, letting my night vision adjust from the lamplight by the front of the building, using the trees for concealment, careful to step only on dirt and moss, avoiding the scattered leaves.

I circled wide again, mirroring the approach I had used on the other side, moving carefully around until I was even with the east corner. In front of the museum, a few people were coming and going. Beyond them, I saw a few more gardeners. None looked at all out of the ordinary.

Where the hell is he?

I don't think I heard the sound behind me as much as I felt it. Or intuited it. Because in a microsecond's insight, I realized Victor hadn't been watching the entrance. Not exactly. He'd known I would approach obliquely, that I would be looking for him in all the stealthy spots. So instead, he'd set up farther out—all the way by the visitors' gate, an approach so obvious he knew I wouldn't dare use it. And he'd spotted me reconnoitering from the west side, known I would repeat the maneuver from this deserted spot on the east side, had cut diagonally across to anticipate, come up behind me—

I flung away the camera and gripped the tripod case, pulling it hard and clearing the sword as I spun, my left hand coming in for a two-handed grip—

And saw Victor, moving in not ten feet away, a gardener's clothes and hat obscuring his identity, a small blade held discreetly at his right side. He pulled up short at the sight of the long length of steel suddenly in my hands, the fading evening light glinting along the *hamon*.

"Typical *Spetsnaz* asshole," I said with a combat smile. "Bringing a knife to a sword fight."

I glanced right and left. I was reasonably sure that, for reasons both logistical and psychological, he would have no one with him. But *Doveryai, no proveryai.* We were far from the entrance and the pathways, and the area was clear. It was just the two of us.

Soon to be just one.

My insult had been calculated. I wanted him to rush me, ideally in a rage, which would be my best chance of exploiting the greater range afforded by the sword. But he didn't. I'd seen before that Victor's self-control could sometimes suppress his insanity. For the moment, it seemed, self-control had the upper hand.

But not entirely. Because a fully sane person, armed only with a knife, would have instantly fled from the sight of that deadly *katana*, hoping to live to fight another day. It seemed Victor had other priorities. He was going to kill me tonight. Or die trying.

Which meant his self-control was only barely in charge. If I could goad him just a little, his demons could easily get the upper hand.

In fact, I had no choice. His willingness to risk suicide gave him an advantage—it would enable him to take chances, to accept even lethal injuries, as the price of killing me. I, on the other hand, determined to live, would be forced to adopt more conservative tactics. Suicidal determination coupled with a measure of control was a daunting combination. There was nothing I could do about the first element. The second, though, I might be able to break.

"What's the problem?" I said. "Oleg couldn't make it? Is he still sick?"

He pulled off the hat and tossed it aside. "You're going to die, fuckup guy. You know this, yes?"

"If I'm fuckup guy, asshole, what does that make Oleg?"

Even in the dim light, I could see his face darken. I pressed the advantage. "Did you know he shit himself as I was strangling him? It's true. The hardest thing about killing your buddy was avoiding stepping in his shit."

I could see his jaw clench, his nostrils flaring. He knew he shouldn't rush me. But he wanted to so much.

"Is that how *Spetsnaz* tough guys usually check out? Shitting themselves?"

But it wasn't enough. He knew what I was doing, and no matter how much the insults must have enraged him, they weren't putting him over the edge. I realized I needed something else—something even more central to his psychology than his military past. I thought of Tatsu's briefing, of the note from the orphanage.

"It's all right," I said. "I'm sure you're tougher than he was. After all, your father was a Soviet general, right?"

He looked at me, a ripple of uncertainty passing across his features, and I went on. "Except he wasn't," I said. "Your father was just some nobody Russian grunt, captured by the Japanese after losing a battle, who raped your peasant-girl mother and filled her belly with you."

"You fucking lying shit piece," he said, his voice practically a hiss.

"Your mother was the liar, Victor. Not that I blame her. She knew the truth would crush you. So she made up a story so you'd think your loser father was a hero." I felt a flash of inspiration. "And Wilson confirmed it, didn't he? Told you he was using his CIA contacts to find your father, the great general?"

He bared his teeth, his eyes burning with hate, and I knew I was onto something. "Does that even make any sense to you?" I said. "How hard is it for the CIA to find a Soviet general? He played you, you dumb shit. Just like your mother. Like everyone. Your whole life is built on a lie so obvious the only one stupid enough to believe it is you. You, Hikaru Yamada. That's your real name, isn't it? Victor Karkov, my ass. What a farce."

He watched me, everything about him feeling like a volcano about to erupt. "And the best part?" I went on. "The best part is, you knew. Deep down, you always knew. It's why you're so desperate for everyone to be afraid of you." I started laughing. "Isn't that right? It's because you're so afraid yourself. Look at you, all it took was the sight of a little sword and you're about to piss your—"

He bellowed something in Russian and rushed me, whether by instinct or some residue of tactical acumen making the move while I was still talking, and therefore inhibited from switching gears to intercept him. But I'd been ready regardless, and as he lunged with the knife, I sidestepped to the left and parried him at the shoulder, raking the *katana* all the way from triceps to wrist like a chef carving off a slice of meat from a shawarma rotisserie.

Blood spurted from the long cut, and he snarled and spun in to me, too enraged by my insults even for a tactical retreat. I brought the sword higher, slashing at his neck, but he parried with his knife hand, enduring another deep gash on the forearm, at the same instant reaching around with his free hand and actually managing to grab the blade of the sword.

I reacted instinctively, jerking the blade from his grasp. Through my adrenalized slow-motion vision, I saw bloody fingers tumbling through the air like spent cartridges from a machine gun, but I realized it didn't matter, he didn't care about his fingers, all he cared about was closing at any cost, and before I could bring the blade in again he screamed and slashed at my belly with the knife. The blade scored across the Kevlar plates, and for an instant I saw his eyes flash with animal triumph at the knowledge he had gutted me. But the look changed to fear as he realized something was wrong, I hadn't grimaced or cried out, the knife hadn't penetrated. Before he could figure out what had gone wrong and regroup for a more effective attack, I sidestepped left again and brought the sword in low across his right wrist. I traded speed for accuracy, and the blow wasn't enough to take off his hand. But it sliced him open to the bone. He lost his grip on the knife, and as he instinctively raised his bloody arms to protect his head and neck, I slashed the sword around low, right to left, connecting with his left knee and nearly severing his leg.

For one weird second, he kept his footing, like a cartoon character racing off a precipice and floating in the instant before gravity asserts itself. Then his leg folded, and he went down. He managed to get out what remained of his left hand and prevent himself from going flat on his face. But there was no question he was done. He struggled to rise, and succeeded only in falling to his back.

I glanced around, ensuring we were still alone. Then I returned my gaze to Victor. I could have moved in and finished him, but for some reason I didn't. I watched for a moment as he continued to struggle to get to his feet. Despite everything, I couldn't help feeling some surprising, reluctant respect for this man, who was so clearly beaten but who refused to die on his back.

After a moment, he managed to roll to his side, get one leg out, and rise to the knee I had just cut through, his good leg extended before him. He shuddered, then somehow stabilized himself, his ruined hands held out in front of him for balance, blood pouring from his wounds.

He looked at me, his breathing ragged but his head defiantly high. For an instant, in his eyes and his posture, I saw that long-ago little boy, who every day had stood with his palms pressed against an orphanage window, hoping and waiting for the mother who never returned for him.

The killing fervor I'd felt so furiously just a moment before was gone. In its absence, I felt the strangest kinship for him. An intimacy. Almost a tenderness.

He nodded at me—just once, down and then up again.

I was suddenly aware of how quiet it was on this part of the museum grounds. There was no one around. No one else who could understand what he was asking. Or do it.

He nodded again, the gesture quicker than the one before, more urgent. This time, I nodded back.

I stepped behind him. He straightened, still on the knee, and tilted back his head, perhaps so that he might have one last look at the sky. I braced myself, left leg forward, right back, and retracted the sword to my shoulder. For a second, he wobbled, and, before he could suffer the indignity of falling, I swung full force into his neck, cutting clean through from one side to the other.

His head toppled to the right and his body to the left, blood jetting from the top of his torso, his limbs twitching. It went on for a few seconds. Then the flow of blood began to ebb, and his limbs settled. A single shiver passed through his body, and then was gone, as he was.

I stood for a moment, my breathing labored, looking down at him in the twilight, that feeling of some strange, poignant bond deepening. It wasn't something I thought I would ever be able to explain to anyone else. I didn't understand it myself. It was as though I had done something that was right, but that was also fraught in ways I could sense but not articulate. Something that felt . . . aligned, somehow, congruent, foreordained by fate or some other force for which I had no name. But whatever that force was, I was aware of its weight. Its consequence. Its irrevocability.

I wanted to wipe the blade on his clothes, but there was too much blood. So I pulled off my jacket, flipped it inside out, and used that instead. Then I turned the jacket right-side out and pulled it back on.

Despite the coolness of the evening, I was sweating intensely, and I would have preferred to leave the jacket off. But that would have looked odd. And besides, there was blood spray on my shirt, which the jacket would help cover.

I retrieved the tripod case, removed the scabbard, sheathed the sword, and laid it next to Victor. In this remote, shadowy spot on the grounds, this late in the day, I doubted the body would be discovered until the next morning. I picked up the camera and slipped the strap over my neck, pausing to confirm I had everything I'd arrived with—camera, case . . . wait, the gloves. The temperature was cool—even cooler on the grounds than it had been on the street—but not that cool. I scrubbed my face in case any blood had hit it, then pulled off the gloves and shoved them into the case.

I needed to go. But I lingered for just a moment longer, watching Victor. I wasn't sure why. It just seemed wrong to leave him lying there like that, so unceremoniously, and butchered, and alone. Still, it had been a good death. The one he'd wanted, when he'd seen there was no alternative. The kind I would hope an enemy might bestow upon me under similar circumstances.

I headed toward the visitors' gate, trying to shake off whatever it was I was feeling. I kept my head down, reminding myself I was just a salaryman returning from a bit of amateur photography. But I was having trouble performing the role. I felt like something else now. I didn't know what.

chapter
twenty

I took a series of cabs to Shinbashi, then walked the rest of the distance to the hotel. I'd stopped at an Ueno Park public restroom to check my appearance on the way out of the museum grounds. The blood on my face and shirt wasn't too bad, and I was able to rinse off the worst of it at the sink, and obscure the rest with the camera and tripod case.

Back in my room at the Imperial, I bagged all the potentially contaminated clothes and gear, showered, changed into my street clothes, and went out, dumping everything that might have incriminated me in a series of storm drains. Thinking of the meeting Miyamoto's boss had instructed him to request for later that night, which I knew was a pretext for the next ambush, I'd decided to keep my homemade armor and Oleg's knife.

The evidence of the crime safely discarded, I felt a little more relaxed. I walked east, toward the waterfront.

It was nearly eight o'clock. Maria's event would be beginning soon. I had told her I would call. But I needed to clear my head first.

I reminded myself that she was all right. The only one who had wanted to hurt her was Victor, and he was dead now. And Sugihara would be safe, too, at least for the time being. If Wilson were still intent on killing him even after losing Victor, he was going to need new cutouts. And that would take time.

I imagined Victor, his body cooling at the dim edge of the museum grounds. I doubted anyone would have found him yet. Or the sword. Or noticed the sword was missing from the storage room, for that matter. But it wasn't impossible. And it would happen eventually, regardless—if not tonight, then certainly tomorrow—at which point Maria would connect the sword to me. I had considered this in advance, of course, and even toyed with the idea of returning the sword to the storage room, or of keeping it. But going back to the museum with the sword following Victor's death felt too risky, and keeping it, though tempting, felt worse than risky—it felt wrong. Besides, if it had been discovered missing, rather than found alongside Victor, Maria still would have connected it with me.

No matter what, though, I was reasonably confident she would say nothing to the authorities, lest our affair come to light. And even if she did, I'd have Tatsu to run interference. But knowing that she would suspect, and might confront me, was sobering. It was one thing to consider it all before the fact. But now . . . I realized I didn't feel the way I'd expected. After killing Wilson's man on the train plat-form, I'd been half-crazed with postcombat lust, to the point where I was ready to take extreme risks just for an hour with Maria. But now, though I still badly wanted to see her, the feeling was tinged with a sadness I didn't fully understand. I wondered if it was connected to whatever had passed between Victor and me in the moments before I killed him.

It didn't matter. She'd told me she would be angry if I didn't call, and, once Victor's body and the sword were discovered, my failure to do so would have looked suspicious, as well. So I found a payphone off the war-ren of streets surrounding the Tsukiji fish market, and dialed her number.

She picked up after a single ring. "Hello," she said in English, a certain coolness in her tone. I felt a little adrenaline hit. Had they found Victor's body sooner than I'd expected?

"Hey," I said. "It's me."

"Yes, I thought it might be. Were you going to make me wait until the start of the reception? In another minute, I'll be late for my own opening."

I felt a surge of relief. "No, of course not. I just thought this would be the best time to catch you in your office. I didn't want to leave word with someone else."

There was a pause. "Ah, I suppose maybe I should have thought of that, and planned a time rather than just a day. You know, I've been sitting here and getting more and more furious at you. I still am."

Imagining her, alone in her office, gorgeous in whatever she was wearing for the reception, and stewing over me instead of thinking about the event, was suddenly an incredibly sexy thought. "What are you wearing?" I said.

She laughed. "Do you not know it's dangerous to trifle with an Italian woman when she's angry?"

"Is it something I can tear off?"

I heard her breathe deeply for a moment. Then she said, "No. But I brought something to change into. For later."

I felt myself stiffening. "Then you can make it tonight?"

"Yes. Probably around eleven. And not for terribly long. My husband has to go out with some work people after the reception. I can come then."

"I'm at the Imperial."

"Good. If you told me another love hotel, I think I would have stood you up."

"You'll like this one. I'll wait for you in the bar, okay? Just come in as though you're looking for someone, then leave. I'll get up and you can follow me up on the elevator."

"Ah, you've thought about this. Very discreet."

"Oh, I've been thinking about it."

"Mmm, good. So have I. I have to go. I should be there around eleven."

She hung up. I blew out a long breath, then waited for my condition to subside before putting the receiver back in the cradle, and rejoining the pedestrian traffic around me.

I found another payphone. I thought about calling Miyamoto, but I didn't need any intel from him, and besides, I didn't want to do anything that might interrupt the meeting at which I was expected later that night. He'd hear about Victor soon enough, and know what had happened.

I did call Tatsu, though. He'd been worried about me, even if it wasn't in his nature to express it with much more than droll asides about my nervousness, and the odd sympathetic grunt.

"Are you all right?" he asked as soon as I'd let him know it was me.

I couldn't help but smile at the concern in his tone. He really had been worried.

"I'm fine," I said. "Though I'm guessing you're going to have another homicide investigation on your hands tomorrow."

"Victor?"

"That would be my guess."

There was a pause. I knew he wanted to know more, but would know not to say too much over the phone. "Would you like to get together?" he said.

"I can't right now, I have something going on. Nothing to worry about. Not that you'd worry about me."

He grunted, returning to form.

"Really," I said. "It's nothing dangerous."

"I'm not sure you're the best judge of such things."

I laughed. "You might be right. How about tomorrow? Same place, six o'clock? I'll have more to tell you then, anyway."

"I'll look forward to it. And whatever it is you're doing tonight, and I'm afraid I can imagine, please be careful. You know the moment following a great victory is when you're most vulnerable to a new attack."

I smiled, feeling good. "I'll be fine."

Yeah. Stupid to the bitter end.

chapter
twenty-one

S tores were open late because it was Friday night, so I went back to Mitsukoshi in Ginza, where Employee Ito helped me select some new Italian clothes—another sweater, slacks, belt, and shoes, and a brown suede jacket. I told myself the right look would help me blend better at the upscale Imperial. But the truth was more that I wanted to look good for Maria. And hell, I had money to burn now. With Victor dead, I had fifty thousand bucks coming from Miyamoto. And steady work to look forward to after that.

Which was good, because the clothes were cheap compared to the next thing I bought: a pair of second-generation, AN/PVS-5 night-vision goggles, at a camera store in Yūrakuchō. The clothes were for Maria. The night vision was for after.

It wasn't impossible they would follow her again. But I doubted it. Wilson's forces were seriously depleted, for one thing. For another, I was expected at Zenkō-ji Temple later that evening.

Still, when I headed down to the Old Imperial Bar that night at a little before ten, I made sure to take a seat at the end of the counter, with a view of the entrance. I ordered a gimlet. It was good, though not quite as incredible as one of Ozaki's. In fairness, though, I had some associations between what I had tasted at Bar Radio and what I tasted after that would be hard for another place to match.

The bar was striking, and I learned from the bartender that many of its design elements were relics from the Frank Lloyd Wright–designed

1923 Imperial, torn down following the Great Kanto Quake that struck on the very day the hotel had opened. I decided it was a Maria kind of place: Oya volcanic stone on the walls, preserved from the original bar; hexagonal fixtures and mirrors and matching chairs; low light, hushed acoustics, an ambience of privacy and class. I had liked it the moment I walked in, but after an hour, I realized that knowing a bit about its history was enhancing my appreciation. I smiled, thinking Maria would be pleased with her student. I had been trying not to imagine her, because doing so made the wait more difficult to endure. But as I nursed my gimlet, I was having trouble distracting myself.

At eleven thirty, as I was torturing myself with thoughts that she wasn't going to come, she stepped inside. Her hair was pinned up, and she was wearing a long, double-breasted tan trench coat and black heels. She was carrying a stylish leather bag, large enough for a change of clothes, and the thought of what might be under the coat made my breath catch. She saw me notice her, and, before I could take in more, she turned and left. The bartender was busy preparing drinks, and it was almost five minutes before I was able to settle the bill—five agonizing minutes. I hurried out to the bustling lobby, but didn't see her. She wouldn't have left, would she? I had only been a few minutes. I knew I was being ridiculous, but still, where was she?

I was suddenly gripped by paranoia. I'd been so confident, but . . . could she have been followed again? Could something have happened to her?

I felt an adrenaline dump kick in and I turned to scope the crowd. No one in any strategic positions, no one who felt out of place or who otherwise set off my radar. But still, where the hell—

She stepped out from behind one of the massive columns supporting the ceiling two stories up. She was looking away, wearing a small but satisfied smile, and I realized she had been playing with me, probably as revenge for my having waited so long to call her earlier that night.

The adrenaline, the alcohol, the sight of her . . . it all coursed through me in a rush. The lobby seemed to melt away, and all I could think about was getting her to my room. But I shook it off, and made sure to look behind her. I saw no one trailing in her wake.

She followed me to the elevator, keeping a discreet distance per the plan. An elderly Japanese couple was already waiting. I got on after them and turned. Still no one in her wake. But damn it, she was too far off. The old man pressed the button for the third floor, then looked at me questioningly. I hesitated, then held the "Door Open" button. "Sorry," I said in Japanese. "I think someone else is coming."

She took her time, and I felt she was taunting me. The elderly couple looked at me, too Japanese to comment on my rudeness in holding the elevator for so long. Finally, Maria walked on. I pressed the button for the eighth floor, where I was staying, and said to her in English, "Floor?"

"Same," she said, barely glancing at me.

The doors opened on three, and the couple got off. The old guy glanced back at me, and for a second I had the oddest sense that he knew what was going on and was amused, or maybe wistful, about it. Then the doors closed, and they were gone.

I watched her, but she kept her eyes on the illuminated numbers over the door, playing the role of a stranger in an elevator. Was she being discreet, or taunting me again? Being enclosed and alone with her, close enough to reach out and touch her, to smell her perfume, and yet to have her ignore me, was maddening.

We got to eight, and the doors opened. I held them with one hand and gestured with the other. "Please. After you."

She gave me the hint of a smoldering smile and stepped past me, pausing to examine a sign laying out the order of rooms, as though reminding herself of where she was heading.

I started down the corridor, then turned to her. "Are you lost?" I said. "Why don't you follow me, I'll help you get where you want to go."

"That's very kind of you," she said, toying with me again with that damn Mona Lisa smile. "If you think you can."

I wanted her so much I was having trouble controlling my breathing. "Why don't we find out?" I said, and turned and walked down the corridor.

It couldn't have been more than fifty feet, but it seemed to take a long time to reach my room. I unlocked the door, stepped inside, then held the handle and waited. A moment later, she ducked in. I shut and bolted the door behind her, then pressed her back against it. In an instant we were kissing. "I want this coat off you," I said, panting.

"What, you don't know how?" she said, her tone mocking. She was breathing as heavily as I was.

It was closed with a knotted belt. Kissing her again, I pulled at the knot. She'd tied it tight, doubtless on purpose, and for a moment I struggled with it, furious that I couldn't get it loose. But then I felt some slack, and pushed the ends through, and all at once the belt was open. I gripped the lapels of the coat and swept it over her arms. She tried to stop me, grabbing at the sleeves, but I pulled harder and got it down, dropping it to the floor at her feet.

I put my palms against the door just past her shoulders and looked down. She was wearing a long black skirt and a ridiculously tight blouse, the top three buttons all undone. Underneath I saw the lacy outline of a black bra, the skin of her breasts pale and insanely smooth alongside it.

"Oh, now in such a hurry," she said, her tone mocking again. "And yet so blasé about making me wait earlier."

I couldn't think of a response. I didn't even want to. I kissed her again, my hands on her face, her neck, her breasts.

"No, maybe now I don't want to," she said, her voice husky. "Maybe I should make you wait, the way you made me."

I gripped the lapels of the blouse, her skin hot against the backs of my fingers, and looked in her eyes.

She grabbed my wrists and shook her head. "No," she said. "I don't let you."

I pulled. A button popped. She gasped and gripped my wrists tighter, trying to squeeze them together. I barely felt it. I pulled more. Another button popped. She looked down at what I was doing, panting, then back at me.

I leaned closer. "Kiss me."

She shook her head.

I tried to kiss her. She turned her head, released my wrists, and tried to shove me away. I might as well have been a tree. I caught her left wrist, swept it behind her back, took hold of it in my left hand, and pressed her back against the door. With my right hand I reached for the back of her neck, where her hair was up, and found a long hair stick. I pulled it out and tossed it aside. Her hair fell to her shoulders and I took hold of her throat.

"Kiss me," I breathed.

Again she shook her head. I took hold of her chin and held her head still and put my mouth over hers. She moaned, and when I felt her tongue against mine I thought my head would explode. With my free hand, I gripped the front of her blouse and ripped it the rest of the way open. She moaned again and squirmed between my body and the door. I reached up behind her and unclipped the bra, then pulled down one side, then the other, and then, still holding her arm behind her back, lowered my head and closed my mouth over a wine-colored nipple. She gasped and with her free hand managed to grab my hair. I didn't care. I barely felt it. I let go of her arm, felt along the top of the skirt for a zipper, found it, undid it, then gripped both sides of the cloth and pulled hard in opposite directions. The sound of the fabric tearing open made me feel crazy, desperate, and she moaned something in Italian and let go of my hair and took my face in her hands and kissed me hard.

Somehow I got my clothes off, or she did. I barely noticed—all that mattered was that I had to be naked with her. I pulled her skirt high and finished tearing it open, then threw it aside. I looked down. She was wearing sheer black panties, and black stockings held up by garters. I didn't know what was more overwhelming—the sight of her in lingerie, or the knowledge that she had worn it for me.

"God," I whispered.

She grabbed me by the hair again. "You don't deserve. To make me wait for your call like that."

"I'm sorry."

"No, I don't think you are. Not sorry enough."

"I'm sorry," I said again. I slipped my fingers inside her panties.

"No," she whispered.

I pulled. I heard the fabric tear.

She gripped my hair harder. "No," she whispered again.

I pulled the other way. The fabric tore on the other side. I tossed the panties aside, lowered my mouth to her breasts again, and started touching her. She was wet.

I let her feel my teeth, and she gave a little yelp. She pulled my hair, hard. And again, harder.

"*Bastardo,*" she breathed. "*Bastardo.*"

I dropped lower, reached under her knee, and straightened, bringing the knee high. I looked into her eyes and pushed against her. She pulled my hair hard again and growled something in Italian. I felt the tip of my cock against her wetness and pushed, not all the way, but hard, and I felt myself slip inside her and God it was good, so good, and I tried to hold back but my body wasn't listening, and she gasped and gripped my hair and swore something else in Italian, and I pushed again, deeper, gripping her leg and holding it high, opening her up to me, and she cried out, and I dropped my hips lower and pressed against her harder and suddenly I was fucking her all the way, as deeply as I could, and I didn't know what she was saying in Italian but I knew it was enraged and filthy, and with my free hand I gripped her ass and fucked her harder and she took my face in her hands and kissed me so fiercely it hurt, and then she was moaning into my mouth, crying out, her arm wrapped around my neck, and I felt her coming and then I was coming, too, my hips pounding into hers and her back slamming into the door in time to our desperate rhythm.

And then she was sagging against me, laughing, and I eased her leg down and settled her back against the door and looked into her eyes, shaking my head in dazed wonder.

"*Oh mio dio*, that wasn't considerate at all."

"Should I apologize?"

She laughed again. "For making me wait earlier? Yes. But I think I wanted to be angry at you. So you would do what you just did."

I smiled. "I'll have to make you wait more often, then."

She punched me in the shoulder. "No, this is not a good idea. Very high-risk for you."

I took her hand and pulled her over to the bed. We got under the sheets and, for a while, just held each other.

"What are you thinking?" she said.

"That I wish you could stay."

"You know I can't."

"Yeah. I just hate knowing how little time we have."

"It's why we have to make the most of it, yes?"

"Ah, a metaphor for life. Still teaching me?"

She laughed. "Tonight, I think I had nothing to teach you. If I'm your teacher, I'm so pleased with the progress of my student."

I smiled. "How was your opening?"

"I have to say, it was sensational. There were many important guests from the world of Japanese art and antiquities, and they were all quite, mmm, lavish in their praise. I was suitably modest in response, of course. But my God, it's a guilty pleasure, to tell you the truth."

I smiled again, loving how alive she seemed as she recounted the evening, at her delight in privately exulting in her obvious triumph. "I'm so happy for you," I said. "You worked hard for this. You earned it. I'd know you were lying if you told me you weren't proud."

"Well, I won't deny it, then. Especially after a whole evening of turning aside compliments."

"What did you wear?"

"A quite stunning Armani in emerald-green chiffon. But I changed in the hotel restroom before looking for you in the bar. If you tried to tear that beautiful dress off me, I would have murdered you."

I laughed. "I wish I could have seen you in it."

"Well, you will before I leave. It's not as though you left me anything else to wear on my way out."

"And your husband was there?" It didn't matter anymore, but I still wanted to know.

"Yes, of course."

"He must have been very proud."

"I think so, yes, but you know Japanese men, it's not as though he could really show it."

"He's out with his colleagues now?"

"Yes, probably for a few hours. But still, I should be sure to get home before him."

I felt weirdly glad he was all right. Granted, I was fucking his wife, but I didn't want to hurt him. And I certainly didn't want to hurt Maria. In another universe, I might have killed Sugihara. But in this one . . . I was just a bullet he had happened to dodge. And he would never even know I'd been there. I'd have no impact on him at all.

We made love again. The second round was different—more gentle, more languorous. But also, for me, less focused. When we'd gotten off that elevator and stepped into the room, the rest of the world had just . . .

evaporated. Now it was coming back, in the form of my early-morning rendezvous at Zenkō-ji.

Maria showered, then changed in the bedroom. I lay on the bed and watched, succeeding to some extent in not thinking about where I had to go next, just reveling in the sight of her getting into that gorgeous green dress. When she was done, she turned and looked at me over her shoulder. "Zip it up for me, yes?"

I stood and put my hands on her hips. "I'd rather take it off."

"Yes, so would I. But I have to go. I've already stayed longer than I meant to."

I did as she asked. She got into the trench coat and belted it closed. I glanced around, not seeing the garters and torn clothes. Then I realized—she had put them in the leather bag, presumably to be discarded somewhere safe. Whatever magic space we'd been inside when we were alone was gone. We were both already thinking of what we had to face next.

I pulled on a robe and followed her as she headed out. She went to open the door, but I reached past her and pressed my hand against it.

"Will I see you again?" I said.

She dropped her head, and for a moment she didn't respond. Then she said, "I'm afraid so. But not for much longer."

"Why?"

"This isn't good. For anyone."

"It is for me."

"It feels good for you. And for me. But that's not the same as being good."

"I don't agree."

"I'm not trying to persuade you. I'm just telling you what's true. But stop, don't make that long puppy-dog face."

I hadn't realized I'd been doing it until she'd said so, but yes, I realized I must have been looking morose.

She smiled. "You're smart, John. And you've seen things outside my own experience. There's something a little mysterious about you, and I think that's part of what makes you so attractive to me. No, that's not quite right, it's the mystery combined with the other thing I was going to say."

"Which is?"

"That you're still young. And in some ways, forgive me, naïve. I think you're more American than you know."

I knew she didn't mean it unkindly, and it was something I was aware of myself. But still, to have someone else point it out felt inherently insulting.

"What do you mean?"

"Americans are such an optimistic people. But so much of their optimism is because they know so little history. They're too young. They haven't lived enough. When you live a little longer, you see the world as it really is. And yes, even then it can be shiny and bright, but also you know it has sharp edges. And sometimes what's shiny is exactly what's sharp. If you want to get close to it, it means you get cut."

"I'm not sure I understand."

"This is what I'm talking about. You don't understand because you're young. In a way, I'm envious, don't you see that? I was once as young as you. But I'm not anymore. And I can't be."

"You can be whatever you want to be."

She smiled sadly. "You don't believe that. You're just being stubborn."

Again, I knew she didn't mean it unkindly. But I knew she was right, and it was making me feel younger by the second.

"I have to go," she said. "But here's a little good news, all right?"

"Please. I could use some."

"Eventually, if we're lucky, this thing of ours . . . it will be good. But not for a while."

"What does that even mean? How can it be good later, and not now?"

"It means you are going to be such a beautiful memory for me." Her voice caught, and she went on. "The only thing I've known since losing Dante that for a few moments could take away my pain, and replace it with passion. I will never forget that. Or stop wanting it back."

"Then why not just keep it?"

She shook her head and a tear ran down her cheek. She wiped it away. "And it will be good for you, too. I've taught you many things, haven't I? And the most important things I've taught you, you won't even realize you've learned until much later. That makes me happy. I'm going to keep unfolding inside you. And what you had with me . . . you'll keep discovering new, mmm, facets, and realizing it was different than what you first thought. Better. More profound. You'll see."

"But don't you—"

She pressed a finger to my lips. "Shh. Remember this. I'm part of you now. Whatever you do next, whatever woman you wind up with, I'll always be part of you."

"It sounds like you're saying goodbye."

She looked down for a moment. "I hadn't meant to. But maybe it's better if we do."

"I want to keep seeing you."

"Of course you do. And if you call me, this will happen again. But at some point, and probably soon, we'll see we can't have what's shiny without enduring what's sharp. And we'll get tired of cutting each other."

I tried to think of a way to argue with her. But I couldn't come up with anything.

She looked at me for a long moment, smiling slightly, but with sorrow in her eyes. Then she reached for the back of my head, pulled me in, and kissed me furiously, her tongue in my mouth, her lips pressed painfully hard against mine.

Then she broke the kiss and reached for the door handle. "Goodbye, John," she said, and was gone.

I stood there for a minute, stunned and confused and bereft. Everything had been going so well, hadn't it? I'd even saved her husband, removed all that as a possible complication. I supposed I knew it wouldn't, couldn't, last with her regardless, but I hadn't expected it to end so abruptly. Or so soon. I wasn't even sure it had ended, exactly. She said she'd see me if I called, right? But did she want me to? What had she meant?

I shook it off. I had to focus. Because the meeting at Zenkō-ji was in less than an hour. And while Victor was dead, there was one more threat out there. A threat I intended to eliminate. That had to come first. I could think about Maria after.

chapter
twenty-two

I changed into my street clothes and the new suede jacket, which was roomy enough to accommodate the Kevlar. Oleg's knife was taped to my left inner forearm, the handle extending into my palm under the jacket sleeve and instantly accessible with my other hand. I picked up the bag containing the night-vision goggles and headed out.

I wasn't sure who would be coming for me. It might have been Yokoyama himself, of course. After all, he was the one who had made Miyamoto set up a meeting. But I had a feeling my rendezvous would be with someone one level higher up the food chain.

Wilson.

Granted, from what I could tell of the man, he preferred to operate behind the scenes, deploying cutouts, seeking maximum insulation and deniability. But the team he'd brought to Tokyo to remove me had been wiped out. Even Victor was no longer available. So if Wilson wanted me gone at this point—and if he was behind Yokoyama setting up this meeting, I had to assume he did—I expected he would try to do it himself.

And why not? From what Tatsu had told me, Wilson sounded like a tough old bastard. Wily enough to have operated in the shadows, killing and surviving, all the way back to the wartime OSS. How many enemies had a guy like that made in the course of his life? How many had come at him? And how many had died trying?

Sobering questions, no doubt. But I'd outmaneuvered a formidable enemy earlier that night. I thought I had a way to outmaneuver this one, as well.

The hotel lobby was empty, and I nodded to myself, pleased I had told Miyamoto we'd meet at such an ungodly hour. If anyone had followed Maria to me, setting up in this deserted space would have been a bitch. And ditto for Zenkō-ji.

I used a side exit and caught a cab. It was nearly two o'clock, but I wasn't worried about being late. In general, the smart—and therefore the expected—approach would be to arrive early. But I had just played that game with Victor, and I didn't want to be predictable. Meaning now it was time to change tactics.

I had the driver stop on Aoyama-dori, northeast of the temple. The area was satisfyingly quiet. I crossed the street, and cut into the Aoyama Kitamachi Apartments, a city-operated public-housing complex built in the fifties and sixties and already beginning to decay. None of the two dozen five-story apartment blocks had elevators; indeed, many didn't even have plumbing beyond toilets and sinks, the residents using the local *sentō*, or bathhouse, instead. The apartment grounds were atmospheric, I supposed. But I wasn't interested in their genteel decrepitude. For me, their most attractive features were darkness, desertedness, and, of course, proximity to Zenkō-ji temple.

I paused for a moment, taking in my surroundings. The only sounds were the buzz of a nearby electrical transformer, and the insects in the trees. It had rained earlier, and the ground was damp, the air moist and cool. But the sky had cleared, and the area was pooled in alternating shadows and moonlight.

I slipped on the night-vision goggles, and hit the power switch. Instantly the shadows were gone, everything around me flaring visible in the goggles' green glow. I swiveled my head left and right, adjusting to my new perspective. The goggles felt right, and not only because they were tactical. The apartment grounds were poorly maintained, the bushes and trees sprawling and overgrown, and all that foliage in night-vision green was Vietnam-reminiscent. I felt weirdly comforted, as though I was visiting a neighborhood I hadn't been to in a while, but remembered completely the instant I returned to it. I didn't know what to expect from Wilson. But I'd sure as shit see it before it happened.

I moved southwest among the units, pausing frequently to look and listen. In about ten minutes, I had reached the southeastern edge of Zenkō-ji, with a view of the entrance. I crept forward for another stop, look, and listen. Not a sound, nor a soul.

I circled counterclockwise, repeatedly creeping in for a closer view, each time seeing and hearing nothing. Once I had finished circumnavigating, I backtracked, pulled myself over the stone wall off Omotesando-dori, and moved in through the small cemetery occupying the southwest quadrant.

I paused at the edge of the markers, overlooking the *hondō*, the main temple hall. I caught a whiff of something I thought for a second was incense, and then realized was sweet tobacco smoke. But the grounds were completely still.

No, not completely. I heard footfalls coming up the main path from Aoyama-dori. They were so audible I assumed they must have been from a civilian, perhaps drunk and seeking some sort of late-night spiritual sustenance.

A moment later, a white guy came into view. About sixty, I judged, with thinning gray hair, a trim mustache, and circular wire-rimmed eyeglasses. He was wearing a heavy tweed suit with a vest, and smoking a pipe. That's what I had smelled.

He paused, pulled a match from one of his suit pockets, struck it against the side of the incense brazier, then cupped it in his hands and attended to his pipe. When it was going to his satisfaction, he shook out the match and tossed it aside, watching the *hondō* as though in contemplation, surrounded in a night-vision-green glow of tobacco smoke.

There was something urbane about him. Professorial. Even affable. All of which, I knew, was a put-on.

Because the man I was looking at was Calloway Wilson.

He looked left and right, puffing on his pipe, so relaxed and casual he might have been standing on his backyard porch, not trying to ambush someone halfway around the world in a Zen temple complex. But was this an ambush? I'd expected a Victor-style approach, an attempt to outmaneuver me with stealth, speed, and subterfuge. This was the opposite. The incongruity, I had to admit, was unsettling. I glanced around, everything clearly visible through the night-vision goggles, looking for confederates. I saw no one. What the hell was he doing?

"Hello, Mr. Rain," he called out, his tone confident, a soothing baritone echoing off the flagstones. "I know you're here. You're watching me from somewhere, probably in the shadows of those monuments to my left."

Well, his tactical instincts were good enough. I remained still, waiting to see if there would be more.

He chuckled. "All right, I'll admit it, I'm cheating. I came by earlier and placed a few radio-frequency motion sensors at the entry points to the temple. That's how I know you're over there. You wouldn't believe what the Science and Technology whiz kids come up with these days. Sometimes I find it hard to believe myself."

Shit. Was he bluffing? I watched him through the goggles.

"You see? I could have outmaneuvered you. No disgrace—you don't have a whole government lab behind you, the way I do. But the point is, I'm not here to outmaneuver you. I'm here to talk. And I wanted you to know that. I wanted you to be comfortable with me."

I glanced around again, looking for the setup, still not seeing it.

"I know how good you are," he went on. "You wiped out a picked team, all former Special Forces. And Victor, who as you know was no cupcake. You're the kind of man who's always looking for an edge, and typically finds one. My guess is, you're watching me right now. Did you acquire some night-vision goggles? If so, I'm impressed. Probably the AN/PVS-5, no? Second generation. But there's third generation now—the AN/PVS-7. Very limited rollout—even the military doesn't have them yet. But we do. Because we're just like you. Always looking for that edge."

I glanced around again. I could see him, and he couldn't see me. I was young, and he was old. And I had the drop on him. And yet suddenly I felt at a disadvantage.

"Here," he said, opening his jacket and doing a slow three-sixty. "I'm not armed. You, undoubtedly, are. I don't object to that. I want you to feel comfortable. We were on opposite sides of the board, but that's changed. There's no reason we can't acknowledge those changed circumstances, and come to some mutually agreeable accommodation. I certainly believe it's in both our interests to do so. And I hope I can persuade you of the rightness of my thinking."

I wondered if he could have a sniper. Not likely—a sniper with night vision could have picked me off at several points while I checked the temple perimeter. That I was still here was powerful evidence no sniper was in play.

But what, then? What was his angle? I could see only one way to find out.

I stood. "Keep your hands where I can see them," I called out. "Walk over here. Slowly."

He looked in my direction. In the moonlight, he was probably just able to make me out behind the gravestone I was keeping between us.

"Of course," he said. I glanced around again, seeing and hearing nothing, the handle of Oleg's knife pressed reassuringly against my palm.

He walked slowly along one of the flagstone paths between the markers. "Stop," I said when he was about eight feet away. "Stay there."

"I understand. I'd want to search me, too."

I ignored the observation and circled behind him, checking in all directions as I moved. He put his laced fingers behind his head, saving me the trouble of having to direct him, and I patted him down thoroughly. The only thing I found was something in a pants pocket—a small electronic device with an antenna and a blinking light. Presumably a component of the radio-frequency motion sensor he had mentioned, though perhaps a transmitter.

"Feel free," he said, as though reading my mind.

If it was a transmitter, he might have placed another close by. In which case, destroying this one would be pointless. Still, I dropped it, then crushed it under my heel.

He started to turn around.

"Don't," I said. "Just talk, if that's what you're here for."

He remained facing away from me. "I'm guessing you'd prefer that I not light my pipe."

"Your intuition is outstanding."

"More an eye for talent and ability than intuition. But of course. Your rules. As I said, I want you to be comfortable."

He paused, then went on. "If you've gotten this far, I think you must know most of it."

If he was hoping I was going to start talking, thereby revealing what I knew and what I didn't, he was mistaken. "What do you think I know?"

"You know who I am. You know I was behind Victor. And you know who's behind me."

"Yeah? What else do I know?"

"You know Victor was a piece on the board in a game being played out on both sides of the Pacific. A rough game. A contact sport."

"Yeah, lot of injuries in your little game."

"Yes, there have been a few. But overall, the game has gone as planned."

I didn't like the passive voice. "As who planned?"

"I'd be disappointed if you didn't already know that."

"Assume I don't."

"All right. Let's just imagine what might happen if there were a split in the president's cabinet. Between, say, the secretary of state and the secretary of defense. If the former were, unfortunately, mired in the past—specifically, his memories of fighting the Japanese in World War Two in the Battle of Angaur. While the latter, by contrast, were able to look to the future."

"You mean Shultz wants to keep Japan disarmed, and Weinberger wants to sell Japan weapons."

"Crudely put, I might argue, but not inaccurate."

"And Casey is Weinberger's man."

"Casey is Reagan's man."

"And you're Casey's."

"Again, crudely put, but not unfair, either."

"You're telling me Reagan knows you guys killed a fucking Japanese prime minister?"

"The president isn't particularly interested in operational details. He sets broad policy—the what—and prefers to delegate the how."

"Then you guys put this thing in motion . . . on your own initiative?"

"I believe Director Casey would say, 'There are things best dealt with through official channels, and others that need to be handled more . . . discreetly.'"

"You mean more deniably."

"However you want to put it. I know you understand there are things that have to happen in the world but that absolutely cannot be attributed to the US government. Those things tend to fall to men like us."

I didn't like the way he tried to pair us. It reminded me of McGraw, when he was trying hardest to sell me. Maybe all these CIA guys took the same courses on manipulation.

"So Reagan wants Nakasone to be prime minister."

"Of course."

"Because Nakasone wants Japan to rearm."

He shrugged. "As Nakasone himself has said, Japan could be America's great unsinkable aircraft carrier. But what good is an aircraft carrier, if it has no planes?"

"And Sugihara was in the way of this, is that it?"

"Sugihara, yes. And a few other pieces that needed to be rearranged."

"That's why you brought Victor over."

"Indeed. Victor was quite a find. His military experience. His status as an outsider. His knowledge of, and hatred for, Japan. One of a kind, I would have thought. Until I learned about you."

"I'm not like Victor."

"No, you're not. You're obviously better."

"But not as deniable."

"True. But perhaps that doesn't have to be quite the fatal flaw I first thought."

"You certainly tried to make it fatal."

"It wasn't personal. Just operational security. Are you going to tell me you never killed a prisoner to make sure your mission could continue?"

I said nothing.

"Of course you did. In fact, it was my agency that saved you from the consequences, by refusing to testify in the so-called Green Beret Affair. But my point isn't to blame. It's to let you know I understand. These are the kinds of decisions no one should be faced with, but that men like us are forced to make all the time. Difficult decisions about how to save the most lives possible. And I made that kind of difficult decision with you. It was ugly, I freely acknowledge it. But it needed to be done. In fact, I won't lie to you, I would do it again—but only under the same circumstances. And these aren't the same circumstances. Not anymore. The pieces that needed to be rearranged are rearranged. The pieces that needed to be removed have been removed."

A little tendril of anxiety snaked through me. Surely he couldn't be saying . . .

"Are you talking about Sugihara?"

"Indeed."

I felt gut-punched. "What? When?"

"A short while ago." He glanced over his shoulder, his expression surprised. "I thought you'd be pleased. You were spared the risk of having to do it yourself, and of course his departure removes a personal complication, as well."

Was this why he seemed so confident he could sell me? Because Sugihara was my bonus?

I thought of Maria. What the hell had she gone home to tonight? What was she doing right now?

"What are you saying?" I managed, trying to buy myself time to think.

"Come on now. I know about his wife. She was how my men tracked you. Well, now she's his widow. Probably in need of some comfort."

When I didn't answer, he glanced back again. This time his expression was concerned. "I . . . assumed your relationship was not very serious. I hope I didn't come across just now as callous. But if I underestimated how much you care for her, well, I would think you would view this as an even more positive development."

"Who did it?" I asked. "Victor's dead."

"We don't really need to get into sources and methods, do we?"

"You?" But as soon as I said it, I knew it didn't make sense. This whole op was built on deniability. There was no way Wilson himself was going to drop a Japanese Diet member.

"Ah, you know better than that."

There was only one other possibility. "Yokoyama?"

"I can neither confirm nor deny."

"How?" I said again.

"Well, Sugihara was out earlier with some colleagues. It seems he suffered a heart attack."

"Like Prime Minister Ōhira?"

"Yes, a pattern we had hoped to avoid. But then Victor hired you, and one thing led to another, and some improvisation was required."

"How did Yokoyama do it? Some kind of poison your Science and Technology whiz kids cooked up?"

"Something like that, yes. And precisely the kind of tool you'd have at your disposal if you were to work with me. I could use a man like you."

I shut down my thoughts of Maria. I would deal with all of it, and doubtless more, later. I couldn't afford to get distracted now.

"What if I don't like being used?"

"My apologies. A poor choice of words. What I'm offering is meaningful work. State-of-the-art intelligence and backing. And compensation the likes of which I doubt you've ever even imagined."

I paused, considering. Whatever he was trying to persuade me of, it seemed he hoped his openness would be his bona fides. I thought I ought to take advantage of that.

"What did you promise Victor?"

"Victor was chafing as a foot soldier in one of the Russian crime families because he knew he was capable of so much more. So I engaged him: 'We have information. You have killing prowess. Two things that go together like strawberries and cream.' We knew about Victor's past, and we offered to set him up in Japan. He correctly saw us as his ticket for a hostile takeover of the yakuza. A way of becoming the czar of the Japanese underworld. And all we asked in return for giving him everything he always wanted was that periodically, when we provided him with a name, a photo, an address . . . that person would disappear with no attribution to us."

"You think that's what I want? To take over the Japanese underworld?"

"No, Mr. Rain. As you said, you're not like Victor, and I wouldn't insult you by suggesting otherwise. What I think you want is independence."

"I have that."

"Do you really? What do you think would have been the result of our encounter here if I had maintained my view that you were a threat, and not decided instead that you were an opportunity?"

"I guess one of us would be dead. But that might still happen."

"Why so pessimistic?"

Cocky bastard. "Why are you so optimistic?"

"Because you're smart enough to know that money always wins."

"Funny, you're the second guy who's told me that."

He chuckled. "Then you keep wise company."

"Yeah, I think what he said was, 'There may be unforeseen circumstances. And frequent setbacks. But in the end, money always wins.'"

"That has indeed been my experience."

"But maybe this isn't the end. Maybe this is one of the setbacks. From your perspective, I mean."

I saw a slight rigidness creep into his spine, and I nodded with satisfaction at the sight of him losing a little bit of that patrician cool.

He turned and faced me. I knew he was unarmed, but still I took a quick step back.

"I told you not to do that," I said.

"Yes, you did. But if you're going to kill me, I'd rather you do it to my face."

Not just cocky. Funny, too.

"I understand we got off to a rough start," he said, his tone extra reassuring.

Extremely funny. I said nothing.

"But I told you, circumstances have changed. Why would you want to give up so much upside, and incur so much downside, over something that was never personal to begin with?"

I shook my head. "You think everyone around you is just a piece on a board, don't you?"

"No. There are the players, too. And I'm giving you the opportunity to become one of them. Why do you think I've told you all I have tonight? Does my information sound like something I would share with one of the pieces? Or only with a fellow player?"

"Maybe I don't want to be either. Maybe I don't like your whole fucking game."

He shifted as though uncomfortable with my response. "I understand how you feel. I once felt the same way. But men like us don't have a choice. We're in the game. We can either be players, or pieces."

I watched him, knowing there was an angle, still not seeing it. "You knew I would kill Victor, didn't you?"

"Well, I couldn't know, of course. But after what you did to my team, I thought you would, yes."

"And you didn't mind that?"

"Victor was unstable. Surely you saw that for yourself."

"Yeah, you're right, he had his disagreeable aspects. But you know what? He looked death straight in the face. You think you could do that?"

"Oh, I have. More times than you know."

"I'm talking about tonight."

"I came here unarmed. Knowing you might be hostile. If that's not looking death in the face, what is?"

Something was wrong. This guy was a survivor. A player, and damn proud of it, too. Tatsu had undoubtedly been right: rather than having

Victor call me off, he'd left me just enough slack to see if I might kill Sugihara—right before his own men killed me. This was someone who always managed the odds. Who always had a plan B. But what?

Something Maria had taught me flashed into my head:

If you want to tell if a man is really well dressed, look down.

I did. And, now that I was looking, noticed the welting on his shoes was unusually heavy.

Heavy enough to conceal some kind of weapon.

Wilson saw me look. Saw the suspicion in my expression, even behind the goggles. There was an electric instant where each of us understood what the other was about to do.

I felt a massive adrenaline dump. Wilson stepped in to close the distance, left foot forward, everything silent now, slow motion, and launched a low kick with his right foot. It was nothing fancy, just a straight shot, the kind that might connect with a shin. Painful, perhaps, but nothing beyond that.

Unless there was some kind of CIA whiz-kid poison involved.

My stance was off. If anything, I'd been expecting a rush. My weight was on my left foot. There was no time to shift my balance and get out of the way.

His foot was arcing forward now, a weird contrail of green light tracking it through the goggles.

I did the only thing I could. Certain I was going to be a second late, I pivoted my hips, moving slowly, terrifyingly slowly, as though the whole thing were the kind of bad dream where you're trying to move through sludge, and I brought my right knee up, seeing that shoe, suddenly so deadly looking, coming closer, slicing toward me . . .

I brought my right foot up from the knee and caught his kicking leg in the calf with my shin. His shoe shot past my left leg like a rattlesnake just missing its strike.

He pinwheeled his arms, having been forced into an unexpected giant step, and before he could recover his balance and come at me again, I snatched a fistful of heavy tweed at the inside of his right knee and yanked it skyward.

He went down hard on his back. I heard the crack of his head on the flagstones and felt the shock of it all the way down his leg. Keeping the knee, I shot a back kick into his balls. He shuddered, and I knew he'd be out of the fight for at least a few seconds. I took hold of his heel with one hand, pulled open his laces with the other, and yanked the shoe off his foot. Close up, I could see the welting around the toe wasn't leather—it was steel, honed to a razor edge. And doubtless covered with some kind of exotic, fast-acting CIA poison.

I stuck my hand inside the shoe and kneeled alongside him. He rolled from left to right, coughing and groaning. When I saw he had recovered his senses, I held the razor edge of the shoe a half inch from his cheek.

"No, no, no," he groaned. "Don't do that. You don't want to do that."

"I don't?"

He groaned again. "We can still straighten this out. Just a misunderstanding, don't you see that? There's so much upside here, for both of us. Don't throw all that away."

"Why not? Because money always wins?"

"Just tell me what you want, then. Anything. I guarantee you'll have it."

I thought of Sugihara. Of Miyamoto's former boss, beaten to death to make way for Wilson's mole, Yokoyama. Even of "Mike," and the other two operators I'd killed.

Most of all, I thought of Victor, whose childhood trauma was just a lever for this guy to pull so that money could always win.

"I want to make you one of the pieces," I said, and slashed the razor edge of the shoe across his face.

He shrieked and his hands flew to the wound. And then his body began to shake and spasm. I stepped back and watched in the green glow of the goggles. His mouth was a rictus now, the shaking and spasms intensifying. His back arched so sharply I thought it might break, his elbows twisting in, his fingers dancing frantically at his throat.

Then his legs kicked once, then again more feebly, and then stopped. A long, gargling hiss went out of him, the sound of a balloon losing the last of its air. And then he lay still, his spine arched like a bow strung so tightly it had cracked at the middle.

I looked left and right. Zenkō-ji was silent again, no one around me but the spirits of the dead.

"You can keep your money, asshole," I said, and walked out.

chapter
twenty-three

Three nights later, I was back at the *izakaya* with Tatsu. I'd called him earlier, and postponed our previously scheduled get-together. There were a few things I wanted to take care of first, and for some matters, it's better to seek forgiveness than ask permission. A bit more wisdom from the late CIA philosopher Sean McGraw.

We ordered *nama* beer, as was becoming our custom. When it arrived, Tatsu lifted his glass in a toast. "To Tokyo's deadly ninja," he said.

We touched glasses and drank. I looked at him, feeling an unsurprising affection. Tatsu wasn't much of a joker, but he was subtle. The ninja crack was his way of telling me he was reluctant to inquire too closely into matters I might prefer to keep to myself.

"Indeed," he continued, "I can't think of any explanation other than ninja for two quite bizarre and identical deaths in the last few days."

Reluctant. But not unwilling.

I raised my eyebrows.

He waited, probably hoping the silence would draw me out. When it didn't, he sighed. "Two mornings ago, the body of a white man was discovered at Zenkō-ji Temple in Omotesando. The body was horribly contorted."

"Any idea what might have caused that?"

"Keisatsuchō pathologists believe it was some sort of paralytic agent, administered in a slash across the victim's cheek. But they have been unable to identify the precise nature of the substance in question. What's doubly strange—literally so—is that last night, there was another such death, on a rush-hour train platform in Akasaka. An LDP bureaucrat named Yoshinobu Yokoyama, slashed across the arm."

"Any leads on the identity of the first victim?"

"He was carrying no identification, and no one has claimed the body. I'm quite confident, however, that in time we will learn he was Calloway Wilson."

"Yeah. I expect you will."

"What a coincidence, then, that I gave you such superb intel on that very man. And on several other men who recently took early retirement, such as Victor Karkov and Oleg Taktarov."

He was reminding me of how much he'd helped me—and how much I owed him. With some justification. I nodded at the subtle rebuke, then broke down and told him what I'd learned from Wilson.

By the time I finished relating it all, we were almost done with a second round of beers. We were quiet for a while as he absorbed the information. Then he said, "Do you think he actually hoped to recruit you?"

I shrugged. "Obviously, I can't be sure. But my guess is, no."

He smiled ever so slightly, and I saw he agreed. "Why?" he said, perhaps not satisfied that I had come to the right conclusion, and wanting to check my reasoning, as well.

I took a swallow of beer. "He wasn't wrong about the upside I might have offered him. But he wasn't wrong about the risk, either. And I think . . . it was probably just his nature to mix a small lie into a lot of truth. That's why he was willing to share so much intel about the plot. Why else would he have done that, if he didn't trust and value me?"

"Well, one reason would be, he was in fact planning to kill you."

"Yeah, exactly. But he knew I'd search him, and of course I did. I gamed the whole thing out, and couldn't see a way for him to get to me. So the idea was, the only explanation for his frankness was that he genuinely wanted me as some kind of junior partner. But the whole time, he was looking for an opening. The truth is, I got lucky. I kept him facing away from me until the end. And when I finally spotted what was coming, it was almost too late. One more second, and he would have connected with that fucking shoe blade."

"Yes, I meant to ask about that. Wilson was discovered with only one of his shoes."

"That's odd."

"Indeed. If I didn't know better, I would think it was the same shoe that yesterday killed Yoshinobu Yokoyama."

He raised his hand and signaled the waitress for two more beers. Yeah, he was subtle, but not too subtle to employ something as obvious as loosening up a subject with alcohol.

Obvious, and effective. I told him that Yokoyama had been Wilson's mole in the LDP—the source of his intel, and of Victor's rise to power. The man who had likely caused Prime Minister Ōhira's "heart attack." And, more recently, Sugihara's, as well.

By the time I had finished, we were mostly through with the third round. He said, "I shouldn't have doubted you about Ōhira. Perhaps if I had taken you more seriously, I could have done something to prevent them from getting to Sugihara the same way."

"It wasn't your fault. It was mine. When I dropped Victor, I thought Sugihara would be safe for a while, at least until I could take out Wilson, too. But of course a guy like him would have had a backup plan. I should have been thinking about that."

He shook his head. "I'm a cop. I was the one who should have been thinking about that. At least next time I come across a death by 'natural causes,' I'll know not to take it at face value. Not even if it's a prime minister."

"Especially if it's a prime minister."

"Indeed."

We sat in silence for a minute. Then he said, "Yesterday, I interviewed several National Museum employees about the sword found alongside Victor's body."

I kept a poker face. "Yeah?"

He grunted. "No one has any notion of how it went missing, or why the killer would have left it as he did, given its inestimable monetary value."

"Maybe the killer appreciated it for some other value, too. And wanted it to reside at the museum."

"I can imagine that, yes. In any event, I don't expect the sword will implicate anyone in anything. I even interviewed Sugihara's wife, by the way."

This time the poker face was more of an effort. "Yeah?"

"Of course, I was especially circumspect, given her bereavement. She claims to know nothing of the sword's disappearance. I have no plans to question her again."

As usual, his intuition was damn near terrifying. I said, "I have no plans, either."

"Perhaps . . . that is for the best."

I knew it was, though I was also having trouble accepting it. I'd spent the last several days tormenting myself with thoughts of what might have happened if Maria and I had met some other way, some way that had nothing to do with her husband. There was some irony involved, of course, because in the end, I hadn't been involved with his death. Very likely, he would have died one way or the other, even if I had never returned to Tokyo.

And yet, I had been involved. And Maria, whose intuition seemed to rival Tatsu's, would sense that. She'd already wondered about me—the military past, the speculation about the CIA, the concern about why I was so interested in her husband. And now there was the sword, which, she had observed—with humor that in retrospect seemed prescient—she would know I'd stolen if it ever went missing.

Maybe that was part of the reason I'd taken it. I didn't need one of Tatsu's Keisatsuchō psychiatrists to know that much. Maybe I'd wanted something that would cut more than just Victor. And maybe it wasn't a coincidence that "cut" was exactly the metaphor Maria had used to describe what we were doing to each other.

It was a shitty way to come to understand what she had meant about the shiniest things sometimes also being the sharpest, but I couldn't deny she'd been right, either. I was never going to have someone like her. I'd learned that ten years earlier, with Sayaka. And Maria had briefly beguiled me into believing that maybe I'd been mistaken. But I hadn't been mistaken. I'd just been trying to find a way not to shoulder the weight of the truth. The weight of destiny.

I shook my head. "You know the worst part?"

He raised his eyebrows.

"Wilson was right. Money always wins. Sure, he's dead, but the real players—in the US administration and over here—they're going to get exactly what they wanted. No, better than what they wanted, because the game is over and even the pieces they used to win are now wiped from the board. It's a better outcome than probably they'd even hoped for."

He nodded. "It is indeed dispiriting, to have fought so hard and accomplished so little. And not the first time for us, is it?"

I shook my head. "No. It's not."

"But what do we do? Give up? Or keep fighting?"

I looked at him, unable to resist smiling. I'd wondered when he'd get around to that.

He finished his beer. "One more?"

I shrugged. "Why not?"

We ordered another round, then sipped in comfortable silence for a few minutes. He said, "What will you do next?"

I hadn't figured all that out yet. Miyamoto had already been promoted, taking Yokoyama's position. He'd promptly paid me fifty thousand for Victor, and told me any new jobs were mine for the asking. What Victor had achieved by threats, he said, I had earned as my right. Victor's dominion was now mine.

I didn't know about any of that, and for reasons I was still too young to fully grasp, didn't want to think about it, either. The only thing I was sure of was that I was heading back to Ginza to buy more clothes from Employee Ito. If the guy hadn't taught me about shoes and welting, I'd probably be dead. The least I could do was throw some more business his way.

But beyond that, I didn't know. I supposed the good news was that, if I stuck around, I'd have steady work. Coming from Miyamoto, a guy I could actually trust.

Maybe I'd do it. Maybe Wilson had been right. How had he put it? *Men like us don't have a choice. We're in the game. We can either be players, or pieces.*

But if I was going to stay in the game, I'd make my own rules. One of which would be, no more involvement. No more attachments. No more Marias, or Sayakas, or anything else. If money was always going to win, I'd get my share and then cash the hell out.

"I think I'm going away for a while," I said, letting him interpret that as he might.

He nodded. "Forgive me for saying so, but I think this would be a waste."

I couldn't help a reluctant smile, because he was just so damn indefatigable. "I know what you want, Tatsu. But I need to figure out what I want."

"I don't know what you want. I only know what you need."

"Yeah? What's that?"

"Purpose."

"Well, I'll let you know when I find one."

He looked down, then back to me. "Do you remember what you said to me the last time we met? About Victor needing to kill you because it was a zero-sum game?"

All at once, I felt uneasy. "Yeah. I remember."

"Have you considered that perhaps that dynamic runs in both directions?"

I tried to think of a meaningful response, couldn't, and managed instead, "I don't see your point."

"My point is simply that 'zero' is not so much to win. Especially after the kind of game you've been playing. Why not play for something more than that?"

All at once, I felt engulfed by a wave of *munashisa*—emptiness, fruitlessness, futility. I waited, hoping it would pass. It didn't.

"I need to go," I said. "Who's buying the beer?"

He bowed his head. "Please. Let me. You buy next time."

"I don't know when that'll be, Tatsu."

"I can wait."

Not as long as I can, I thought.

He put some yen on the table and we stood to go. *"Jaa,"* he said, meaning, in this context, *See you again.*

I almost replied with *Sayōnara*—Goodbye.

But I didn't. Because the truth was, maybe he was right. Maybe I did want more than zero. I just didn't know how to get it. Or if I ever would.

Notes

Chapter 3

For more on the two percent of soldiers the US government considered "aggressive psychopaths" in World War II, I recommend Lt. Col. Dave Grossman's *On Killing: The Psychological Cost of Learning to Kill in War and Society.*

http://www.killology.com

Rain's thoughts on how recognizing something is dangerous automatically makes it less so are courtesy of Marc MacYoung.

http://nnsd.com

And for a conversation between Rain and MacYoung on violence, personal security, and tradecraft, along with a few other tales about life out at the edges, I recommend *Campfire Tales from Hell.*

https://www.amazon.com/Campfire-Tales-Hell-Survival-Bouncing-ebook/dp/B0083XYSWM

Chapter 4

The original Hotel Okura was torn down in 2015. I'm glad I saw it before then. Here's more on its history and on what made it special, including a wonderful photo slide show:

http://www.travelandleisure.com/slideshows/hotel-okura-tokyo
http://www.japantimes.co.jp/life/2015/06/06/style/refusing-check-hotel-okura/#.V_Gv1jKZN3k

Chapter 5

It seems that recently, love hotels are being increasingly promoted and used for activities not strictly amorous. Obviously, Rain has been all over the additional benefits for decades.

https://www.theguardian.com/world/2016/dec/24/no-sex-please-were-japanese-love-hotels-clean-up-their-act-amid-falling-demand

Chapter 6

The quote Rain refers to is from Reinhold Niebuhr's *Moral Man and Immoral Society*, where Niebuhr writes, "Self deception . . . is the tribute which morality pays to immorality; or rather the device by which the lesser self gains the consent of the larger self to indulge in impulses and ventures which the rational self can approve only when they are disguised."

Treasures of Azuchi Castle and Nijo Castle was a 2016 exhibit at the Tokyo National Museum. I hope I can be forgiven for moving it back in time a bit.

Chapter 8

Some of my favorite *izakaya* are the really old-school, under-the-tracks variety. Here's a nice photo blog of Yūrakuchō, home to some great ones.

https://lifetoreset.wordpress.com/2013/06/06/tokyo-neighborhood-izakaya-under-the-train-tracks-at-yurakucho/

Chapter 9

One of Tokyo's best bars (which is saying a lot), Bar Radio has been through several incarnations since its 1972 debut. I described it as it appears today—which works in a story set in 1982 because the bar is timeless. If you're in Tokyo, visit and see for yourself.

http://www.tokyofoodlife.com/?p=708

Chapter 10

Here's a good photo of the street in Shibuya were Rain gets ambushed—a part of town called Hyakkendana. I post my research photos on my website, but this one's better quality and really nails the nighttime feel of the area.

https://www.flickr.com/photos/sbisaro/7562779568/in/photostream/

For more about the Church and Pike Committees and the assassination, domestic sabotage, and human experimentation programs they uncovered, Wikipedia offers a good primer. Fortunately, these sorts of abuses are ancient history and could never, ever happen now.

https://en.wikipedia.org/wiki/Church_Committee
https://en.wikipedia.org/wiki/Unethical_human_experimentation_in_the_United_States

More on Project Gamma and "the Green Beret Affair"—the "termination with extreme prejudice" of a suspected South Vietnamese double agent by US Special Forces in Vietnam.

https://en.wikipedia.org/wiki/Project_GAMMA#Capture.2C_ interrogation.2C_and_killing_of_Chu_Van_Thai_Khac

You can't take the kind of urban-ops course "Mike" mentions to Rain as the source of his ability to blend in Tokyo. But here's one you can take, and it's at least as good—Violence Dynamics.

https://www.facebook.com/violencedynamics/

Chapter 11

The intelligence adage, *First, tell me what you know. Then tell me what you don't know. Now tell me what you think*, is courtesy of a man called Slugg, whose untimely death early this year is an immeasurable loss for everyone who knew and learned from him.

Chapter 15

The programs Tatsu describes—Operation Paperclip, Operation Gladio, Operation Mongoose, Operation Chaos, Project FUBELT, and MKUltra—and others like them, all really happened. Google the names and see. Of course, the government would never, ever engage in such activities today.

For more on the history of soapland, I recommend Nicholas Bornoff's wonderful book, *Pink Samurai: Love, Marriage and Sex in Contemporary Japan*.

https://www.amazon.com/dp/B01N9LTLAZ

And here's a great article from longtime Tokyo resident and *Japan Times* reporter Mark Schreiber on Yoshiwara then and now.

http://www.japantimes.co.jp/news/2017/03/04/national/media-national/japans-magazines-get-misty-eyed-showa-era-brothels/#.WL2cWBjMzkF

Chapter 16

An interesting video on Kevlar's effectiveness against knives.

https://vimeo.com/8502720

Chapter 18

Tokyo's famous Imperial Hotel—repeatedly damaged, destroyed, torn down, and rebuilt—has an incredible history, including opening on the day of the Great Kanto Quake of 1923—and surviving it, though not unscathed.

http://www.fdtimes.com/2016/01/13/imperial-hotel-tokyo/

More on CIA stockpiling of shellfish toxin, cobra venom, and other poisons.

http://www.nytimes.com/1975/09/17/archives/colby-describes-cia-poison-work-he-tells-senate-panel-of-secret.html

The CIA had a heart-attack dart gun, too. Because it's the government, they called it a "nondiscernible microbionoculator."

http://www.military.com/video/guns/pistols/cias-secret-heart-attack-gun/2555371072001

Acknowledgments

Thanks to Koichiro Fukasawa and Yukie Kito, who yet again were invaluable in answering my questions about all things Tokyo and Japan: new and old; native and foreign; cultured and *gehin*.

Thanks to Michael Kleindl of Tokyo Food Life, who introduced me to Bar Radio and quite a few other Tokyo standouts, as well.

http://www.tokyofoodlife.com

Any shortcomings in the judo Rain uses in the subway struggle are entirely the fault of Tom Schinaman—a great judoka, *jiu-jitsuka*, and teacher—who helped me choreograph the scene one memorable night in Tokyo. ☺

To the extent I get violence right in my fiction, I have many great instructors to thank, including Massad Ayoob, Tony Blauer, Wim Demeere, Dave Grossman, Tim Larkin, Marc MacYoung, Rory Miller, and Peyton Quinn. I highly recommend their superb books and courses for anyone who wants to be safer in the world, or just to create more realistic violence on the page:

http://www.massadayoobgroup.com

https://blauerspear.com

http://www.wimsblog.com

http://www.killology.com

http://www.targetfocustraining.com

http://www.nononsenseselfdefense.com

http://www.chirontraining.com

http://moderncombatandsurvival.com/author/peyton-quinn/

Thanks as always to the extraordinarily eclectic group of "foodies with a violence problem" who hang out at Marc "Animal" MacYoung and Dianna Gordon MacYoung's No Nonsense Self-Defense, for good humor, good fellowship, and a ton of insights, particularly regarding the real costs of violence:

http://www.nononsenseselfdefense.com

I like to listen to music while I write, and sometimes a certain band or album gets especially associated with what I'm working on. This time around, the band was Godspeed You Black Emperor! and the album *F# A# ∞*.

Thanks to Jacque Ben-Zekry, Blake Crouch, Gracie Doyle, Meredith Jacobson, Mike Killman, Lori Kupfer, Dan Levin, Genevieve Nine, Laura Rennert, Michael S., and Ted Schlein for helpful comments on the manuscript.

Most of all, thanks to my wife and literary agent, Laura Rennert, for doing so much to make these books better in every way. Thanks, babe, for everything.

About the Author

Barry Eisler spent three years in a covert position with the CIA's Directorate of Operations, then worked as a technology lawyer and startup executive in Silicon Valley and Japan, earning his black belt at the Kodokan Judo Institute along the way. Eisler's bestselling thrillers have won the Barry Award and the Gumshoe Award for Best Thriller, have been included in numerous "Best Of" lists, have been translated into nearly twenty languages, and include the #1 bestseller *The Detachment*. Eisler lives in the San Francisco Bay Area and, when he's not writing novels, blogs about torture, civil liberties, and the rule of law. http://www.barryeisler.com

"The most charismatic assassin since James Bond."

—SAN FRANCISCO CHRONICLE

Returning to Tokyo in 1982 after a decade of mercenary work in the Philippines, a young John Rain learns that the killing business is now controlled by Victor, a half-Russian, half-Japanese sociopath who has ruthlessly eliminated all potential challengers. Victor gives Rain a choice: kill a government minister or die a grisly death. But the best route to the minister is through his gorgeous Italian wife, Maria, a route that puts Rain on a collision course not only with Victor but with the shadowy forces behind the Russian's rise to dominance—and the longings of Rain's own conflicted heart.

It's a battle between kingpin and newcomer, master and apprentice, a zero-sum contest that can only end with one man dead and the other the world's foremost assassin.

ISBN 978-1477824467

51595

9 781477 824467

f THOMAS & MERCER